# RISE
## OF THE
# SEA WITCH

Stacey Rourke

# Dedication:

*This book is dedicated in loving memory to Walter Elias Disney. Thank you for inspiring countless generations to believe that magical things can happen when we follow our hearts and chase our dreams.*

# PROLOGUE

*I* admit that in the past I was a princess. They weren't kidding when they called me ... well, a spoiled twit." Tentacles rolling and churning beneath me, I turn to the newest member of my little garden with effortless grace. Arms thrown out wide, I grant the shriveled polyp a beguiling smile. Those around him tremble in fear, pulling as far away from him as their roots deep within the ocean floor will allow. "Through rather unfortunate circumstances it became mandatory I mend my ways. And, yes, some of the techniques I employed earned me the title of villain."

"Never, my Queen," Floteson murmurs. Coiling around my upper arm, he drapes himself across my shoulder.

Jetteson's oily scales lovingly brush my cheek. "Every one of them was deserving of your wrath."

Shoulders curling in, I pucker my lips which are freshly glossed by a crimson sea-flower and tenderly scratch each of them under their chins. "How horrible can I be to be so adored by such sweet babies?"

"She shows us nothing but love," my darling zebra sharks chorus.

Their unwavering dedication soothes me, allowing me to expel a calming breath that bubbles in a wreath around my face.

"I am not the horrible beast many think me to be. Yet I feel it is your own misconceptions that brought you here, and led to ... well, you know." Floating passed my ornate vanity mirror, which seems out of place in the dreary cave I call home, I suck in my cheeks. Turning my head one way and then the other, I inspect my reflection. A smug smile curls the corners of my lips. The woman staring back at me is positively voluptuous with power, mayhem swirling within her clay-gray eyes. "Undoubtedly, you've heard rumors of my banishment."

Hitching one eyebrow at my newly planted polyp, I watch him squirm under the weight of my attention.

# Rourke

"Do you even know my true given name, I wonder? Before hateful whisperings from the farthest reaches of the Seven Seas dubbed me The Sea Witch, I went by another name: Princess Vanessa of Atlantica. I harbored dreams of bringing peace and happiness to the kingdom … as their noble queen."

Jabbing my hands on to my ample hips, I turn in a swirl of black and purple. "I'm not sure if that pitiful pout is caused by your deep longing to hear more, or if you're mourning the loss of your shriveled limbs. But," with a theatrical roll of my wrist, I snap my fingers – my cauldron sparks to life, an ethereal green glow simmering from within, "I choose to think the former because it's about me … and all of my favorite things are.

"It would be predictable for me to say it all began with the death of my mother. Predictable and false."

Water rushes beneath me with one mighty flap of all my tentacles. The power of the act propels me over to my alchemy shelves, where my fingers flick over the exposed vials. Some days I seek to terrorize my captives, calling out each ingredient or dangling it over their heads before tossing it into my brew.

Tongue of porpoise.

Eye of cuttlefish.

Shell of sea turtle.

I won't lie and say watching their complexions green and bug eyes bulge isn't a guilty pleasure of mine. For the moment, however, a wave of generosity – brought on by the mention of my mother – prompts me to toss them in without my usual theatrics. Each is received into the cauldron's wide-mouth drum with a puff of smoke and spray of sparks.

"As much as I loved my mother, losing her didn't drive me to madness as some would have you believe." Hearing the melancholy in my tone, I bristle. "Far from it, in fact. I would have subjected myself to an abysmal existence of the mundane in honor of her memory. No, it was after the black flags of mourning had been strung through the kingdom, after the spectacle of her funeral procession had passed, that my descent began."

Throwing one final ingredient into the cauldron, a veil of greasy smoke wafts from its rim. Images begin to form within the haze: the king's regal quarters, and a formidable frame seated in a high-backed chair behind a massive stone desk.

Crouching down, I position myself eye level with the miniscule scene unfolding. My tentacles coil into tight knots beneath me. "This was the night … the night when I was touched by magic for the very first time … and loathed it to my very core."

Within the ghostly image, the curtain to the king's quarters is pushed open. A heavy set nursemaid with stripes of gray in the messy twist of her *bun swims in. On one hip she balances a cherub-faced baby that's only two months shy of his second birthday. Blond ringlets halo his head. Both his eyes and cheeks are ruddy from crying. The frazzled servant's other hand clings to that of a raven-haired princess who rubs at her tired, violet eyes with a chubby, toddler fist.*

"If you aren't following along yet, that princess is me," I explain to my captive audience. "The maid softly shushing my younger self is Loriana. Oh, how dear she was to me. She was a servant in the castle, tasked with tending to my brother and I. That little sunset orange tail poking out from behind her belongs to her son, Alastor. He was Triton's best friend and would become much more than that to me ..."

"Sire," respectfully bowing her head, Loriana readjusted her hold on Prince Triton, "I hate to interrupt."

My father, King Poseidon, pushed his chair back from the desk in a swirl of water and sand, and rose in greeting. To the rest of the kingdom, he was known as simply the supreme ruler of Atlantica. To me, and my juvenile ignorance, he was the God of the Sea who towered over us all. I envisioned all of his enemies, and anyone that ever wished me harm, falling to their knees and trembling before his commanding presence. His hair and thick beard were the red of Precious Coral. Muscle rippled over every inch of his exposed torso. His narrow waist tapered into an emerald green tail that perfectly matched the shining jewels of his eyes. Countless times I had examined the lines of his face in search of some similarity between the two of us. None could be found. Triton had his smile, and later—when adolescence hit—he would inherit his strong chin. Me? Every inch of me was a lackluster shadow of my mother's regal beauty. Where her eyes and tail sparkled like freshly polished amethyst, mine seemed dull by comparison. Or, perhaps the lighting from the pedestal I'd built for her in my mind shone for her with a more flattering shimmer.

"The hour is late. I welcome the interruption." Poseidon set his fish bone quill onto the desk top, and positioned its stone cradle on top of it. "How can I be of service, Loriana?"

"It's the children, Your Highness." Her face a mask of maternal sorrow, Loriana gave my hand a quick pulse of comfort. "This is the first night they have ever tried to go to sleep without a lullaby from their dear mother. I'm afraid I can't seem to calm their troubled little hearts."

Poseidon's broad chest expanded with a deep inhalation, and tipping his head he exhaled a flurry of rushing water and bubbles. "This is a troubling time for us all," he agreed. Crossing the room with one stroke of his tail, he extended his hands to receive Triton. My brother waved his arms in eager delight, wriggling into the security of Father's strong embrace. Inching forward, I blinked up at the mighty king. He floated past without so much as ruffling my hair. "I'm afraid I don't have your mother's gift of song, but perhaps we could sit a spell and find peace in our togetherness."

Honoring her position outside of the room, Loriana gave me a gentle push forward to follow my father. Casting a tentative glance over my shoulder, I did just that. Poseidon swirled Triton around, eliciting a giggle that crinkled the corners of his ocean blue eyes, before the king collapsed on the sea sponge sofa with his darling son on his lap. I perched on the very edge of the far cushion, uninvited and unnoticed.

Before that moment our father had been more of a … hmm, how to put this delicately? A *figurehead* in our lives. We knew *of* him and regarded him fondly, but unfortunately his kingly duties allowed our primary interactions to be those staged for political potency. Our mother, the lovely Queen Titonis, spent her days caring for my brother and I with only Loriana to aid her. Now, Poseidon had no choice but to pick up the yolk. For Triton this transition seemed to be going swimmingly. I, however, was getting as much attention as the Orca-bone end table.

Hands under the little prince's pits, Poseidon turned Triton to face him. "I was *so* proud of how you behaved during the processional today," he gushed. "You honored not only me, but your mother's memory when you clasped your tiny fist over your heart and held your head high as her carriage passed."

"Follow Nessa." Triton looked to me with love, his tailfin a muted clap when connecting with Father's lap.

"Your sister has *two whole years* of further training and experience than you, my boy." Poseidon's shoulders raised, his voice dropping to a conspiratorial whisper. "*You* exhibited the poise of a true leader."

My lips clamped shut to stifle a sob, his words stinging like a slap. I had just as much right to the throne as Triton, but this was the first moment I became painfully aware of who he longed to see succeed him. It would not be the last … or the most painful.

"She held her curtsy so long, merfolk threw flowers!" Alastor, a year and a half older and *far* more eloquent than Triton, darted into the room to brazenly interject. Mahogany waves curled over his earlobes, adding dimension to his round little face that resembled a bubble. The boldness of his gesture quickly shriveled under Father's menacing glare.

"The son of a servant entering the king's quarters?" Father boomed, one eyebrow raising in question. "One *might* question your upbringing, lad."

"A thousand apologies, Your Majesty!" Loriana blushed from her neck clear up to her earlobes and snapped her fingers at her wandering boy. *"Alastor, come here at once!"*

Shoulders sagging like a stone cast to the depths, Alastor returned to his rightful place in the hall. The heat of his topaz stare bore into me as he paddled along, searching for even the slightest acknowledgement of his noble deed.

I had none to offer.

My own gaze had drawn away from my brother, laughing while Father tickled his cheeks with his beard, to scan the items neatly arranged on father's desk. Inanimate objects which earned his attentions daily just by *being*. On the right side, closest to his scrawling hand, sat the quill. Its fat little ink pot was perfectly positioned perpendicular beside it. In the center of the desk, weighted by stones carved with the royal crest, rested a stack of scrolls awaiting the king's notice. On the left-hand corner, Poseidon's late night snacking needs were met by a plate of rolled and seasoned seaweed puffs.

The ink pot lured my attention back as if calling to me.

I had never had to work for attention in any capacity. My mother had always given it freely, and in limitless supply. Since she had been taken from me, I had unquenched needs: hugs, stories, and all of that … drivel. So, yes, I thought about acting out. I toyed with the idea of knocking over that little clay pot and letting the ink flow to ruin the staged perfection of father's space. More than that, I *wanted* to. I wanted to hear him shout out my name in his menacing vibrato, because at least *then* he would have to acknowledge me. While my hands stayed folded neatly in my lap, as the good little mergirl I was, *something* within me I had never felt before reached out. Palpable energy, only I seemed privy to, crackled through the water to cradle the pot in its hold. I could feel it, poised and ready, awaiting *my* command. Biting my lower lip to fend off a threatening grin, my essence gave barely a nudge and the ink pot tumbled. A thick black cloud exploded over my father's desk, staining the scrolls and ruining the once delectable wraps.

"*Vanessa!*" thundered my father, rocketing off the sofa. "*Look what you've done!*"

I turned toward him with feigned remorse … and screamed. The howl of terror tore from my chest until my gills ached and my throat was raw.

There was a buzz of activity: Poseidon calling to the nursemaid, Loriana swimming in as fast as her fins could carry her, Triton wailing in fear, Alastor trying to shush his friend from the doorway to which he'd been banished. I neither saw nor heard any of this.

Floating in the center of the room, bobbing with the current, was my mother.

Not the serene vision of loveliness I had known her to be that was full of life and love. Heck, I even would've happily settled for the slumbering beauty she appeared to be during her funeral. In vast contrast, the entity hovering before me had chunks of flesh gnawed away by assorted sea beasts. Cracked, ashen lips curled into a snarl. Black ooze bubbled through her teeth, dripping from her chin and clouding the water. My scream reached a fevered pitch, spots dancing before my eyes. The ghoul, who in life sang me to sleep, reached for me with one hand that had been gnawed to bone.

You see, by using magic I opened a door and allowed the darkness in. The cost being more than I could bear, I vowed to myself—as my consciousness waned—never, ever to dabble with such things again.

Oh, the lies we tell ourselves …

# Chapter One

*L*et us skip ahead nine years into our tale. Why? Because this is my story and you're ... well, botany. Sure, I could lament about my childhood. Daddy never paid me enough attention. All I did was study and train for a throne which would never be mine. Boohoo. We've established I wasn't my father's favorite; let's skip over that other drivel. It was the eve of Triton's eleventh birthday, marking a monumental day for us both — even though only one of us seemed to view it as such. When the second born to the king reached the age of eleven both contenders to the throne were treated to their Initiation Rite. That's just Atlantica's fancy way of saying that we were allowed places within the palace we hadn't been before. These newly opened doors were to help further our understanding of kingdom politics to help prepare one of us to rule. I was giddy at the prospect. Triton? He was nowhere to be found ...

Soaring pillars lined the expansive hall, each draped in seaweed garland decorated with bushels of blush-pink sea anemones. Shell chandeliers hung over head, and the bioluminescent plants lighting them cast a soft blue glow over the space. Diamonds danced over the sand dollar mosaic floor beneath me, acting as the only sign that in the world above us it was a bright and cloudless day. I only noticed these things in passing as I swam down the hall at a reckless speed.

Bursting out the side servants' entrance, I kicked on toward shallower waters. The ocean lightened around me from a deep sapphire to a dazzling turquois. Bright coral of every hue of the prism waved my welcome to the outskirts of Atlantica. There, trilling sounds of laughter led me right to my target.

Jabbing my hands onto my hips, I tipped my head and cast a disapproving glare in my brother's direction—not that he noticed, or cared. The only son of Poseidon was rolling and frolicking with a herd of manatee calves. Nuzzling their noses with his, he spun them in barrel rolls that made their tiny flippers flap merrily.

"*Triton!*" I called, doing my best to emulate father's booming tremor. Even I heard how far short my attempt fell. "By chance do you remember a previous commitment you have today?"

"Vanessa!" My brother's face tipped in my direction, his beaming smile spread from ear to ear. His baby weight, like my own, had melted off. A lifetime of swimming everywhere can be thanked for that. Unfortunately for Triton, and my own sense of sight, it had left him a mess of knobby arms and a scrawny torso. At the time I often mused that if he ever grew into his ears and teeth, and reminded *everyone* he met that he was a prince, some of the less discriminate mermaids *might* find him appealing. "Look at all the manatee pups! I'm calling them my mana-minis! This is what happiness looks like! *Get in here and give them a smoosh!*"

"I would love to, *really*," I lied, my full lips pursed in disdain, "but I actually *care* about who chooses me as their apprentice. I want to be there the very moment they wave us into the Summit Room. Punctuality and enthusiasm are of utter importance to Fleet Master Neleus, and I want him to *know* the second he sees me that I'm to be his selection! The last *eight* rulers of Atlantica all apprenticed with the Royal Guard. That *can't* be a coincidence!"

"I know you're talking," Triton giggled, twirling around with yet another calf, "but all I can hear is '*Blah, blah, blah, I need to hug a manatee'*."

"Hey, Nessa! Nice dress!"

My head swiveled at the chirp of a familiar voice.

*Okay, we're going to pause and talk fashion for a minute here. Mermaids of today swim around in those teensy shell bras which leave*

nothing *to imagination. During my time at the palace, dressing was an event. Saying the dress I wore that day was "nice" was like saying the Great Barrier Reef contains a little bit of coral. This was a garment that commanded respect with its high neckline, and sweeping skirt that parted just above my tail for mobility's sake. Conch shells, positioned on both shoulders, added stature to my slight frame. Delicate threads of kelp, dyed to a deep-sea violet with a mixture of squid dye and crushed flowers, wove together a bodice decorated with tiny sand dollars and pearls. Flowing out at the waist, it tapered out to drip its elegance down the length of me. Costuming and pageantry, kids, it's what separates us from the Sea Cucumbers. Now, where was I? Ah, yes ...*

Turning, I found Alastor seated on top of one of the larger manatee bulls, attempting to ride the animal, much to its *extreme* indifference. Adolescence was being slightly kinder to Alastor. He was just as sinewy as Triton, but somehow it looked ... *better* on him. Jerking his entire body forward, he attempted to coax the bull to move. Long blinks while munching on a mouthful of musk grass was as taxing an activity as the manatee intended to partake in.

"Not you, too, Alastor. Really, one *might* question your upbringing." An audible lilt of humor drifted into my stern tone at the opportunity to utilize our long running joke at my father's expense.

"It's all in the name of science!" Alastor countered, slapping his tail against the side of the manatee. "They're known as sea-cows. Perhaps, if we can train them, we could ride them into battle. Or, more likely, we could transport Atlantica's elderly and feeble around without even blowing their hair back."

The last fin slap was the one which annoyed the manatee into action. At a speed that a snail would find tiresome and dull, it began rolling to its side.

Alastor disappeared behind the manatee's girth, nothing but his flapping orange tail visible. "Oh ... *ow!* There's a boulder back here! He's still rolling ... may not be able to breathe much ... longer. Little help, please?"

"In the name of science, I think you need to see this experiment through to fulfillment. What will you learn if I help you?" My glossy black hair hung down my back in a curtain. Loriana had caught just the sides and pulled them back in a delicate braid resembling a waterfall.

Flipping the end of that braid over my shoulder, I once again focused my attention on Triton. "Now, we don't have time for you to change into fitting attire, but if we hurry we can still make it before the curtains to the Summit Room are drawn back."

Popping up next to a nursing manatee, Triton rested his elbows on her back and cradled his chin in one palm. "You know, I hear other girls in the town square talking about which member of the Royal Guard they find to be the dreamiest. Are you capable of such musings?"

"Neleus's name is mentioned often," Alastor's muffled voice came from behind the bull, who appeared to be smiling victoriously. "They say his eyes are as bright as freshly sprouted sea grass."

I couldn't have fought off that eye-roll if I tried to—which I didn't bother. "*Most* girls aren't contenders to the throne. Who I apprentice with is a crucial undertaking. If not directly with the Royal Guard, I need someone who can help me form solid relationships with Atlantica's dignitaries. Triton, if you have any desire to be king, you'll strive for the same."

"That's where you're mistaken, dear sister!" Triton's eyes twinkled mischievously. "I have *no* desire to rule today, tomorrow, or ever! By all means, give my regards to Father and his Council."

Patience waning, I slapped my tail against the water. "Triton!"

If I showed up without my brother, *I* would be the brunt of Father's fury. I would sooner fish-hook Triton's cheek and drag him back to the palace flailing and kicking than to allow that to happen.

A grunt, a shove, and Alastor squirted out from behind the manatee. Tawny hair stabbed off his head in disheveled spikes, his amber eyes bulging. "What did I miss?"

Crossing my arms over my chest, I twisted my lips to the side in wry smirk. "Oh, nothing much, just Triton relinquishing all rights to the throne."

"We haven't even had breakfast," Alastor mused, his lips pressed together in a thin line. "That seems like a big proclamation to make on an empty stomach."

"Oh, but it's true!" Throwing his arms out wide, Triton swan dived backwards. Calves scurried out of the way to avoid being clobbered by his back flip. "Vanessa can be Queen of Atlantica! I'll be King of the Mana-minis!"

Finding himself face to snout with a calf, Triton caught it in his arms. Cradling its face in his hands, he puffed his cheeks and mimicked its expression. The mother of the calf scowled her disapproval and whacked Triton with her tailfin. Erupting in a fresh fit of giggles, he rolled away from the herd.

"Your subjects seem less than enthusiastic about this prospect," Alastor pointed out to my slow-witted brother and playfully bumped my elbow with his.

Letting my head loll to the side, I stared up at him from under my lashes. "You speak his language. If I apologize for letting you get squashed, will you *please* help me wrangle him?"

"For you?" Alastor's eyes narrowed in contemplation for a fraction of a second before a smile bright enough to light the farthest reaches of the ocean's depths spread across his face. "Okay, but you owe me a favor to be named later. Anything I ask."

"*Within reason*," I countered, hitching one brow.

"Agreed." He nodded, then raised his voice to be heard over my brother's babbling baby talk directed at the infant manatees. "Triton! Your birthday banquet is tomorrow. They're sure to have those seaweed-wrapped scallops you adore. If you don't participate in your Initiation Rite, you know your Father will have you mucking out the porpoise stalls instead of feasting with the rest of the nobility!"

Triton's head burst up like a surfacing orca. "I *love* those scallops!"

"Well, of course you do!" Raising his palms skyward, Alastor let them fall to his sides with a slap. "They're delicious! Little bit salty, little bit sweet, it's delightful! A true culinary treat, so let's go!"

Repelling off the nearest bull, Triton fired past us, stirring up a strong current in his wake. Spinning around, he paused to toss back a winning smile. "You two coming, or what?"

Without waiting for a response, he swam off, leaving only his echoing laughter behind.

Alastor tried, and failed, to hide his victorious smirk. Turning one hand palm up, he shrugged as if he was as surprised by his talent as I was.

"You think you're clever? If I do become queen, I'm assigning *you* to be his handler. You can spend your days preventing him from irritating Blue Ring Octopuses or being devoured by Great Whites."

"Oh, come on! I'm only one person! Albeit an insanely charismatic one, but *still*!"

Offering him little more than an indifferent lift of my shoulder, I kicked off with the intention of following Triton. I hadn't made it one flip of my tail before Alastor's hand caught my upper arm and turned me back to him.

"My one favor; I want you to answer a question for me."

A hot blush warming my cheeks, I self-consciously pulled my arm away. "What's that?"

Alastor's eyes darkened with a wisdom beyond his years, the intensity of his stare causing my heart to lurch in a spastic stutter-beat. "You work extremely hard, deprive yourself of much, and for what? We consider our culture to be evolved, yet some of our practices are still archaic and rooted in tradition we can't *begin* to understand. You work and you slave for that throne. Do you ever stop to think, I wonder, that on the day of the Choosing Ceremony all the tireless tolling could be for naught? It will come down to the Trident and the Ursela shell. One will choose *you*, and not the other way around. If the shell picks you, it will grant you its power. You will become the Royal Alchemist, resigned to a life of science … *and magic.*"

A noose of fear tightened around my throat, choking me with its looming threat. The all too vivid memory of my mother's reanimated corpse flashed behind my eyes.

"That *can't* happen." Forcing the words through my constricted throat, I turned tail and kicked for Atlantica. But it was too late. Alastor had seen the tears of fear welling in my eyes at the prospect of such an abysmal fate.

# CHAPTER TWO

*I* couldn't tell when you came in if you actually were a pauper, or just had some sort of aversion to mirrors and good taste. Regardless, I should give you a bit of backstory on the politics of Atlantica so you can follow along. As I have made abundantly clear, my father was the king and held ultimate rule over the seas. Even so, like any quality leader, he needed trusted advisors to help him see various sides of the issues Atlantica faced. To keep matters as fair as possible, one representative was chosen from each of the Seven Seas; the Gulf, Arctic, Caribbean, Indian, Mediterranean, Atlantic, and Pacific. By the votes of their own people, these select seven were chosen to sit on the Council of the King. They were an intricate part of our government ... and were surfing my last nerve with their tardiness. The Summit Room couldn't be opened to Triton and me until all of them arrived, and some stragglers had yet to make their appearance. Therefore, we were being dragged through the same tour of the Temple of the Kings that we, and every other child of Atlantica, had been subjected to every year since our first schooling. That said, I took my role as princess and future queen seriously. With my hands folded behind my back and my posture stiff and regal, I floated behind our guide, listening intently to historic tales I could have recited by memory.

"This is Thetis, of the twelfth empire," the records keeper, a reed-thin merman with a hook nose and overbite which rivaled that of a swordfish, explained in a monotone cadence sure to cure insomnia. "She followed her grandmother, Tethys, to the throne.

She was sculpted in wedding attire from the day she married the notorious war hero, Peleus. It is said the jubilance of that day radiated so far and wide, it created the first red sunset human sailors now gauge the weather upon. Positioned at the foot of Thetis you will see an exceptionally oversized pearl. Legend says Thetis was gifted that pearl on the eve of her wedding by the gods of Mt. Olympus. Each laid their hands upon the precious stone and bestowed upon it a glimmer of their power. It was believed the artifact would grant a surplus of magic to whomever possessed it. As queen, Thetis so feared its power, and the threat of it falling into the wrong hands, that she commanded it be protected by guards at all times and *never* touched. Now, it or a replica there of, sits here for us all to appreciate. And we're moving on! We're swimming. We're swimming." Curling his fingers, he swam backward and motioned for us to follow. At the foot of the next statue, he spun around to gaze up at it like a familiar old friend. "And we're stopping."

From behind me I heard a muffled snort of laughter. Let me state up-front I didn't want to look back. I knew nothing good would come of it. That being said, my doofus of a brother was behind me. If I had learned *anything* growing up with him, it was that it was better to risk a glance than to be hit in the back of the head by whatever trouble he had stirred up. Pulling up short, I glanced back in time to see Triton pluck the giant pearl from the foot of the Thetis statue.

Tossing it up with one hand, he caught it with the other, and offered me a toothy grin. "Hey," he whispered, flipping the pearl onto the back of his hand, he let it roll up his arm and onto his back, "do you think I can roll this into the Hall of Records from here? There's quite an angle at the archway, but if I put the right spin on it—"

"*Triton, no!*" I hissed through my teeth, my head whipping in the direction of our guide.

If he had heard anything he didn't let on, but continued his well-rehearsed spiel without interruption. "Here we have Pontus, who was *quite* a character during his reign!"

"*Put it down before you break something!*" I demanded in an urgent whisper, my hands balling into tight fists at my sides.

"This is fragile?" Triton asked, momentarily frozen. Flaxen brows rocketed into his hairline, his face a mask of mock innocence. "Then, I *really* shouldn't do this."

Letting the pearl roll down his spine and onto his tail, he gave it a bump with his fin and flipped it over his head.

Diving to catch it, a yelp escaped my parted lips. The second the pearl settled into my waiting palms, a warmth I hadn't expected radiated over my skin in relentless waves. My fingers — sliding over the flawlessly smooth surface — prickled, a shiver of awareness shuddering through me.

Righting myself, I gaped in Triton's direction with bulging eyes. "Did … did you feel that?"

"*Princess Vanessa!*" our guide snapped. Appearing over my shoulder, he glared down his dorsal fin of a nose at me. "Perhaps you could put down the *priceless work of art*, and repeat back to me what I just said?"

With a dutiful nod, I returned the pearl to its rightful place. Stone scraped over the treasured jewel as I situated it back into the shallow cavity Triton had plucked it from. Cold, as cutting as that of the sea's most formidable depths, bit into the morrow of my bones the instant I released my hold on the artifact.

"Actually, sir —" Swimming forward, Triton attempted to do the noble thing and fess up.

If I didn't think it would land him in a boiling spring of trouble he couldn't handle, I may have let him speak. Instead, I caught him by the elbow and pushed him behind me.

"Shut up, Triton," I commanded. My stare flicked passed the tour guide to formulate my best guess of which statue he had stopped at. Flicking my tongue over my bottom lip, I began, "Well, sir, you were introducing us to King Pontus. It is said that he personified the sea more than any other king or queen before him, or since. As a fierce leader he could embody the most dangerous elements of the oceans. Yet he was still a just and kindly leader, like the lapping sea on a calm day. Rumor has it he became so enraptured by the sea, that he never found a true love of his own. He never married. Never had children. Such things were impossible when he felt his soul mate was the essence of Mother Ocean herself."

The guide simply stared, blinking his astonishment.

"Was that right?" I asked, knowing full well that it was. Catching the end of my braid, I twirled it around my finger. "I could work on my execution for next time."

"*Nessa*," Triton tried to interrupt.

Unfortunately, this ball of sass was on a roll.

"Maybe I should juggle?" I ventured at the expense of the aghast guide. "Make it a bit … showier."

"*Vanessa!*" my father boomed from the expansive archway behind me. "*Apologize at once!*"

My gusto washed out like a riptide, the cause for Triton's dire warning suddenly blazingly obvious. I didn't try to argue, didn't omit a peep of protest. Chin dropping to my chest, I mumbled a brief apology to the guide. Turning to my father, my entire body tensed in anticipation of his fury. Triton edged in closer, offering support in the simple form of his arm brushing mine. My only saving grace? Poseidon had an audience, and in the eyes of his people he always strove to appear considerate and kind.

Pulling himself up to full, menacing height, Poseidon tipped his head and glared me down from under his brow. "This is *my* palace. Gillian is a member of *my* court, not yours. I shall *never* hear you speak to anyone within my kingdom with such blatant disrespect. Is that clear?"

Something within me wilted in upon itself, like a land plant deprived of the sun. "Yes, Father," I croaked, blinking back the hot rush of tears that stung behind my eyes.

Father nodded as if appeased. "It would serve you well to follow your brother's lead in what is *acceptable* conduct. For now, you shall conclude your tour here. With our thanks to you, Gillian," the king nodded to our tour guide, who dipped in a respectful bow in return, "the Atlantic representative has finally arrived and we are about to call the Council to order."

Heart aching, I hung back for a pause, catching Triton's hand as he swam past to follow Father out.

Eagerly he spun, his apology already forming on his lips. "I'm so sorry! You didn't have to take the blame for me!"

Stare locked on our father's retreating back, I batted his words away with a flick of my wrist. "We'll talk about that later. I fully intend to put a poisonous jellyfish in your bed tonight. But the pearl, Triton, did you feel anything when you touched it?"

Triton's lips screwed to the side as he considered it. "Cold, kinda slimy, heavy ..."

"Dig a little deeper, simpleton. No tingling warmth, like touching an electric eel, only *nicer*?"

Clapping a hand on my shoulder, Triton pulled me closer and pressed his forehead to mine. "Maybe that was the thrill of doing the first fun thing in your life. It'll be less jarring if you don't space those moments out as much."

Laughing, I shoved him away with more force than necessary. Triton fell into a back roll then kicked off after Father, jerking his head for me to follow. I paused for a beat, casting a quick glance back at the pearl. The once still stone had come alive, swirls of opalescent color dancing within it. Curling my hands into fists tight enough to slice half-moons in my palms, I fought off a pull—almost magnetic—to reunite my twitching fingertips with its hypnotic pulse. Its glow beckoned in a siren song for me alone.

From my first trip to the Temple of the Kings, I had always figured King Pontus to be mad for his romantic feelings for the ocean. I mean, it was a *thing*; it could never reciprocate that affection. Then, I entered the Summit Room. If the Summit Room was a person, I would have written our names in the sand with a big heart around them. I would've waited in the hall to stage an accidental encounter where I flipped my hair and batted my eyes coquettishly. I would've ... well, I think you get the idea.

It wasn't a particularly impressive space—modest in size and sparing in decoration—yet power and purpose dripped from the walls. Triton and I sat in the second row of the two lines of seating which circled the perimeter. Massive columns separated the spectators from those with position and prestige. Golden Angler fish had been carved into each column, the lures that bulged from their heads irradiated by luminescent plankton. In the center of the room, a stately stone table spouted from the earth like a massive whale's tail. Eight high-backed thrones were situated around it, none as elegant or kingly as that of Poseidon's.

Perched on the edge of my seat, I listened intently while the dignitaries from each of the Seven Seas discussed Atlantica's ongoing battle against the humans.

"The cargo we have claimed from the humans' sunken ships has furthered the way of life for *all* of us," the Indian Sea representative stated. Humbly covered from neck to tail fin in the customary black garb of his people, he exhibited their desire to showcase the strength of their minds over that of their physique.

"Be that as it may ..." The enchanting, olive-skinned specimen from the Mediterranean Sea leaned over the table in his direction, granting him an eyeful of her bountiful curves. Blushing ferociously, the Indian Sea rep snapped his head in the other direction. The Mediterranean beauty flipped silken black locks over her shoulder with a winning smile. "... we have neither the resources nor the soldiers to launch attacks to sink ships for their booty as some of our brother seas have." Glancing in Poseidon's direction, she raised one brow. "Surely, you don't mean to make such acts *mandatory* to ensure a place at this table?"

Father didn't respond, but leaned back in his chair; one arm folded over his broad chest, the opposite hand stroking the length of his thick beard.

The representative from the Pacific rested his elbows on the stone table, the intensity of his stare could have bore holes through Miss Mediterranean if such a thing was possible. "If the rest of us are risking the lives of our own people for the cause, wouldn't it only be fair for your district to act in turn? That is, if you still want the combined protection and good favor of the entire brethren."

His people viewed various forms of self-mutilation as signs of strength and valor. Squid ink tattoos, bones or sharks teeth embedded in their skin; these things were the norm within their community. The Pacific delegate represented his culture with the thin bone fragments fished through both his cheeks, jagged teeth of a Great White protruding from each end. The way they twitched when he spoke made each word seem a viable threat. The majority of the soldiers in the Royal Guard could be traced back to the Pacific, their panache for teaching various forms of combat from the day of hatching could be thanked for that.

Bone white hair swept down the back of the representative from the Arctic like an avalanche, a headdress of icy crystals fixed across her head like a crown. The sharp cut of her cheek bones and pointed chin were a customary trait among her people, a physical attribute that seemed to warn of their bitterly harsh personalities. Steepling her fingers beneath her chin, the water chilled by roughly ten degrees the moment she spoke. "And what of those of us who have a thick ceiling of ice between ourselves and the ships? They use tools to chip away the ice and allow their ships passage. Tools *we* do not possess. How would you have us combat that obstacle?"

Beside me, Triton folded in half with a *humph* of boredom. Catching one of the shells dangling from the bottom hem of my gown, he pulled the strand back and let it fall into place, connecting with the other shells in a series of muted claps and clicks. I slapped his hand away, not bothering to tear my gaze from the scene unfolding.

Only then did the russet-skinned mer from the Caribbean, who had been listening intently with her chin to her chest and her hands folded in her lap, tip her head and gaze up at the others from under a wild array of sun-bleached, twisted braids. The gleam in her eyes could be described only as conniving, bordering on predatory. "The Caribbean Sea has the highest population of mer. Our bounty of soldiers and potential soldiers is plentiful. I would *happily* send troops to assist any district requiring them ... for fifty percent of the bounty claimed."

Father's face remained a mask of neutrality. "That fifty percent share customarily goes to the king," he stated, his tone calm and bordering on disinterest." You would have *me*, the patriarch of the Seven Seas, take a smaller cut than that a serving dignitary from the Caribbean of all places?"

"A dignitary with the resources to bring down ships where others cannot," she practically purred. "A fraction of a ship's hold is better than full claim to an empty hold. You know more than anyone, my liege, that you can't get something for nothing. I need to be compensated for risking the lives of my mer."

With the knuckle of his index finger pressed to his top lip, Father nodded his understanding and appreciation. He seemed on the verge of reaching a decision—be it good, bad, or indifferent— when the braided kelp curtains to the Summit Room were forced aside in a rustling of foliage. Father bolted from his throne, the rest of the room respectfully following his lead.

"My wife?" His voice rose at the end of his acknowledgment ever so slightly, making it more of a question. Not that anyone could blame him for his confusion. The newly crowned queen used her magic to glamour her appearance and never wore the same façade twice. No one willing or able to speak of it had ever gazed upon her true face—that they knew of. It was public knowledge that she considered such a revelation the *ultimate* act of vulnerability.

I suppose I should offer a bit of backstory here. My father went through the Choosing Ceremony alongside his brother, Hades, just as I would with Triton. The Trident chose Poseidon, the Ursela Shell selected Hades. The brothers served the kingdom alongside each other for years. Then, for reasons my young mind couldn't begin to decipher, dear Uncle Hades requested a new assignment in another realm. It was shortly after my mother's funeral that he took my face in his hands, kissed my forehead, mumbled a brief apology, and said his good-byes. Did I miss him? Yes. Did I blame him for leaving? No. I was certain my father's obstinate streak had something to do with the rapid departure. For years the kingdom was without the services of an alchemist, the search for a worthy replacement dragging on. At the time I was not privy to the talks and negotiations. I learned, along with the rest of the kingdom, that a marriage had been arranged to an heir from one of the most magically inclined blood lines under the sea. Her name was Amphrite, and I had only shared the same space with her a handful of times: the day the announcement of their betrothal was made to the kingdom, their wedding—which redefined extravagance, her coronation day—that managed to make the wedding look tame, and this very moment.

Each and every time, she had appeared as a completely different person.

Her current guise made a wry smile curl across my face. "Brilliant," I marveled, and slapped Triton's hand away from my dangling shells once again.

In a room full of self-serving negotiations and ulterior motives, she was the vision of innocence. Hair, the beguiling pink hue of Harbour Island, flowed around her in mesmerizing waves. Her bra was compromised of the most delicate looking Lion's Paw shells I had ever seen. Eyes, the warm, welcoming shade of the ocean on a clear day, sparkled sweetly as she batted impossibly long lashes at her husband. Squinting to get a better look, I noticed that the shape of her eyes was a touch too wide, and a bit too round to pass for natural. That was just another fine detail of her costume thought out to make her appear the virtuous damsel.

One flip of her golden tail propelled her into the room.

Addressing her king and Council, she curled one shoulder in a deliberately coy fashion. "You started the meeting without me. How disappointing not to be included."

"She should wear that every day," Triton sighed dreamily, suddenly upright and attentive.

Nose crinkling, I shot him a disgusted grimace. "She beds your father. Stop being gross and … go back to playing with the shells or something."

"There was no insult intended," Poseidon replied, dipping his head in a gesture of apology. "We were deliberating over the seven districts sinking passing ships in order to claim their bounty. Do you have anything to add, my Queen?"

Nodding her head as she mulled over the matter, pink curls bobbed up around her flawless face. "Wasn't it humans who killed your first queen?" she asked, batting her lashes.

Father flicked his tailfin once, the only visible sign of discomfort at the sensitive topic, and jerked his chin for the lot of us to be seated. "You know that to be true."

"Yet you wish to intensify our current war by sinking their ships and stealing their wares?" Amphrite tipped her head and twirled one lock of hair around her forefinger.

Members of the Council exchanged tight-lipped scowls at the queen's expense. She was new. She was flighty. She was young. What could she possibly know? I couldn't understand how it was that they failed to see the challenge in her stare as she peered in my father's direction. It reminded me of a circling shark, bumping its prey to test it before the attack.

"In turn," Amphrite continued, "they will seek us out and kill any of our kind they can find. And for what? Treasure we have no real need for that will rot on the ocean floor in heaps of once sparkling baubles? That hardly seems worth the lives of our people."

"It actually makes a lot of sense," the representative from Atlantic agreed, eliciting a groan from the other members. Midnight blue hair faded to turquoise, turquoise to sea foam, as her waist-length strands stretched down her back. Squid ink blended with purple sea flowers lined her dark eyes with dramatic violet swirls.

Atlantic mer possessed a flair for the flamboyant I could appreciate. They wore their hair and make-up in every conceivable color, and designed extravagant clothes that made my mouth water. Still, their panache for costuming had earned them a reputation of being erratic and unreliable within the Council.

"I couldn't agree more," the representative from the Gulf chimed in. Shirtless and rippling in the all the right places, he leaned forward with his elbows on the table. The glow of the lights glistened off his sun-kissed skin. "Our culture is a deeply rooted tree that shields and protects us. It makes us who we are. We needn't bring in items from the outside world when we have all that we need here, under the sea."

Around the table lips twitched, stares were deliberately averted, yet no one else risked speaking for or against their king *or* the newly placed queen and Royal Alchemist.

Fighting off boredom, Triton had returned to messing with the seaweed strands of my gown. Sneakily as he could, he attempted to braid them tight around my tail in hopes I'd flop to the ocean floor the second I rose from my chair. Absentmindedly, I shoved him away and kicked the braided strands free. Returning the act of sibling love, he pushed me back hard enough to knock me off my seat.

"Vanessa," my father's head whipped in my direction—the potency of his glower froze me mid-scramble back to my chair, "did you have something to add?"

Glancing in the opposite direction, Triton casually rubbed one hand over the back of his neck. "Don't say anything," he quietly coached.

Swallowing hard, I stalled for time. "No, Father, I—"

"Can't be bothered to pay attention?" Poseidon finished for me, with an accusatory sneer.

"Ah, crap," Triton grumbled. His head fell, forehead slapping against the cradle of his palm.

Straightening my spine, I pulled myself up to my full, unimpressive height. "Please excuse my clumsiness, Father, but rest assured I absolutely *was* listening. Enough to state that I agree with Queen Amphrite." If I really did, I couldn't say. Desire to come out against *him* spurred the words from my lips before I had time to weigh their full consequence. "Our way of life existed long before we began pilfering wayward ships. We can do without such extravagances."

"Says the spoiled princess," Fleet Master Neleus scoffed. Many a mermaid throughout the kingdom would be giddy at the prospect of the golden Adonis of the Royal Guard acknowledging them in any way. *That* was my first actual interaction with him. Political goals aside, the guy was the slimy underside of a Hagfish.

"You disagree with the princess's views?" Father ventured. Pivoting his upper body, he addressed Neleus and Doralious, the Command Master that flanked him, with interest.

"Yes, Your Majesty, I do," Neleus stated. Clasping his hands behind his back, his bulging pectorals flexed. "It's my opinion that if the princess ever hopes to find a mate, she should realize that in Atlantica it's she who holds her tongue that gets a man."

A scalding current of embarrassment flooded my face. Biting the inside of my cheek hard enough to taste a rush of coppery warmth, I mentally willed my father to come to my defense. To scold and belittle the commoner who *dared* speak to the princess of Atlantica in such a way.

The silence of the king was deafening.

It was Doralious who countered on my behalf. While his rigid posture matched that of Neleus, his features were warmer, and far more welcoming. "That seems to be primitive thinking for a man that could be beached at that same maiden's command. It may serve you well, Fleet Master, to remember she could be the future ruler of Atlantica. Although I would enjoy stepping into your position when you're demoted to a stable hand."

His gaze flicked my way for a moment, to cast me a conspiratorial wink and smile.

At the snickers which bubbled through the room, Neleus rolled his shoulders. The tendons of his neck straining in annoyance. "The day you replace me is the day I voluntarily beach myself."

"And what of you, Triton?" Father inquired. Ignoring the verbal sparring of his soldiers, he lifted one brow at his treasured boy. "What say you on this matter?"

Clenching the edge of his stone seat in a death grip, Triton's head snapped up. "I ... *uh* ... agree with the Council majority, and you, Father."

*Such* a tail polisher.

While I was certain he had no idea what the conversation had actually been about, his dismissive answer was enough to make father's chest puff with pride. *"That's my boy!* Willing to make the hard choices to preserve the way of life for his people! Aye, Neleus?"

"That he is, Your Majesty," Neleus agreed. Swimming around the edge of the table, he peered up at Triton with a smug smile. "Exhibiting insight and intuition such as that, it is my honor to offer *you* the apprenticeship with the Royal Guard, Prince Triton."

Black swirls tinged the corners of my vision, my pulse roaring in my temples.

My dream.

My studying.

My training ... all dissipating like a stirred up dust cloud.

It was my own fault. If I hadn't disagreed with Father; if I was capable of holding my tongue— *No!* Raising my chin slowly, I watched Father give Doralious a jovial elbow to the ribs before clasping forearms with Neleus in a handshake of brotherly solidarity.

Four words from their muted conversation floated my way, spearing my heart. "... *mustn't ascend the throne.*"

I may have thought I imagined the exchange, had Doralious not picked that moment to peer my way. His features clouded by a blend of regret and pity.

*Nothing* about this had been spontaneous. Father had decided whom *he* wanted to get that position long before any of us entered the room. To my great regret, it had *never* been me.

# Chapter Three

The second we were dismissed from the meeting, I swam from the decomposing corpse of my fallen dream as fast as my fins could carry me. The Temple of Kings passed in a blur, the novelty of seeing the Hall of Records all but forgotten. Fighting off tears, I kicked through the throne room with my chin to my chest. The only thing that could make this day worse in my mind would have been for my moment of such extreme vulnerability to be viewed by the servants or milling members of the court. Diamonds of light danced over my skin as I burst from the castle's gold-etched grand entrance. Working my hips rapidly side to side, I tore down the pillar-lined entryway until it spat me out in the middle of the bustling town square.

Weaving between bodies, I forced my way through the crowd. While each of the Seven Seas had its own distinct customs and styles, all were represented in the melting pot of Atlantica. I dodged around one merman, who had blended the easy, natural style of the Gulf district with a fish-bone barb pierced through his eyebrow like those of the Pacific. Ducking past a lass with flowing fuchsia locks, I noticed with little interest she had swirled the extravagant Atlantic flair with the contradictory stoic fashions of the Indian Sea. Barely keeping my threatening tears in check, I paused to let a dreadlocked mermaid holding the hand of her snowy-haired beau pass.

From behind me I faintly heard Triton holler my name over the buzz of the crowd. I could've talked to him like a mature, well-adjusted member of the royal family, *or* I could forego manners and shove my way through the sea of bodies with no consideration to the well-being of others. I went for the later.

Outside the heart of the kingdom, through the coral gardens, my belly skimmed along the ocean floor as I plunged into the abyss of the deeper waters where light dare not venture. A few quick blinks and my burning, red-rimmed eyes adjusted to the darkness. Where I was headed, I didn't know. My only goal was to swim the pain away … if such a feat was possible.

I only slowed when a stitch in my side made doing so a necessity. With two fingers, I pushed back against the cramp, bending in half to steady my rapidly fluttering gills. A quick glance around and I was struck with the realization that I had ventured farther into the chasm than I ever had before. Poseidon's unlimited rule was the propaganda he boasted for all to hear. But here, in the depths, a far different truth existed. One where the biggest fish, with the sharpest teeth, reigned. In that moment I dared the worst of them to come. No physical damage could compare to that of my shattered hopes … or so my sheltered little mind thought.

Breath coming in rapid pants, I forced myself upright and turned in a slow circle. Down the ridge from me laid the yawning maw of a cave. It was dark. It was foreboding. And it beckoned to me in a truly ominous way I simply couldn't resist.

Glancing in one direction, then the other, I half-expected a reasonable minded adult to materialize and warn me away. When no such rationale argument was interjected, I set my jaw and swam straight into the pitch-black cavern. The rush of the forbidden altered the nervous drumming of my heart into an alluring chorus that spurred me on. The stagnant stench of mildew welcomed me to the primitive grotto. Creeping inside, I skirted between the looming stalagmites which dangled like ravenous fangs. Prickles of foreboding awareness awoke, dancing up and down my spine. The rising hair on the back of my neck warned I wasn't alone. Something lurked in the shadows … and I longed to look it in the eyes.

Deeper still, I slunk. The farther I wandered, the more enthralled I became by this forbidden world forgotten by Father's confining reach. Inch by wicked inch I ventured into the hollow. The spell of the unknown was broken by the snap of hungry jaws followed by the cold slap of a slimy tail against my hip.

Frozen by fear, my head slowly swiveled toward the cave's *other* inhabitant.

The shimmer of light that managed to filter through the blackness illuminated the silver silhouette of a hungry barracuda.

Self-preservation *should* have kicked in and sent me rocketing from the cave in a blur of elbows and tailfins. And it probably would have ... had my gaze not flicked to the two wriggling baby zebra sharks left behind in an otherwise ravaged nest. The rest of the family was most likely somewhere in the digestive tract of the carnivorous fish.

Before I could even think to swim away, the predatory beast turned on me in a blur of fins and teeth. My hands rose defensively, every muscle in my body tensed for the moment those jagged jaws sank into my flesh. Magic was *not* my intention. Knowing of its horrifying side effect, it never was. Even so, green shimmering tendrils instinctively licked from my fingertips in the same type of fear response in which others would simply shudder or cringe. The rampaging fish was reduced to a defenseless clam that collapsed to the ocean floor and bounced twice before settling into the sand.

In a perfect world that would've been the end of it. Crisis averted. Unfortunately, the icy quivers wafting up from tail to brow whispered that the worst was yet to come. Body convulsing in terrified tremors, I crumbled to the ground, curling my fins to my chest. Cocooning myself with my arms, I tried to block out the nightmare that *always* came next.

"*Vaaaanessa.*" Stale breath, reeking of decay, assaulted my cheek.

"*No! Go away!*" I forced the words through chattering teeth, the sea swallowing each tear that slipped passed my tightly squeezed lids.

"*My sweeeeeet girl,*" the gravelly version of my mother's voice, made raspy by death's rough touch, murmured. Something cold and coarse stroked the back of my head, tangling in the loose strands of my hair. "*I only wish to care for you.*"

A choked sob caught in my throat, leaking out in a plaintive whimper. "Please. *Please,* just leave me alone."

"*My baby ... left all alone with no one to protect her tender heart.*"

Swallowing hard, I pried one eye open to risk a peek around my arm. The once exquisite Queen of Atlantica knelt beside the remnants of the egg casings the sharks hatched from. Fingers, gnawed to knobby bone, gently stroked the backs of the orphaned pair of hatchlings. Bones creaking, she gradually turned my way.

For a moment my gills clamped shut with fright.

Vacant amethyst eyes provided a startling contrast to her putrefied, ashen complexion. Decayed flesh dangled from her perfectly sculpted cheekbones, exposing the time-rotted teeth beneath. Black hair rode the current around her face, each roll granting glimpses of festered patches where hair had fallen away to reveal bare skull beneath.

"*Just like* them." Stare shifting back to the sharks, she considered them with a tilt of her head. "*You need friends, my darling girl, and they need protection.*"

Sea bugs skittered out of a slash in her cheek and reentered through her ear canal, causing bile to scorch up the back of my throat. My churning stomach made averting my eyes a necessity. I chose the shark babies as my visual safe haven. There was no denying they were newly hatched. Their scrawny black hides, dotted with white spots, were barely the length of my palm. Mother was right, left to their own devices they didn't stand a chance. Without help, they would be a meal to some passing creature before night fell.

Biting my lower lip hard enough to experience a bark of pain, I shook my head in hopes of waking from that dismal reality. "No, I can't. If I help them …"

The words trailed off, some part of my whirring mind still afraid to offend my long dead parent.

Mother sank back on her tail, hands folding in her lap in a chorus of snaps and creaks of putrefied tendons. "*If you use your magic to help them, my presence will linger. And, in your mind, that is the worst fate of all.*"

"You … aren't supposed to be here," I stated in place of an explanation, my tone a blend of apology and fear. When dealing with an entity that, if angered, could rip her face off and throw it at me, the importance of manners and conduct seemed crucial.

"*And* you *aren't supposed to fear what you are.*" Head snapping in my direction, accusation narrowed her eyes to deadly slits. "*Magic is a part of who you are, just as it was for me. Deny* it *and you deny yourself.*"

"I–I can't." Face crumpling, my eyes pleaded with the ghoul for a bit of understanding.

"*Vanessa*," with a lift of her chin, she glared down the bridge of her upturned nose, "*do you wish for me to become cross?*" Voice eerily hollow of emotion, the underlying threat was potently inferred.

Suppressing a whimper by clamping my teeth on the meat of my palm, my breath came in ragged pants. Seeing no other alternative, I reluctantly waved one hand toward the sharks.

Tiny bodies jerked, vibrated, and began to swell. I didn't grant them an abundance of size or maturity, just enough for them to handle themselves in that area of volatile sea.

Two little heads poked over the edge of the rocky were they huddled, their mouths slightly agape as if they had just finished a snarky punchline and were awaiting my guffaw. Despite my macabre companion, an almost smile tugged at the corners of my lips, prompted by their sweet faces. The sharks responded with giddy appreciation. Fervently snapping their whip-like tails they darted my way as fast as they were able, their frames now measured about the length of my arm from wrist to elbow. Their gracious thank you came in the form of one coiling around my neck while the other brushed his clammy hide against my cheek.

"*Yessss*," Mother purred, the intensity of her gaze making me even more leery of her intent. "*Your new friends need names to make them ... real. To make them allies.*"

With the sharks twining their way up my arms, my thoughts ventured to the accident that stole my mother from me. The unfortunate catastrophe which robbed her of life and beauty, and left behind that deteriorating form with skin drooping below her left eye to expose a bony socket and strings of tendons.

Two separate pirate ships, with their cannons thundering and crew plundering, were oblivious to the regal merqueen paddling beneath their ongoing battle. She was departing the island of Lemuria where she visited frequently on diplomatic missions of goodwill — or so I had been told for years. The swashbucklers were so distracted by the severity of their battle that they had no clue a member of mer royalty struggled for life beneath them. She found herself trapped between a rocky crest and the sternpost of one of the ships. Her cries for help went unheard. Her final gasps were drowned out by the petty scuffles of air breathing *filth* that weren't worthy to bow before her, much less snuff the life from a beloved noble. Yet while they and their ships ventured off into the horizon, Queen Titonis was reduced to a rotting pile of parts that would plague her eldest offspring by simply existing. Her life could have been spared by one careening canon ball striking at that pivotal moment.

A scattering of floating wreckage and cast off cargo would have equated one treasured life …

"Floteson and Jetteson," I murmured, my voice cracking with emotion.

The young sharks squeezed my arms in a delicate embrace of approval.

"Are you okay?" a meek voice inquired from behind me.

At the sound of the intruder, Floteson and Jetteson darted behind the nearest boulder, peeking out in the interest of self-preservation.

Mother sucked in a shocked breath that reeked of sorrow and decay. Her crumbling hands clasped over her long-stilled heart. *"My boy, look at how handsome he's become."*

My own fear and well-being fell clear out of my head. Bolting off the ground, I cruised straight for my brother, needing nothing else in the world except him out of there. *"Get out of here, Triton!"* I yelled in a tone as sharp as a blade's edge. "You should've taken the hint I didn't want company when I ignored your incessant shouts in the courtyard!"

"I was worried about you. I didn't want you to be alone—"

"Even though that's *exactly* what I want?" I snapped.

The pain that etched itself into his features would have squeezed my heart in a constricting fist, had our mother not picked that moment to close the gap between her and her unsuspecting son. I cursed my own weak inadequacies for not toughing out the horrific aspects of her jarring spirit to learn more about her. I didn't even know if she could *actually* harm anyone. What I *did* know was that I had no intention of acquiring that knowledge at my brother's expense. Bristling as her clawed hand rose, I recoiled at the seemingly loving gesture of her gnarled knuckle tracing over his jawline.

Taking another approach, I softened my tone to a nurturing hush. "Triton, I beg of you. Leave … *please*."

Crossing his scrawny arms over his bowed chest, Triton shimmied on the obstinate smirk of pre-pubescent wickedness. "Or *what*? I'm not afraid of you, Vanessa."

A normal day, a passing fancy, and I would have used my sass to cut him to the bone until he turned tail and fled. Such a thing wasn't even taxing. I knew all his deep dark secrets: like he still sucked his thumb during thunderstorms, and he was terrified of blowfish because I once told him they only inflated after sucking the soul from a nearby mer. Be that as it may, I didn't have it in me to snip and exchange words. My only goal was to spare him from the poltergeist that could turn on us *both* at any moment.

Flicking my tongue over my bottom lip, I did the best impression of someone unphased and unaffected as I could muster. "If the only kind of help you came to offer is mulish drivel and a nasty attitude, I'll decline. Thank you."

"You don't need to be harsh," Triton countered, his face folding into a pout.

Mother's face had morphed into a flare of such hatred it made my pulse pound with terror for him.

"*My baby boy,*" leaning in, she breathed him in with a deep inhale—the unsuspecting Triton batted at the water beside him as if shooing away a bothersome shrimp, "*it pains me to see so much of his loathsome father in him.*"

"It's not *my* fault that things didn't go your way today," he continued. "*I* want to play with manatees and you—"

"*Need* to become the next ruler of Atlantica," a sharp female voice interjected from the cavity of the cave entrance.

Triton and I spun to found Queen Amphrite leaning one shoulder against the jagged cave wall, her opposite hand jabbed onto her hip.

Sucking water through her teeth, Mother withdrew from Triton's side as if she had suddenly been scalded. Tilting her head, she exposed a gaping wound oozing with brown sludge.

"*Atlantica's replacement queen,*" she mused through blackened gums and browning teeth. "*I would despise her if I didn't view her only as little more than next victim of Poseidon's false promises and twisted sense of affection.*"

I wanted my brother out for the sake of his own well-being, and instead we were drawing a crowd. As heroic endeavors went, this one was a disaster.

Oblivious to the criticisms from the beyond, Amphrite lifted one brow at Triton in candid indifference. "Leave," she stated, in a tone that left no room for discussion.

Mouth opening and shutting, he stammered, "I-I was just t-trying to—"

One delicate hand raised to halt him. "Don't care. Didn't ask. Get out."

Mother's cracked lips curled back in a predatory snarl. "*Pink hair, an overabundance of skin, and she dares to speak to my child that way? The things I would do to her if she wasn't Poseidon's bride. That in itself is a cruel enough fate … for now.*"

Grateful for the assist, I nodded my encouragement to Triton that he should obey the reigning queen.

Reluctantly, he turned to leave, gazing back with the protruding lower-lip of a pitiful-guppy. He wanted me to change my mind, of that I was well aware. However, considering I was riding high on a tidal wave of relief at that growing distance between him and our corpse mom, any sort of interjection would *not* be happening. Dejected, he hung his head and paddled from the cave's mouth, undoubtedly to linger nearby.

A heavy silence swelled in his absence. Amphrite flitted around the perimeter of the cavernous space, inspecting it with what seemed to be genuine appreciation. Mother matched her kick for kick, stroke for stroke, always positioning herself between the new queen and myself. While still a notably uneasy situation, my inner protective beast had been satiated by Triton's departure. It was far less stressful knowing I could freak out accordingly. I'm not too proud to admit I fully intended to leave Amphrite to fend for herself if Mother so much as said boo in an untoward tone.

Swallowing hard, I shattered the crushing hush. "If the purpose of you tailing me was to suggest I pursue becoming queen, you should know I've written of nothing else in my private scrolls since I was four years old. Unfortunately, that particular dream died this very day. I believe you were there for its execution."

"I saw nothing that should diminish your hopes or aspirations in the slightest." Amphrite's dainty fingertips brushed over a notched-out section in the cave wall. She rubbed the algae collected by the swipe away with the pad of her thumb. "That said, your little outburst made it appear as if seeking your father's approval is of greater importance to you than that gilded trident."

"*I may smite her just for the fun of it.*" Mother's pointed, gray tongue pressed against her top teeth, as if envisioning exactly where she would begin her games.

Hitching one brow, I contemplated encouraging her sport. Thinking better of it, I crinkled my nose and bitterly deadpanned, "If you had known my father longer than a moon cycle, you would know the throne would be easier to attain than his good favor."

"So target the easier mark ... and claim it," Amphrite countered, letting one slender shoulder rise and fall in a casual shrug.

"*Infuriating little ambergris.*" Spinning on me, Mother's irises dilated to manic, black pits of carnage. "*Let me talk you through how to disembowel her. You'll find the process therapeutic.*"

"Maybe another time."

"Pardon?" Pink brows pinched in confusion.

Clearing my throat, I forced an awkward smile. "Catch in my throat. Apologies, Your Majesty. What I meant to say was, with all due respect, Triton received the apprenticeship with the Royal Guard. If you know your Atlantica history, you are aware that the last *eight* rulers have—"

The darkness morphed Amphrite's hair to a violet veil which fanned around her angelic face. "Apprenticed with the Royal Guard. Yes, I know. But eight in a line of how many?"

"*You come from a family of glorified magic peddlers.*" Lurking behind the unsuspecting queen, the words seeped from Mother's lips in a sinister hiss. "*What could you possible know of royal matters?*"

Raising my hands, I let them slap to my sides in exasperation of the fickle moods of the living and dead. "Are you suggesting an alternative that could break the long running streak?"

Tossing her hair, Amphrite granted me a smile that would make the stars envy her sparkle. "By finding yourself a far better tutor ... namely, *me*."

I felt Mother bristle beside me. Yet before she could utter further off-color, overly descriptive commentary, I interceded on her behalf. She may have been a deteriorating shell, prone to homicidal inklings, but she was *my* deteriorating shell prone to homicidal inklings.

"Is this the part where you offer to be the mother I never had? What is it you think you could teach me? How to braid my hair and apply sea flower to my lips without any bothersome creases?"

In a blink Amphrite floated in front of me, the rush of water and bubbles from her breath tickling over my cheeks. "Your mother ended up dead on the humans' shoreline. I have no desire to be her.

I wish only to be your teacher, coach, and," the corner of her mouth curled up in a carnivorous smirk, "… *friend.*"

"And what do you hope to get in exchange for this invested time and effort?" A flap of my fin and I rose to match her in height, if for no other reason than to hint that it took more to intimidate me than a painted sea siren.

"If all goes according to plan?" Scooping the water with cupped hands, she pushed back to a less intrusive distance. "I get the ear of the queen when you take the throne."

As inconspicuously as I could, I let my stare flick to my mother.

*"Do not trust her,"* she warned. *"Such a young, vibrant beauty that agrees to a union with a man at your father's station in life has motives all her own. Mark my words, she will use you to further her own cause. No throne is worth that."*

Looking back, I had no solid proof that the putrid form haunting me actually *was* my mother—Mother Ocean knows she didn't look *or* smell like her. Even so, she made a valid point I couldn't ignore.

Raising my chin, I stared down my nose at Amphrite in the same haughty fashion I watched Poseidon address his subjects with countless times. "You have the ear of the king—among *other* things. I'm afraid you're going to have to make do with that."

"We shall see about that," Amphrite glowered, and kicked from the cave without another glance back.

# CHAPTER FOUR

My mother sang me to sleep that night. It was not the tender moment I remembered. Her jaw unhinged mid-melody and sent her scrambling to reattach it. It wasn't until the early morning sun waved down in softly waving diamonds that the lingering effects of magic wore off, and Mother faded into nothingness once more.

Heavy eyes had finally claimed sleep's sweet serenity when I was gently swatted awake by Loriana's tailfin.

"Rise and be well, Princess!" she chirped, fluttering around the room on one task or another. "We have lots to do for tonight's celebration and limited time to do it! The staff is all abuzz about the preparation details! It seems your father is determined to make this a gala unlike anything Atlantica has ever experienced before. I do wish it was *your* apprenticeship we were celebrating, along with Prince Triton's birthday. Even so, that gives us further motivation to make sure you appear the resilient, enchanting royal you are!"

"Too many ... words." Grumbling, I ground the sleep from my eyes with the heels of my hands but refused to budge from the sanctuary of my bed.

"Get a decent night's rest and mornings won't be so unbearable." Face folding in a maternal frown, she dangled a whale hide canteen in front of me to lure me from my cocoon of covers. "Fresh spring water infused with a hint of water lily ... it should chase away the drowsiness."

"Nectar of the gods," I murmured, grabbing for the much needed beverage.

Loriana, clever minx that she was, kept it just out of reach until I sat upright to seize it. Before I could flop back down, she swooped in to slather a clay mud mask under my eyes.

"Sneaky." Bringing the canteen to my lips, I shot her a sideways glance.

"You will be more than appeased when you see what I have in store for you today." Nudging me to the edge of my giant shell bed, Loriana positioned herself behind me with a basket of goodies. "I saw some kids in the square with a fun new look inspired by the Atlantic Sea mer. After a bit of conversation, and coaxing, they explained how to create it!"

"Let's make this quiet time until I get to the bottom of this canteen." Cradling the supple leather between my hands, I gazed lovingly at the soothing liquid.

"Always such a blowfish in the morning." A hint of laughter could be detected in her tone. Still, she granted me my peace.

Working in a comfortable silence, her hands flew around my head with flawless accuracy. Dividing my hair into sections, she traveled the length of it with a salve made of diluted squid ink and ground flowers. The end result was a savage, wild mane of black and fuchsia stripes. She finished her task by fixing a headband — spiked with sharks' teeth — across the crown of my head.

Turning my head one way and then other in front of my vanity mirror, I sucked in my cheeks and admired her handiwork.

"Father will hate it," I giggled. "What kind of respectable princess attire can even accompany such a bold look?"

Squeezing my shoulders, Loriana's reflection locked eyes with mine. "I have laid out a choker for you with an aquamarine stone. It's said that the gem can ward off evil spirits. You will wear that, your *stylish* headband, and a shell bra. That's it. Be *you* without apology *or* explanation. None is needed, Princess, and *don't you forget that*. Do you hear me?"

My only response was to squeeze her hand and offer her a thankful smile.

My own mother was molting, but at least I had Loriana.

Human architecture is limited by stairs, heights, and other such hindrances. Mers had no such limitations obstructing them when the Atlantica ballroom was designed. The soaring tower, perched high over the tallest point of the castle, crested over the city as a stately beacon of nobility. Every inch of surrounding wall space within it was lined with open current windows, allowing the peasants of the town to gaze up at the regal elegance that lingered out of their laboring reach.

Father spared no expense on the banquet. Two long tables overflowed with scrumptious culinary extravagance. A raw bar of shrimp, salmon, squid, and eel filled one table. The other was lined with seaweed puffs, and entrees cooked over a hot spring for the less adventurous guests. A plethora of tables filled the space to accommodate all the guests deemed worthy to attend. In the center of each sat coral candelabras illuminated by glowing sea plants which danced and waved in the day's relaxed current. Overhead, a collection of the largest sand dollars I had ever seen had been suspended from the ceiling. Rumor had it, Father sent guardsmen to scour the farthest reaches of the ocean floor in search of them. Spiraled tendrils of kelp dangled from the middle of each shell. Each masterpiece was then painted with luminescent plankton until they shimmered like live, bobbing jellyfish. The effect was stunning, if not a tad ostentatious.

As the first member of the royal family to arrive, I was immediately whisked from one pompous guest to the next. Smile fixed in place, I played my part of the demure princess impeccably, *and* suppressed each dramatic eye-roll that threatened during the frightfully dull conversations—and there were a lot of them.

That's *true* talent.

"Had it been up to me, I would have selected *you* to succeed Poseidon to the throne." Snow white lips pinched tight, the delegate from the Arctic Sea cornered me at the hors d'oeuvres table. The crab puff had been my undoing in that conversational sink hole. "With this latest development, the unlikelihood that your rule will come to pass disappointments me."

Covering my mouth with my hand, I talked around my mouthful. "My deepest apologies for letting you down."

Yes, bits of food spraying from my lips was rude. The same could be said for practically every word that came out of the emotionless, ice-mer's mouth. So, at least in that regard, I figured we were even.

"Your brother seems to be a doofus," she stated. Clasping her hands behind her back, she squared her shoulders in her usual snooty posture. "I once observed him attempting a staring contest with the tailfin eyespot of a damsel fish. They use those to fool predators and the simple-minded. It's safe to say there were no winners in *that* particular situation. This concerns me for what kind of king he would be. I anticipate him flipping a sand dollar to resolve perplexing political issues."

I wanted to argue and stick up for my brother in some way. Unfortunately, I remembered that day and how Triton pouted over his loss and what it meant for his staring abilities.

Gulping down the rest of my shrimp fritter, I tried to think of some acceptable proclamation to appease the frosty politician. Thankfully, three sharp conk shell blasts spared me from any lackluster sentiments. The trumpeters, positioned on either side of the sweeping archway, announced the king's arrival in the customary formal fashion.

I heard the sharp intakes of breath before seeing the imposing spectacle that triggered them. Normally, Father arrived to such occasions in the royal chariot pulled by four of his strongest porpoise bulls. This particular happening demanded a bit more wow factor, one that any history buff would be anticipating. Judging from the frightened squeals and panicked gasps that resonated through the ballroom, I was clearly *not* in the presence of such scholars.

In their defense, the gnashing rows of teeth that burst into the room *were* a bit off-putting. It's not every day that a massive Great White invades a formal gathering, his wide head flipping side to side in a vicious fight for freedom from Poseidon's taunt rein. The onlookers had no idea the king had spent months scouring the shallower waters off the shores of Lemuria in search of specimen docile enough to be tamed—to a certain degree—for the sole purpose of this pretentious display.

Suppressing an eye roll, I joined the applause of the startled merfolk nervously clapping their mandatory appreciation as Father rose from his over-sized Chestnut Turban shell chariot and threw his arms out wide. Tossing the reins of the gnashing shark to Neleus, Poseidon floated down to be swallowed by the tittering crowd that swelled around him. Diplomats slapped approving hands to his back; members of court bowed and curtsied in search of Poseidon's favor. The display was nauseating, really. The members of court were like well-trained porpoises, feeding off a nod or acknowledgement from their king.

Jerking at the reins, Neleus tugged the head of the snarling beast around. Only when the chariot began to lurch back toward the exit, did Triton's head poke up from where he hunkered. Face ghostly pale and glossy with sweat, he darted from the chariot and swam straight for me with the driven purpose of a land bound hurricane. Pressing my fist to my lips, I tried with little success to stifle the snort of laughter that threatened.

"The future King of Atlantica," the Arctic mer scoffed with a disgusted shake of her head. Clucking her tongue against the roof of her mouth, she swam off to avoid Triton, her silvery locks trailing out behind her.

Not that I could blame her. He was a hot mess.

Someone—*Father*—had forced him into the imperial armor of the Royal Guard. The armor, which had been designed for grown mermen who spent their days training through rigorous physical activity, hung off his scrawny physique. If I never received another gift in my life, I would have remained blissfully satisfied by the image of him in that ill-fitting garb. The walrus skull helmet sat slightly askew on his head. The mighty tusks, which protruded from the front to shield the soldier's face during battle, would find little use from Triton. Except, perhaps, if he used them to try and catch calamari rings as the night progressed. The breast plate, twice the width of Triton's narrow chest, was comprised of the shoulder blade from a Humpback Whale. Rows of walrus ribs were strung beneath that, each covered with teeth from Bull, Mako, and Great White sharks that threaded together in a lethal brand of chainmail. Odds were good that at some point he would impale, slash, or mutilate himself with his own armor.

"*He hooked the chariot to a bloody shark!*" Triton exclaimed. His bulging stare snapped over his shoulder, as if anticipating the shark sneaking up on him. "*Why? Why? Why, would he do that?*"

"Other than tradition?" A lilt of laughter fluttered through my tone, mingling with a healthy dose of mocking. "The only other motivation I can think of would be to get *this* reaction out of you. It's really quite inspiring for a potential future leader. Really, Triton, how can you be even *remotely* shocked by this? We discussed this entire spectacle in school *four moons ago!*"

*"You know I don't listen!"* he countered, his hands raising in exasperation and then falling to his sides to slap against his tail. "I doodle on my scrolls! Speaking of … did you see the starfish I sketched in the Arctic Sea headdress? He was jaunty."

Tilting my head, I considered him through narrowed eyes. "How are we not yet discussing your ensemble? I feel it demands a conversation … amongst other things."

Triton's shoulders sagged under the weight of his getup. *"Ugh,* I feel like I have a lion seal strapped to me. How do the soldiers wear this and not sink straight to the ocean floor?"

"Well, most of them have these things called muscles. Shall I tell you how to acquire them? Word of warning? You can't get them by floating with manatees. Actually, maybe you should take notes."

Rolling his eyes skyward, Triton gave me a playful shove to the shoulder with the heel of his hand. "Ha-ha. Seriously, though, truth time. On a scale of high tide to still waters, how stupid do I look in this?"

Folding one arm over my mid-section, I rested my opposite elbow just above my wrist. Raising one eyebrow, I pinched my chin between my thumb and forefinger and focused on formulating my answer with the optimum level of snark. "If a tidal wave were to—"

"Tidal wave?" Alastor interrupted. He appeared as if from nowhere, seemingly conjured by the need for further sarcasm. Balancing a serving tray on the palm of his hand, his arm brushed mine with a whisper of a touch. "I think what we have here is more of a fashion disaster perfect storm."

"During a raging tsunami," I giggled, taking great pleasure in the rosy hue that filled my brother's cheeks.

His gaze self-consciously flicked side to side in hopes no one else was looking his way.

He was a prince with a walrus skull on his head. *Of course* people were looking.

"You guys are a couple of blow-holes," he grumbled under his breath.

Letting my raised hand fall limp, I feigned a mask of aghast realization. "You know … I think we might be."

"Someone *might* question our upbringing," Alastor chuckled. Catching a lock of my hair with his free hand, he gave a gentle tug. His gaze appreciatively traveled the length of me. "Vanessa, on the other hand, is killing it tonight. You look every bit the fetching mer princess."

"Gross," Triton's face crumbled with disgust, "She's not fetching. She's my sister."

Our banter came to an abrupt halt the moment Poseidon swept over and clapped a hand on Triton's shoulder. "Alastor, need I remind you *once again* that servants are to keep a respectful distance from royals?" He sneered down his nose at our blushing friend.

Alastor yanked his hand away, his sheepish gaze cast downward. "A thousand apologies, your highness."

A snort of appreciation and Poseidon whirled Triton toward a cluster of eager guests without so much as glancing in my direction. "Come, my boy! It is time for our festivities to begin!"

"You can see me, right?" I asked, tilting my chin in Alastor's direction. "I didn't go all Demersal fish and blend with my surroundings, did I?"

"No surroundings could ever capture your beauty." Stare still locked on the shell-tiled floor beneath his fins, Alastor's blush spread to the tips of his earlobes.

Letting my head list to the side, I glanced up at him from under my lashes. "You've been listening to the Royal Guards chatting up townies in the square again, haven't you?"

Head snapping up, a stray lock of chestnut hair tangled in his lashes. "Possibly, but that doesn't make it any less true."

Staring down at my hands, my thumb fiddled with a hangnail. "I liked you standing where you were before," I admitted. Throat parched by my brazen declaration, I giggled and tagged on, "it made it easier to get to the seaweed puffs.

Huffing a wry laugh, he bumped my arm with his and offered me the tray.

"*My treasured guests!*" Poseidon shouted to be heard over the hoopla, which promptly fell into a respectful hush. "I could not be more thrilled to have you all here to celebrate with me today! Not only does my son, Triton, turn eleven years of age this day, but I also get the great honor to announce that he has been selected for the apprenticeship with *the Royal Guard!*" The excitement of his exclamation grew with each word into a grandiose crescendo that burst from the chest of the beaming king.

Merfolk, dripping in their extravagant finery, erupted in rousing cheers and heart-felt applause. Even the Arctic mer, with their emotional constipation, politely clapped. This time, I couldn't bring myself to join in. Smile fading to more of pained grimace, I watched as my now unattainable dream was paraded before me.

Adjusting the helmet which had slipped forward and blocked his eyes, Triton visibly tensed at the sight of a dozen strapping members of the guard circling his chair. Unlike my clueless brother, I knew *exactly* what was coming next, and it made the sting of rejection burn through my veins with a potency that paled to the most venomous Stonefish.

"This is a high honor drenched in tradition," with a flip of his tail, Poseidon dove into an elaborate back flip and kicked toward the wall, granting the guards and their new recruit center stage, "and that tradition begins … *now*."

His statement was punctuated by the ballroom being plunged into darkness, every light extinguished in a blink.

A wave of nervous whispers tittered through the room—understandable after the shark-infested interlude.

One light, a lowered coral candelabra braided with luminescent kelp, flickered directly overhead of where Triton had been positioned. Forced down into a chair by Doralious's firm hand, he grasped the sides in a white knuckled grip. Seizing the base of his seat, six guards hoisted an ashen-faced Triton high over their heads.

Building in a low, gruff chorus, the lot of the attending guardsmen joined their voices in on a time-honored tradition I had only ever read about:

*"To be the king Atlantica needs,*
*The ocean ye rule must first concede.*
*We, the guards of y'er chosen realm,*
*take up task to follow the helm.*
*A ruler needs courage, a ruler needs might,*
*Like the Great White, they have to fight!"*

Chair bobbing up and down as he was twirled, Triton's turquoise eyes bulged from their sockets at the mention of the ravenous fish that escorted him in. Helmet sliding off his head, it spiraled to the ground and landed with a dull lump.

*"Through a series of trials your character we'll test,*
*Be a good lad an' give it ya'r best.*
*How do we determine the strength you will wield?*
*By ya muckin' the stable, and polishin' our … shields!"*

Party goers lost in peals of laughter, the guards lowered Triton to the ground where he was further welcomed into the brotherhood with hair rufflings and pats on the back. Hovering alongside, one hand jammed on his hip, Poseidon radiated with pride. I envied the way he gazed upon his son, with the corners of his mouth twitching in his attempt to maintain his trademark stoicism. Never had he ever looked at me with anything resembling that degree of delight.

Biting my lower lip to squelch the wash of tears that burned behind my eyes, I averted my gaze to the elaborate buffet display.

"There's to be a Harvest Moon tonight."

I jerked at the sound of Alastor's voice, having spiraled so far into my own pity party that I forgot he was there.

"I've been floating here for quite some time, eating the appetizers I'm supposed to be distributing to the guests, and not a word has been said about it." Lips set in a downward C of contemplation, that brilliant servant boy offered me exactly what I needed in that trying moment. "No one here is taking notice. It would be simple for me to slip out and go enjoy nature's splendor. I wonder, though, how hard it would be for a princess to make her escape?"

For a beat I could manage only a befuddled stare. That he knew me *that* well, could pick up on my precise emotion with such ease …

"What do you say?" he asked, his topaz eyes twinkling with mischief. "I could tell the staff I'm feeling ill and be out of here before the guardsmen ramp up for another sing along. We could meet in the square as soon as we can both break away. Think you could swing it?"

Go against what was expected of me?

What a strange and alluring concept.

Did I dare?

"Don't be long," I jabbed, reveling in the thrill of my act of rebellion.

Head held high, I swished toward the exit, riding a ripple of my own trumped up sass.

"Vanessa!" Triton yelped from amidst his crowd of admirers.

Slowing my kicks, I tossed around the idea of stopping.

It was an option.

The proverbial *right* thing to do.

I acknowledged it.

Accepted it.

Then, pretended I didn't hear him, and swam on.

My goal driven momentum came to an abrupt stop when a large, unyielding mitt caught my upper arm in a vise grip that gouged divots in my flesh. Whipped around with a force which cracked my neck with a painful *snap*, I found myself staring into the face of Fleet Master Neleus. The majority of mermaids throughout the Seven Seas candidly gushed about his chiseled jawline, muscular build, and wide-set seafoam eyes. All I could see was the cruelty of his soul.

"The future King of Atlantica spoke to you," he growled. "You *will* acknowledge him with the respect he deserves, *girl*."

My gaze darted to the table where my brother held court. Triton's mouth swung slack, apology bleeding from his stare. Doralious's chest puffed protectively, his eyes narrowing in Neleus's direction. Father floated beside him. It *should* have been considered a high offense for a soldier to speak to a royal in such a fashion, yet Poseidon remained unresponsive on the matter. Until our little show drew an audience, he wouldn't bother with it, or me.

Jaw locked, I glared the soldier down with the heat of an underwater volcano. "My title is *Princess Vanessa*, and he is *not* the king yet. Upon last inspection of Atlantica traditions, I have *just* as much claim to the throne as he does. It may serve you well to remember that."

Neleus attempted a charming smile, but it landed closer to the terrifying scowl of a Northern Stargazer. If you haven't witnessed those elusive little buggers, they are a species of fish that *sound* adorable, but look like the face of demon emerging from the ocean floor.

"He has the entire Royal Guard preparing him to rule. What do you have, little Princess?" Grabbing one strand of my hair, Neleus gave it a rough tug before letting it float from his fingers. "Who would even accept such a pointless cause?"

"And what makes it pointless?"

Conversation ground to a halt. All eyes turned to the queen who drifted through the hall, weaving between bodies, to inject herself in the dispute. That day she opted for ebony hair pulled back in a severe bun. Her demure gown resembled that of the Indian Sea mer, starting high on her neckline and falling in loose folds at the bend in her tail. Lips, stained a deep chum red, pursed in distain. Black eyes, lined with intricate red swirls that matched the glistening scales of her glamoured tail, narrowed. Tilting her head in the Fleet Master's direction, she fixed on him with a predatory stare.

Neleus dipped into a deep bow of respectful. "I speak of past accounts alone, Your Highness. It is common place for the heir that trains with the likes of the guard to one day claim the trident."

Folding her hands behind her back, Amphrite's sharp gaze traveled the length of the bold soldier from top to tail, and back again. "Aw, yes, the trident. That enchanted artifact which decides the fate of—well, if we want to be specific—*all* of Atlantica," leaning in, she stage whispered, "and who, exactly, do you think enchanted both that and the Ursela shell?"

Neleus pulled himself up seahorse straight. "You cannot possibly expect me to believe that *you* enacted such a powerful incantation *centuries* ago. Do you think me mad?"

Releasing her hands, Amphrite tapped one dagger-like nail to her chin. "Hmm," her lips twisted to the side, "if I actually were a haggard old wretch that *would* explain my panache for disguises."

The high ranking warrior floundered for the correct response; glancing over his shoulder he beseeched his fellow officers. They offered only mystified shrugs and sympathetic cringes.

"Or, in an alternative that keeps me young and beautiful," Amphrite shielded her mouth with the back of her hand, "perhaps the trident and shell were enchanted by one of the most magically inclined families under the Seven Seas. Or, as I like to call them, Nana, Papi, Mom, and Dad."

Neleus's jaw swung slack. "You can't mean ..."

"That one of the most potent magicks ever known, that the very *structure* on which our government was based, was invoked by *my* family? Yes, my dear, sir. That is *exactly* what I mean."

Prior to that moment, I thought Amprhite to be a frivolous nit—father's narcissistic arm-accessory that flitted her days away with pageantry and costuming. The assertive version trending before me pulled back the curtain of that façade, exposing the ravenous beast beneath. She was truly an enigma that no solitary label could define. Somehow, it made me appreciate her an inkling more.

Clearing his throat, Neleus forced a tight smile to save face in front of their audience of onlookers. "I appreciate the gift of your powers and what they bring to your role as the kingdom's alchemist, my Queen. That said, I hardly see what that has to do with deciding Atlantica's next ruler. The Royal Guard knows how to train a king … or a queen, and we have selected Triton. But Vanessa … well, there have been no volunteers to instruct her."

"I expected someone of your high ranking to have bit more foresight," she sighed, as if exasperated by his ineptitude. "If she is willing, the princess will be *my* apprentice."

Shocked gasps echoed through the hall.

My mouth fell open, vexed by the mermaid that was proving herself to be a diabolical genius. I told her no, quite emphatically in fact. Yet there she was, establishing herself as my public heroine. I would be viewed as an ungrateful brat if I said no to her now. Conniving as she was, I marveled at her brilliant execution.

Goaded on by the unease moving through the room in a potent wave, Neleus barked his discord, "*You are queen*! Such a thing is unheard of!"

Instead of matching his agitated squawk, Amphrite dropped her voice to a silky whisper. "I am also the Royal Alchemist. The most powerful one to ever hold the title, and that is *not* boasting. According to the historic scrolls, by law it is written that the *alchemist* may take an apprentice. However, as martial harmony is of utmost importance to me …" With one swirl of her tail, which glittered like rubies, she addressed her husband with humble reverence, "Dearest husband, may I ask for your blessing on this arrangement?"

The room fell silent.

Faintly, the distant squeaks of the stabled dolphins could be heard.

Water shifted, Father's massive frame rising from the seat he had claimed beside Triton. My heart forgot how to beat as a slow smile spread across his face, yet never quite reached his eyes. "If such a thing will make my queen and daughter happy, who am I to deny such a request?"

Alastor, who had found someone to relieve him of his post *and* plate of hors d'oeuvres, picked that moment to skirt behind Poseidon on his way to the exit. Father caught him with one giant flipper of a hand slapped to Alastor's scrawny shoulder. Yanking the bewildered servant boy tight to his side, the king's rough fingers dug into his flesh with enough force to make Alastor wince.

Face dead of emotion, Father jerked his chin in my direction. "Of course, I leave the final decision to Princess Vanessa. It is *her* future we are speaking of. Answer truthfully, child. Does this arrangement *please* you?"

To anyone else, Poseidon's act probably seemed a casual gesture of mer solidarity. I saw it as the silent, yet palpable threat that it was. His fingers squeezed hard enough to pucker the skin, Alastor's shoulder sagging in search of relief.

I had no desire to study under Amphrite's tutelage. As the vision of my mother pointed out, the young queen was *not* to be trusted. Still, I found my father's fervent desire to keep us apart compelling. One corner of my mouth curling in a defiant smirk, I made the reckless decision to call his bluff.

Dipping in a deep curtsy, I peered up at Poseidon from under my lashes. "Nothing would please me more, Father, than to train under your *wise* queen."

I thought myself so slick, a true rebel—right up until I shot a sideways glance to Amphrite. Triumph played across her features, sharpening them to a blade's gleaming edge. Chewing on her lower lip, she couldn't suppress a gleeful grin. Icy awareness of the mistake I made doused my sense of a pre-teen revolution.

"Then so it shall be," Poseidon professed, sealing my fate.

Amphrite extended her hand to me, her gaze shifting back to Poseidon. "If it pleases Your Majesty, we will take our leave to discuss the terms of our arrangement privately."

Swallowing hard, I forced myself to place my hand in hers. There was no warmth in her touch, just cool, clammy indifference.

"Very well." Poseidon's jaw flexed, his teeth clenched to mask his annoyance. "You have my blessing, unless Vanessa has any … *hesitations* she wishes to discuss?"

If Father could have shook Alastor, like a shark seriating its prey, to make his threat more blatant, he would have. Ever mindful of the crowd, he released his grip and drummed his fingers against Alastor's bruising shoulder.

I couldn't look Alastor's way; the guilt was too stifling.

Taking another route altogether, I flashed Poseidon my most beguiling smile. "None at all, Father."

Alastor's stare burned into me. Betrayal wafted from him.

I would make this up to him, beg his understanding.

This could be repaired.

It *had* to be.

Squeezing my hand hard enough to grind my knuckles together, Amphrite dipped in a final curtsy. "Thank you, Your Highness. We shall work hard in your honor."

Tugging me along, she flutter kicked toward the exit without looking back.

"Keep up," she muttered, for my ears only, "and do *not* look back. Whatever you feel for that boy, for the moment think of him as nothing more than particles of sand flittering over your fins. Your father must think he means *nothing* to you."

She saw it.

She saw the threat and manipulated it to get what she wanted. And now, I was bound to her at the expense of Alastor's trust.

*Mother Ocean, what had I done?*

# Chapter Five

"D o you have a favorite?" Cradling his jowls in her palms, Amphrite nuzzled the snout of Anchor, Father's prize bull dolphin that pulled his carriage in every parade.

She had led me to the stable without explanation, not that I felt one was needed. Many teachers tried the tactic of making Triton and me muck out the stalls as a way to humble us. The lack of originality disappointed me. I expected more creativity from someone capable of her elaborate glamours. Not that I minded a trip to the stable. It was a majestic cavern carved out of rock with a private fresh air pocket tucked into its ridged peek. Nature's helpful attributes to the design made me a believer that Mother Ocean had a special place in her heart for her bottle-nosed beauties. Whenever time allowed it, I loved to watch the royal pod swim, swirl, and dive to their hearts desire, surfacing whenever they pleased.

A smiling gray face poked out from between the stable's stalagmite bars, nudging my hand for a chin scratch. I happily obliged his tender request.

"This is my boy, Gully." Scratching my knuckles over his forehead, my tense expression softened at his merry little squeaks. "He was the steed of a member of the Royal Guard until he reached retirement age two years ago. Father, charitably, let me keep him. We don't go out for swims often, because he tires easily. But, we do enjoy our visits. Don't we, boy?"

Gully trilled his agreement.

Arching her arms behind her, Amphrite released her tightly wound bun and let it tumble down her back.

"They're so loyal," she wistfully mused, "so trusting."

"Only if they are trained properly," I interjected. "Gully had never been—"

"*Come with me!*" Suddenly perking, Amphrite turned tail and swam off. Flipping onto her back, she gestured for me to follow her out the back of the stable.

"Sure, why not," I grumbled under my breath, giving Gully a final pat. "I was totally done talking by the way. It was really more of a philosophical statement, *'Gully had never been.'* Ponder that."

"What?" Halting in a tight spin that made her hair cyclone over her head, the young queen blinked in my direction.

"Nothing," I countered with a forced smile. "Just excited to get started."

For reasons I can't explain, I thought stabbing my fist forward with my elbow crooked, would demonstrate my mock jubilance further.

"Does that have some sort of meaning?" Amphrite's locks, slightly more titanium than onyx in this light, fell around her face like a lapping waterfall as she stared down at my outstretched hand.

Cheeks burning, I let my arm fall to my side. "I have no idea. I saw some of the soldiers do it once. I thought it was a thing."

"Let's move past the awkward gesture, shall we?" A flip of her hair, and she swam on at a speed that would make a Sailfish tip its hat in appreciation—if fish wore hats.

Pushing off the pocked sidewall side of the stable, I worked my hips as fast as I could to catch up. While following the blur of her shape, I darted between coral, reeds, and waving plankton. Pulling up short at the base of a towering rock wall, I came a breath away from slamming into the back of my new mentor.

"Do you know what lies up there?" Tipping her head to peer up the embankment, Amphrite's hair swayed across the small of her back.

Assuming I knew what she was hinting at, I furrowed my brow, pursed my lips, and did a dreadful impression of my father. "*Humans. Barbaric, mean-spirited, fish-eaters!*" Deflating under the heat of her questioning stare on my face, I bit my lower lip and tagged on sheepishly, "According to my father."

"Careful, catfish," she warned, clucking her tongue to the roof of her mouth, "your whiskers are showing."

Dropping my chin to my chest, I immediately folded into a reverent bow. "My apologies, my Queen. I meant no disrespect."

"Bah!" she exclaimed, with a toss of her head. "What's the point of *any* of this if we can't poke fun at the uptight turtle-turds, like your father, behind their backs?"

A brash, and particularly un-princess-like, guffaw burst from my lips. Slapping a hand over my mouth did nothing to magically reel it back in. No matter, I really wasn't terribly concerned. My mind was occupied toying with the notion that I may have been wrong about Atlantica's chameleon beauty. If she shared my views on some of the kingdom's haughtier members—her own husband included—it seemed she couldn't be *all* bad.

"Our first lesson is that you need to relax around me. We're partners now." One shoulder rising and falling in a nonchalant shrug, she glanced up the steep embankment. "What I was actually referring to, was the large patch of Milleporadae nestled into the reef at the top of that ridge."

Momentary appreciation for mommy-in-law was smothered by a blanket of unease. "Fire coral," I murmured in a barely audible whisper.

"That's right!" she bubbled with a winning smile. "Its calcified external skeleton can scrape away the skin, allowing hundreds of tentacles protruding from *countless* pores to inject their venom *directly* into the bloodstream of their victim. Isn't Mother Ocean *fascinating?*"

Swallowing hard, I forced down the lump of fear constricting my throat. "I fell into a patch when I was younger. It's not fascinating. It's dreadful. For hours every inch of my skin burned as if wrapped in the pulse of an electric eel. No tonics or cool compresses could offer even a moment's relief. I called out for my father. He never came. Triton did, fluttering in with his stubby toddler tail, which barely allowed him to swim a straight line. He took my hand, curled up beside me, and didn't leave my side until the writhing finally relented." Dread snaked through my tone, morphing it into an ugly panic. "I know all too well the anguish that species of coral can cause. What I *don't* know is what you plan to do with it."

"Well, that depends on you." She turned the full effect of her onyx stare my way. The glamour she cast blacked out her irises, giving her the vacant stare of a predator. "You have magic. I saw it in the cave when you saved those zebra sharks. I want to see how potent it is."

My blood ran as cold as the deepest trenches of the sea. "N-*no* … I don't know what you *think* you saw, but I—"

"Oh, yes!" Her hands came together in a sharp clap that prompted a jerk from my tightly-wound nerves. "Let's waste time by pretending to be something we aren't. *You* be a non-magical lump and *I'll* be a cod fish. It'll be like improvisation, except … frightfully dull. So, yes, just like improvisation."

"You d-don't understand," I stammered. The shark's tooth headband fastened across my hairline weighed on me like an anchor, dragging me down for the fraud that I was. I wasn't strong. I wasn't confident. I was a little girl terrified of a part of herself she didn't understand. "I have magic. I admit that, but … I can't use it."

Holding out one hand before her, Amphrite inspected her dagger-sharp nails. "Does Triton have magic?"

Sensing where that line of questioning was headed, I mashed my lips together and scrambled for a viable excuse to detour her. "No, he doesn't. However, with my skills and education—"

Curling her hand in, she jabbed it to the curve of her hip. "You mean the skills and education Triton has been subjected to same as you? *That* will not get you the throne. *That* will get you a heaping dose of disappointment, and the unquenchable desire to go back in time and listen to me at this very moment. I don't know what your grievances against magic are—" She held both hands up to halt me the second my mouth opened to form an explanation. "*Not asking. Don't care.* I am simply stating that with your magical attributes you can float above your brother, who currently has the advantage of being the male heir under a bigoted patriarch. You could be queen. He could be chosen by the Ursela shell and bestowed with just enough magic to deem him *moderately* useful within the kingdom. Therefore, allowing *him* the sort of lackadaisical existence he longs for, and *you* to assume your rightful position. It's win-win. That said, how about if we stifle the whimpering and excuses, and actually do what it takes to get you that trident?"

So many horrible visions.

So many sweat-drenched nights squeezing my eyes shut as death tickled my back and sang me sweet songs.

How could I explain, when she spoke the truth? Only by embracing the side of me I had stifled for too long would I maintain *any* chance of ever having that golden crown placed upon my head.

Gazing down at my anxiously wringing hands, I questioned *myself* more than my new mentor. "How could I *begin* to tap into that energy now without losing complete control?"

"I'm *so* happy you asked." Lacing her fingers, she let them swing down in front of her. "What sort of effect do you think a rock slide of Fire Coral would have on your beloved team of dolphins?"

Pulling back with a start, I blinked rapidly, trying to wrap my mind around what I *hoped* was a random topic change. "The reef is *quite* secure. I don't think—"

Her hand shooting through the water in a wide arc cut off my contention. Violet tendrils sparked from her palm, darting through the water in zealous wisps and rolls. Bonding together, the formed a potent bolt of purple lightning that struck the rock wall with a *crack* violent enough to shake the ocean floor. A zigzagged split traveled down the side of the wall, sending pebbles raining down. Stone shifted with an ominous creek. A chunk of the reef, nearly matching the stable in size, shifted ... shimmied ... tipped ... and teetered on the edge of the plateau it was no longer connected to.

"*Wha – what did you do?*" I gasped, eyes bulging in disbelief.

"I've started you on a path." One blink and her eyes altered to a serene blue; the hue conjuring images of the sun beaming down, and a light breeze lapping over the water. Dipping her head in a maternal fashion, the corners of her mouth pulled up ever so softly. "One there is no turning back. That rock *will* come down, showering those poor, unsuspecting dolphins with Fire Coral. Unless *you* stop it. You want to be queen, Vanessa? You want to rule? Channel what's inside of you and use it to save those that trust and believe in you."

Vanishing in a swirling cloud of purple, Amphrite reappeared on top of the reef.

"Your future begins now, Princess," she shouted down at me, "and only *you* can decide what it shall be."

As if moving in slow motion, her fire-red tail curled in front of her, then slapped down against the teetering rock. The ground trembled. A dusty haze clouded the water. Rumbling, like distant thunder, heralded that the boulder broke free and was skidding down the steep incline on a collision course with the stable.

Alarms trumpeted through my head. My every impulse screamed for me to swim away. All that kept me buoyed to that spot was the sweet chorus of squeaks behind me. The dolphins knew nothing of the boulder careening toward them, ready to crush their home and pelt misery down on them. All they wanted was play time and belly rubs. The alternative of pain and woeful torment had been ushered in, thanks to me.

Cursing my daring attire, which offered up a bounty of my exposed flesh for the voracious coral to feast upon, I brought my hands up in a defensive posture. "*Please*," I pleaded to Amphrite, "don't do this. You don't understand the cost!"

Catching one lock of hair, she twirled it around her finger, her dreamy gaze cast toward shallower waters. "Cost-shmost! You want the avalanche to stop? Make it! And you should probably hurry, panicked dolphins may turn on you. You know, I *think* there was a reversal spell for situations such as this, yet for the life of me I can't recall it."

Shrapnel from the rock broke off, spitting sand and coral grit down on me. Shielding my face behind my arms, I yelped as the poisonous bits sizzled and hissed against my skin. The pain pierced into me like the prickles of a thousand sea urchin spikes.

Still, the needed part of me held back.

"*Amphrite, help me!*" I forced the words through clenched teeth, my heart hammering against my ribs. "Don't let them die for *my* inadequacies!"

"Is that what you are, *little mermaid?*" Amphrite's hand fell, swinging to her side as she sized me up through narrowed eyes. "*Inadequate*? If that *is* the case, you have no place on the throne and never did. We can end this charade right now without wasting a moment more of each other's time."

"*No!* You don't understand!" The words tumbled from my lips, freed by my growing desperation. "The magic I possess … it comes at too powerful a price! *I cannot harness it!*"

Water roiled around me. The ebb and flow of a sudden and demanding current formed a massive replica of Amphrite's face hovering over me.

"Pay it. Own it," the watery bust sneered. "*Claim your birthright!*"

The watery image of Amphrite was sliced in two by a hunk of the boulder that broke off and pin-wheeled down, end over end.

My effort to dive out of the way fell short, the edge of the rogue shrapnel slicing across my forearm. The threatening scream wedged in my throat, held there by the scorching, venomous heat which contaminated my blood and seeped through my veins. Slapping my opposite hand over my pulsating arm, my stare tore up in time to see the same coral-laced shard winging straight for where Gully's head poked out with interest.

Instinct stabbed my good hand out. I didn't think. Didn't agonize over the outcome. Nostrils flaring, I kicked open the creaking gate within me and freed that long stifled force. The influence of my essence licked from my palm in emerald tendrils that latched onto the splintered rock with ease and batted it aside. Retraining my focus, I whirled on the larger, looming problem. Filling my gills, I relaxed the rein of my will and let the power within fling its head high, and bare its teeth. Sapphire water lightened to luminescent turquois as a fresh onslaught of vining magic bloomed from my palms. Eager to do my bidding, the vines latched onto the boulder. Skin cracking and blistering at the crumbs of coral that fell, I arched my back and leaned into the rock with every ounce of strength I had. The pull of the boulder's momentum crushed down, promising to snuff me out if I failed. Just as I squeezed my eyes shut, anticipating that bone crushing crunch, it skidded to a stop in a mushroom cloud of sand. It receded a beat later, pulling back the curtain with flourish to unveil my victory.

Exhausted arms dangling at my sides, my tail failed me and I crumbled to the ocean floor. Staring at the rocky catastrophe I prevented, my gills labored to reclaim my breath.

"*You did it!*" Amphrite applauded, materializing beside me in a violet fog. "Granted, extreme measures were taken to coerce you, but that is a bothersome detail to be dealt with later. For now, enjoy your victory! Now that you have accepted this side of yourself, things will only get easier!"

Her words reached my ears like muffled cries resonating to the depths of a trench. The scorching pain that should have been pulsing through me held the lackluster punch of a skinned elbow. Coral dust wafted into my eyes, swelling them to slits—even this failed to register. My entire consciousness was consumed by every wave that lapped past, every current that eddied by. Each contained a face, the tortured mask of a long dead soul. They lashed around me, moaning my name in plaintive pleas. A choked sob tore from my chest. Head falling back, the weight of my greatest fear being realized trampled my soul more than the boulder ever could.

Hoovering on the ravaged reef ledge, my mother glared down. The flesh across her cheek and jaw hung loose, exposing time-weathered bone.

"*Vanessa*," her haunting rasp drifted down, a bubbling brew of disappointment and seething betrayal sharpening each word, "*what have you done?*"

Amphrite flittered around me — fluffing my hair, wiping muck from my cheeks — oblivious to my private purgatory. "I can't very well send you back to the palace looking like *that*," she harrumphed. "Your face is swelling like a Pufferfish. Your father isn't the *most* intuitive mer, but I'm guess this wouldn't escape notice."

Rubbing her hands together, she produced flares of purple between her palms.

"This won't hurt a bit," she said with a soft smile, a faint dimple dipped into her cheek.

"*Stop!*" I recoiled, frantically slapping her hands away. "*Don't touch me!*"

Hands raised, Amphrite pulled back. She stared at me with the same aghast horror one would a sea slug that had wandered onto their breakfast platter.

Rubbing my blurring eyes with the back of my hand, I mumbled, "Take the pain ... leave the scars."

Amphrite's gaze flicked over the angry gash on my forearm. Pride cast its divine glow over her delicate features, crinkling the corners of her eyes.

"It would be my honor, Princess," she declared, and bent her head once more to conjure the healing energy.

I trained my gaze on her task, willing myself to ignore the restless spirits writhing all around me. Their presence would not be ignored, each prickling through me with ghastly fingers that beckoned me to glimpse their eternity.

"*I begged you to stay away from her,*" my mother voiced in ominous warning. "*To trust me. To believe in me. Instead, you've thrown open a door that cannot be closed. This is just the beginning, Vanessa. Believe me when I say, in no way are you prepared for what is to come.*"

# CHAPTER SIX

Where do you seek sanctuary when your prison is in your own mind? When every shadow has eyes and every corner whispers your name in a taunting reverberation? Amphrite sashayed back to the queen's quarters bolstered by what *she* considered a triumph. My journey, sulking through the halls and wincing at every noise, was a far more jarring one. The castle — more specifically the corridor which held my room — had always been my safe haven. When the seas of life raged, that was where I could batten down the hatches and weather any storm. Opening the door to magic welcomed the darkness in along with it. Now, unseen talons swiped at my flesh. Teeth snapped just behind my ear. Both faded into nothingness the second I spun on them.

Behind the pillar closest to my room, a form moved. Blinking hard, I tried to distinguish eerie visions from reality. The water rolled, Neleus's formidable stature materializing from the ocean's murky blue abyss. His critical sneer, which traveled the length of me, seemed undeniably real. Or was it? Herky, jerky flashes distorted his eyes to smoldering ruby embers. Another flicker, and they reverted back.

"Fleet Master Neleus," clearing my throat, I did my best impression of someone *not* gradually losing their mind, "did you need something? Or is stalking around the quarters of young, impressionable girls a hobby of yours?"

Cinders sparking in his lethal stare once again, Neleus tipped his head and swam a slow circle around me. Words rumbled from his chest in a menacing growl, "Such courage you've shown. Such bravado." His cheek brushed my hair, the rush of water from his exhale tickling across my earlobe. *"What a fine leader you could've been."*

Shriveling under his glare and proximity, I found myself robbed of my last shred of valor. In my mind I saw my body crinkling inward, cowering to the earth until I was nothing more than a gruesome reed with bulging sacks for eyes.

*I'm no leader*, I mentally berated myself. *I'm nothing short of a damaged mess.*

"What do you want?" Forcing the words through my constricted throat, I gritted my teeth at how they broke and trembled.

Leaning down, he curled one finger under my chin and tipped my face to his. "I want *you* out of the way."

My chin betrayed me by quivering. Tears of frustration burned behind my eyes. I would sooner have dug the treacherous orbs from their sockets than to allow such a display of vulnerability in front of *him*. "I didn't realize a thirteen-year-old mer-girl could do *anything* to hinder the plans of a military legend such as yourself."

"My military merit bears no weight on this matter, but who I am willing to serve under as my future ruler *does*," he snarled, his top lip curling from his teeth.

A rush of awareness straightened my spine, yanking my shoulders back. "You actually view me as a *threat*."

"Don't confuse proactive measures with *concern*," he sputtered, turning into a tight barrel roll with one flick of his tail. "You're no *threat*. You're nothing, *little mermaid*."

He was the second mer that day to call me that. I didn't know where the new nickname came from, but I hoped it didn't catch on.

"You can't believe that entirely," I pressed, "elsewise you wouldn't be here."

My gaze instinctively darted to the sword looped at his hip, as if my subconscious sought to remind my sharp tongue that he was armed.

Neleus shook his head, chuckling at a joke only he understood. "Your brother will work tirelessly. He will be bruised, he will be battered, but he will persevere. Do you know why?"

"His glowing golden locks?" I jabbed. "They *are* magical."

My attempt at humor didn't penetrate his callous demeanor, not that I believed it would. "*He* will succeed because he has the protection of the Royal Guard." Swirling to face me, he scoured the lines of my face for a shred of weakness to feast upon. "Who will protect you, young one? Not the queen. She cares only for her own agenda, I promise you that. Only one fate awaits you. One in which you will train alone, you will fight alone, and — if you dare stand in Triton's way — you shall *die* alone."

"Triton would *never* let harm come to me." There were few things in my life I counted at certainties; trust in my brother was top of that list.

Curling in a final lap around me, Neleus caught one strand of my hair between two fingers and gave it a rough tug. "Triton will see what *we* want him to. Keep that in mind as you scheme and plot."

Kicking away with broad strokes of his tail, the ocean's obscurity swallowed Neleus bit by bit. Reduced to nothing more than a shadow, he turned to offer me a curt bow.

"May Poseidon's blessing flow upon you, *Princess*," he said, his smirk audible.

Letting the sentiment bob in the water between us, he vanished from sight.

A cold, clammy hand seized my shoulder, causing a shiver to jolt through me. "*I never liked him,*" Mother croaked, manifesting behind me. "*He takes liberties above his station.*"

With a forceful roll of my shoulder, I shrugged off her unnerving touch. "Like tormenting those around him by pretending he's alive long after his death?"

Mother pulled back, one side of her disintegrating face tugging up in a lopsided grin. "*Such a sharp tongue for a girl that's seldom heard. I may be too proud of your resilience to be offended.*"

"Glad to hear it." Shoving the makeshift curtain-door to my bedroom aside, I escaped inside. While the wafting verdure fell back into place, I collapsed against the wall beside it. My breath came in rapid pants that made the water boil around my face. Thankfully, Mother didn't follow. At least not yet. A glorified sheet wouldn't keep her, or any other spirits, out. Nothing would. It was only a matter of time until …

"*One went behind the bed!*" My reverie was interrupted by Loriana ambling across my room as fast as her fins could carry her, a hand-weaved net hoisted over her head. "*Get it!*"

Alastor's head poked around the side of my bed, my blanket draped over his forehead. "What do you think I'm doing under here? Diving for pearls?" Noticing my arrival, his face blanched. "Princess Vanessa! We were … *uh* …"

"Oh, for the sake of Mother Ocean, Alastor, be honest with the lass! Humor me into thinking I've at least taught you that much." Loriana dropped her hands, adjusting her grip on the net. Her face creased in a cringe of equal parts regret and disgust. "My deepest apologies, Princess. I know it's incredibly inappropriate for a boy to be in your quarters under *any* circumstances, unfortunately I needed his aid. It appears we have an … *infestation* of sorts in your quarters."

Puffing my cheeks, I blew the hair from my eyes. "Of course we do," I grumbled. "What is it? Some nasty little sea bugs that cause scabies and make your hair fall out? Because that would be quite apropos in the scheme of things."

Floteson and Jetteson's tiny faces peeked out from under my pillow. Their speckled little bodies wriggled with excitement the second their beady eyes found me.

"There they are!" Alastor exclaimed. Scrambling off the floor, he lunged for the zebra shark tots.

"*No!*" Shoving off the wall, I dove between them. "They're my friends!"

Riding his wave of momentum, Alastor flopped onto my bed. He wasted no time righting himself, his posture pulled up urchin quill-straight. "They're your friends and you stood up for them. Huh, I wasn't aware you were capable of such things."

"Alastor!" Loriana chastised, cracking the net's reed against her open palm. "She is a *royal*! Remember your place!"

"No, Loriana, he's right," I corrected. Settling onto my bed, I absentmindedly scratched the sharks under their chins. "I'm sorry, Alastor. If it makes things any better—and I'm sure it doesn't—I knew Poseidon would never hurt you. Not with all of Atlantica watching."

Dreading the justified accusation I was certain would be scrawled on Alastor's face, I filled my gills and forced myself to meet his stare.

My imagination failed to accurately represent the sting of the reality.

Glancing from me, to her son, and back again, Loriana dropped her net and eased herself on to the bed beside me. Taking my hand, she cradled it between hers. "They put so much pressure on you and your brother. In many ways they rob you both of your youth." Her chin tilted in Alastor's direction. "A fair amount of understanding should be granted by those who cannot begin to fathom those kind of expectations."

Alastor cast his gaze to the tips of his tailfin that were tracing designs in the sandy floor. "I didn't go to see the Harvest Moon," he admitted, glancing up from under lush lashes. "It lost its appeal without my best friend there."

"I thought Triton was your best friend?" I ventured, screwing my lips to the side to suppress a smile.

"I have to let him think that," he deadpanned. "He's actually quite emotionally fragile. Beneath the bumbling, happy-go-lucky façade beats the heart of a poet."

Simultaneously we erupted in snorts of laughter.

"That boy is a ray of sunshine, and you two are merciless little beasts for poking fun of him," Loriana scolded, the edge stripped from her tone by a hint of amusement. "Now then, Alastor tells me the *queen* took you as her apprentice! How exciting that must be! Tell us of your first training session!"

Laughter dying on my lips, I flicked an anxious glance toward my arm. Keeping it tucked firmly to my side, only one corner of the angry red slash was visible.

True to nature, Loriana missed nothing. Following my gaze, she sucked in a shocked breath. "Sakes alive! You're wounded! Alastor, fetch the salve! Quick, now! I'll get some bandages!"

As she spoke, the shadows in the room began to elongate, wriggling and writhing into spectral shapes.

"*No!*" Emphatically I shook my head, my headband slipping loose and falling around my neck like a noose. "I'm fine. It doesn't hurt. *Don't go!*"

One rogue tear slipped from my lashes, followed by another. In a sudden rash of hysterics, I dissolved in a fit of wailed, hopeless sobs.

"There, there now," Loriana soothed. Cloaking my quaking shoulders with one plump arm, she drew me to her. She smelled of sandalwood and water lilies; a comforting, maternal mix that eased my battered soul. Fingers combing through my hair, she paused to remove the headband lassoing my neck. "Nothing has been done that can't be *un*done with a little patience and fortitude."

How wrong she was.

Curling his tail under him, Alastor settled on the floor beside us. His gentle hand pressed tentatively to the bend of my fin, voice dropping to an uncertain quiver. "Mada, what can we do?" he asked, fear causing him to forget his place and use the mer slang for mother—a no-no in the presence of royals.

Dotting a kiss to my forehead, Loriana held me in a snug embrace. "We will look out for her as we would want her to look out for us when she's queen. And I truly believe with her pure heart, she *will* be." Pulling away, she met my stare and swiped a tear away with the pad of her thumb. "Is there anything I can get for you, my dear? Something warm to drink before I turn down your bed, perhaps?"

Risking a glance to the shadows, I noticed my metaphysical followers still lingered but had yet to solidify.

"*Please don't go!*" I pled, both my hands encircling her wrist. The spirits held back for some reason with the two of them there. I feared their departure would throw me to the mercy of every lingering wraith. "*D-don't leave me alone.*"

It was a sign of weakness Poseidon would have scoffed at, lifting his nose at such a pathetic display. Loriana, however, read the fright etched into my features with a mother's compassion.

Deep divots of concern sliced between her brows. "Alastor, swim to our room and retrieve my blankets. I shall accompany the princess in her quarters tonight." Gently extracting one hand from mine, she tenderly pressed her palm to my cheek.

Shoulders collapsing with grateful relief, I leaned in to her touch.

# CHAPTER SEVEN

## SIX YEARS LATER

*I*'*ve walked on land. I've felt the earth squish beneath my feet and been assaulted by the nauseating onslaught of pungent odors that waft in on every breeze. I've sat shoulder to shoulder with strangers who seemed to have a distaste for water or cleanliness, and watched grown humans play make-believe as a form of entertainment for their audience. If my life in the three years that followed my partnering with Amphrite had been one such predictable satire, there would have been a musical montage of my training. It would have begun with me awkwardly bumbling through drills, and progressed – through a series of clever snippets – to reveal me as an exquisite, polished warrior by the end. Hours spent together would have bonded Amphrite and me in a deep and spiritual manner. My father and his Royal Guard would have witnessed how hard I was working and developed a sense of appreciation and respect for my efforts. The kingdom would have been frozen in a state of serenity, calmly awaiting the day a future ruler would be named.*

*But this was no such parody.*

*No jester stood on the side of a plank board stage cuing the good people of Atlantica when they were to applaud, laugh, or gasp in astonishment.*

*This was real life, and real life was … messy.*

Our swords met in a rapid-fire succession of claps. Weaponry of the mer was truly beautiful to behold. The skulls of swordfish claimed by the sea were cleaned and polished. The eye sockets then removed, and the cheekbone whittled down to shield the user's hand. The parietal bone was filed down and crafted into a hilt which perfectly fit the grip of the mer who would wield it. The swords had a touch of flexibility, but the raw potency nature provided trumped that of any man-made metal contraption.

Parrying back, I allowed Triton to lunge in on the attack. With each of his strikes, I let the block of my weapon drop a hint lower, drawing his guard down without him realizing it. His last blow hit at waist-level, my counter landing a touch of the tip of my foil to the dead-center of his chest. Knocked off balance, he fell to the floor. The water clouded from the sand storm he kicked up.

"My match." While my voice came muffled from behind my walrus skull helmet, the smile it held was audible.

The blast of a conch shell confirmed my win.

Holstering my sword in the loop on my hip, I offered my brother a hand up. Tugging off his helmet, he dragged a hand through his golden sunshine locks. Beside the fencing arena, a school of his adoring admirers—Tritonites as I liked to call them— squealed and clapped their appreciation like a giddy pod of seals. Time, training, and his status as a prince had earned him his own little fan club. They viewed him as a sculpted god, especially since maturity struck and granted him a surplus of father's strength and intimidating stature. To me, he would always be my guppy of a brother.

"Fantastic match, Nessa." His hand closed around my forearm, allowing me to yank him upright. "Your form is exquisite."

Chewing on the inside of my cheek, I pulled off my helmet and cradled it between my hip and forearm. My mind ticked over his technique, in search of *something* nice to say. "You strike quite forcefully, even if your body does announce your move *before* your sword, and you don't maintain your guard."

*There, that was supportive – ish.*

"I'll work on that." His blue eyes crinkled into a grin, his palm rubbing over the stubble of his chin that was thickening into a fuller beard by the day.

The simple gesture made the Tritonites swoon and fan themselves.

"Great job, Princess!" Doralious shouted from alongside the fencing strip. Time grayed-hair knotted at the base of his neck, he threw me a beaming smile and thumbs up. "Thanks for going easy on our boy!"

Glancing his way, I caught a glimpse of fluttering movement behind him. Even as I forced a tight smile in response, my body bristled. Fingers drumming against the hilt of my sword, I watched Amphrite swim into view. She chose a pale shade of icy blue for her hair that day. It floated and danced over her shoulders like a gentle snow-flurry. The enigmatic queen borrowed inspiration from the Caribbean merfolk when she opted for a sun-kissed complexion and an eye shade matching their serene, crystal waters. Thanks to her constant glamours, she hadn't aged a day since I met her. Raising her hand in a wave, she offered me a soft smile I made no attempt to return.

"Tomorrow, same time?" I raised my eyebrows in Triton's direction.

"Until I finally win," one muscular shoulder rose and fell in a casual shrug, "then I'm going to stop challenging you and remain the victor forever."

"It's good to have goals," I snorted, slapping a hand on his back.

I turned toward my dressing room, swimming one stride before I was halted by Triton self-consciously calling out, "Vanessa? Would you ... I mean, I know our schedules are insane, but I ... miss you. Do you think we could dine together tonight? Maybe catch up a bit?"

Hesitating, I floated where I was. My gaze flicked around the room. Neleus hovered on the side of the room, critiquing his protégé by jotting down notes on a scroll. Amphrite peered my way in anxious anticipation to unload whatever criticisms she had of my performance. The Tritonites called out to their imperial idol:

"Triton, look over here!"

"I love you, Triton!"

"Will you sign my shells?"

Somewhere along the way our worlds had aligned like oil on water, overlapping yet never mixing.

Glancing back, I offered him a tight smile which couldn't quite make it to my eyes. "Another time, brother. I think your admirer means to take off that shell bra for you to sign it," my chin jerked in the direction of the buxom brunette, "and I'm already seeing more of her than I care to."

Disappointment registered in the sinking corners of his mouth. "Another time," he muttered. "I'll hold you to that."

"Please do." Even I heard the dismissive nature of the statement and cringed. Expression softening, if only marginally, I nodded to the sword at his hip. "Maybe I can teach you how to actually use that thing."

With that as our parting sentiment, I kicked off to change out of my armor.

I didn't have to look back to know Amphrite was following me. Her prize seahorse had just come off the track. She needed to make sure my joints were oiled and I got my cool down swim. Okay, maybe that was a bit harsh. I couldn't recall a specific situation where she had ever been *intentionally* cruel to me. Demanding, scattered, bi-polar, persistent, unforgiving, and a bit flighty? Yes. Cruel? Not deliberately. Then again, how else could you describe someone who inadvertently brought your most vile nightmares to life?

"You didn't enchant your sword before the duel," she stated. Leaning one shoulder against the wall of the changing room, she crossed her arms in front of her.

Shrugging off my breast plate armor, I shook out the sharks' teeth chainmail and hung it inside a large wooden armoire one of our fleets had claimed from a ship they sunk off the coast of Bora Bora. The item had once been a lovely show piece that the retrieving mers had been anxious to bring before their king. The sloped peak of the structure was garnished with a pair of intricately carved chubby, human babies with dimples and wings. Apparently, humans do not find their children attractive enough and have to add fantastical elements to them to make them more appealing. It's sad, really, but I digress. Like any other land-based treasure, the cabinet had not fared well under the sea. Its once rich cherry hue had been infected by rot's dull, gray pallet. Barnacles grew up its sides, morphing the wooden babies into monstrous mini-beasts.

"The day I have to enchant my sword to fence against Triton is the day I give up our training and become a stable hand." Reaching in to situate my helmet on the rickety hook opposite my armor, my wrist was seized by a grim, bony hand within the cabinet.

Its claws punctured my flesh to the bone, spurting blood of crimson sprays that were instantly gobbled by the ravenous ocean. My arm wrenched to the side at a harsh, unforgiving angle. The force yanked me farther into the makeshift locker. Instinct screamed for me to fight, to pull, to heave at the expense of my trapped limb until I claimed my freedom. Nonetheless, I had played this particular game before. I knew how to end it. Filling my gills with a deep, calming breath, I expelled a wreath of bubbles through pursed lips.

"Vanessa? Are you okay?" Amphrite asked, concern sharpening her usual chirp.

My arms went limp. My body leaned into the anguish. A beat. A tightening of the unyielding grasp made me think that *this time* I'd made a horrible mistake. Then ... the ghoulish hand vanished, and I was free.

Pulling back, I rubbed my wrist. Not a scratch. Not a blemish. Not a surprise.

"I'm fine," I lied, holding my wrist up for her to see. Trying to force a smile, it landed somewhere closer to a pained grimace. "Thought I caught myself on a shark's tooth. Must have been a shell."

Her pouty lips puckered into her "thinking face". I had long since given up trying to predict what gibberish would follow that look. Her moods ran as rampant as the ocean current.

"You're getting stronger and aren't relying on your magic as often as you used to."

Turning to the mirror, I adjusted my opalescent shell bra and smoothed my hands over my hair. Loriana had knotted and braided my onyx locks until they ran down the center of my skull like a sleek Orca fin. I couldn't help but adore the vicious look. Most of the other mermaids in Atlantica possessed a soft, radiant appearance. Their features were delicate, their bone structures dainty and petite. Not me. I was my father's daughter. I favored him with my strong jawline and wide shoulders. Unlike the other girls' wispy frames, training for days on end had sculpted me into a rock of pure muscle. Convention be damned. I was comfortable in my skin. My *mind* may have been a bottomless pit of despair, but my bod was fierce. That was one silver lining I appreciated.

Running a finger alongside my lower lashes, I wiped away a bit of the squid ink liner which had gotten smudged during the duel. "Correct me if I'm wrong, but wouldn't that be considered a good thing? I'm getting stronger, don't need to cheat."

"It can be good," catching a strand of blue hair, she twirled it around her forefinger, then pressed it to her lips, "unless you're neglecting your magical training. An unused muscle weakens, and with the current state of Atlantica—"

My palms slapped against the vanity table with a loud crack, the mirror and its pedestal quaking at the impact. All that time, all those hauntings, and I had never told her the truth. Any time I tried to she accused me of making excuses. So, when it came to her, I suffered my episodes in silence.

Glancing over my shoulder, I caught her stare and held it firm. Filling my gills, I fought for a calm tone. "When it comes to magic, few under the sea can match your talents. Be that as it may, you are not trained in the way of battle techniques. It would be foolish of me to focus on magic, with all its unpredictabilities, alone. Let us agree that my *other* strengths have merit as well."

Amphrite pulled herself up to full height. A haughty lift of her chin allowed her to glare down her nose at me, magic sparking from her fingertips in an open threat. "Let us *also* remember that while we *are* working together, I am still your queen and you *will* show me the proper—"

Her declaration was cut off by six long conk blasts blaring through the castle and reverberating off every wall. Spinning on the indignant queen, I seized her forearms and forced her to the ground.

"*What is that? What are you doing? What's happening?*" she prattled off her questions in a short, clipped tone which rose a panicked octave with each syllable.

Throwing myself on top of her, I shielded her body with mine. "*Those* would be the trumpets of war, my Queen. If you had the battle training I mentioned, you would know that." Raising my head, I screamed for the guards, "*Here! The queen is in here! Come quickly!*"

It took only moments for them to respond, a chorus of clapping swords and banging bone armor announcing their arrival. The dozen soldiers who flooded in immediately formed a protective circle around us as per their standard protocol.

"It's clear, Princess," Doralious prompted, his fin nudging my side.

Shifting aside, I allowed him to help Amphrite up and floated upright beside them. While Doralious never dared to *publicly* align himself with me, through years of mutual respect I considered him my closest ally in the Royal Guard … and a friend.

"Take her to her quarters, and do *not* leave her side," I commanded. Shoving my way in between a cluster of soldiers, I reclaimed my sword from the cabinet. "Where are my brother and father?"

"Your father is being rushed to the Summit Room." Doralious circled one finger for his men to surround the queen, then nodded to the doorway for them to escort her out. "Your brother was last seen in his quarters."

"Then that's where I'll start looking for him." My sharp rebuttal acted as a dismissal. He started to follow his men out, only to be stopped by my barked intervention, "Commander Doralious?"

Turning back, his brows hitched in question.

"See to her yourself. If any harm finds her, the king will hold us *both* personally responsible."

"On my life and honor, Your Highness." A respectful bow and he trailed his troop out.

Weapon in hand and pulse racing, I swam hard to answer the call to war.

My course led me first down the hall to the sleeping quarters. Once a regal display of extravagance, it had since been deprived of its former splendor. Open arches that once allowed diamonds of light to filter through from above were now sealed off by impenetrable rock walls. The ornate chandeliers had been removed and stowed away for safe keeping. The only light in the space came in the form of the sickly green glow of luminescent sea moss wrapped around thick reeds, which were then stabbed between the gaps of the mosaic shell floor. Sometimes I felt that the castle saw what fun the spirits were having haunting me and made the decision to join in by setting the mood for the lurid nightmares plaguing me. This was one such moment.

Lights flickered, elongating every shadow.

Dark recesses of the hall whispered my name.

Overgrown patches of seaweed morphed into wraith-like hands that clawed up the walls, sprouting and stretching to envelope me.

Hands clenching and unclenching at my sides, I focused on the sand and swam on.

"It's not real," I chanted. "*None of its real.*"

As if the ocean itself longed to prove otherwise, a loud *boom* shook the castle, trembling the ground beneath me. It was immediately followed by a second, which sent pebbles of rock skittering down the massive bellies of the boulders that encapsulated the hall. The Summit Room temporarily forgotten, I huddled to the ground and pulled my tail in tight to my chest.

"*Not real!*" I shouted hard enough to strain my voice as yet another explosion shuddered the sea around me.

The faces would float in at any moment. Their hands tearing at me, vacant eyes pleading with me to hear the tales of woe that prevent their wayward spirits from moving on.

"*Vanessa!*" Alastor's voice was a fog-horn through the chaos, guiding me back to safer shores.

I wanted to reach for him, or — at the very least — sit up. Unfortunately, another jarring explosion anchored me where I was, whimpering whilst the hilt of my sword dug into my gut. Not my finest hours, kids, but also *far* from my worst.

Alastor dove alongside me, gathering me protectively in his arms as his belly skimmed the ocean floor.

"Hey, hey," he soothed against my ear, "I'm right here. I've got you."

My fingernails scraped red streaks across his well-muscled chest, scrambling to cling to him. "Alastor! Is it real? *Can you see it?*"

I will say this for the servant's son, he aged well. The sharp set of his features gave him a dangerous allure. His hair had darkened to the sky's deepest shade of amber right before the sun bows its head for the night. Most merman let their locks flow long and free. Alastor kept his knotted at the base of his neck. He used the edge of his hand-me-down sword to keep his threatening beard at little more than a rough stubble across his jawline.

Water rushed over our fins, yet another ear-piercing strike blowing a chunk from a neighboring boulder. Cradling the back of my head, Alastor held me in the secure cocoon of his embrace. Bubbles from his exhales tickled over my cheeks, still I dared not move.

"I can see it," he assured me in a raspy whisper. "It's really happening."

Alastor knew my secret. He was well aware of the cost that came with my magic. The decision to tell him had *not* been one I made voluntarily. His mother had been ill. Despite royal decree, and her better judgement, she sent Alastor in her stead one night to turn down my bed. He found me cowered in a corner, openly sobbing, after a particularly horrifying vision. I was only fourteen at the time. Since that moment, he had truly become my best friend, the one I trusted him above all others with the ugliest parts of myself. Only he despised my magic as much as I did.

Confidence building that this *wasn't* a freakish apparition, I risked a glance up. My gaze traveled the length of the hall, searching for clues of the cause of the ruckus. "What is it?"

"It's the humans. If I had to guess, I would say Lemurians followed a fleet back to Atlantica." As he spoke, he turned over one of my arms and then the other, inspecting me for signs of injury. "We are no longer the myth beneath the sea to them. We have now become the menace that sinks their ships and pillages their bounty. Really, we left them no choice *but* to attack. Which they are doing by training their cannons directly into the water and blasting for all they're worth. I wish some of them would dive in and go head to head with us, even the odds a bit."

My nose crinkled at my suddenly insufficient sword. "They can rain fire from the sky and we can counter only with pointy sticks. If only someone had warned the Council of such an outcome. Oh, wait … *I tried.*"

Alastor's arm flung up to shield my head as another rumble sounded and bits of stone pelted down. "Such boisterous judgment from the girl I found hunched on the ground."

Ignoring his barb, my hands seized his arms with a forceful desperation that could bruise flesh. *"Triton! Where is he?"*

Extracting one arm from beneath me, Alastor laid a comforting hand onto my white knuckled grasp. "He wanted to wait for you, but I forced him on to the Summit Room with the assurance I would usher you there the moment I found you."

Reluctantly, I released my hold and brushed his arm aside. Steeling my spine, I rose from the ground with one flick of my tail. "You can't. You must find your mother, and stay with her. I don't like her being alone at such a time. She must be worried sick not knowing where you are."

Gliding to my side, Alastor's fingers linked with mine. "She knew without question where my heart took me the moment that first trumpet blasted." The emerald glow of the room hugged the rise and fall of each and every taut muscle of his chiseled chest, concern sharpening his features with a dangerous edge. "Promise me you will offer the Council your opinions, *not* your magical influence."

Jaw tensed, I managed a nod. "Believe it or not, I don't enjoy my visits with the dearly departed. The warning against magic is a moot point."

My rebuttal was punctuated by three back-to-back blasts. One of which tore through the wall to our left, allowing beams of red from the fiery attacks above to brighten the hall with a hellish spark.

Enveloping me in his embrace, Alastor shielded us both under his arms. "You're sure you won't let me escort you to the Summit Room?" he ventured, his lips brushing my ear, "Even if it's to ease my own mind?"

Pulling back, despite the pleas of my heart, I forced the mask of neutrality years of training had perfected. "Your mother needs you, and I couldn't dare show up with a bodyguard and maintain even an iota of respect from delegates."

Alastor's hands fell to his sides, the temperature of the water plummeting at his retracted touch. Anguish and a begrudging understanding sliced deep creases between his brows. "As you wish. Just promise to be safe, Vanessa, and hurry back to me."

Unable to promise such lofty things, I turned away from his expectant stare and swam on with hot tears burning behind my eyes I would never dare shed.

"Princess Vanessa, so kind of you to join us in the midst of a raging attack," the newly promoted Chief Master Neleus snarled the moment I swam into the room. "If you're going to be *this* late for an emergency gathering, you should be dead or dismembered."

Have you ever disliked someone with such intensity that the simple act of talking to them left a sour taste on your tongue? That sums up how I felt about Neleus. "I'll try harder to accommodate next time." Screwing my lips to the side, I tapped my chin with one fingernail, feigning innocence. "*But* … if I hurry, how will I keep up pretenses that I'm allowing you boys to figure out matters on your own?"

Over his shoulder, my mother shimmered into view. A shiver skittered down my spine. What skin was left on her face was stretched tight over protruding bone. Pressing one gnarled finger to blackened lips, she shushed my disrespectful tone. A blink, and she was gone.

"Vanessa!" Poseidon thundered, cracking his trident against the ground. "In what way is insulting our most decorated soldier considered *helping* this situation? Apologize this instant!"

Dragging his tongue over his top teeth, Neleus stabbed his hands on his hips and waggled his eyebrows suggestively.

Grinding my teeth to the point of pain, I forced the vile words passed my lips. "My deepest apologies, *Chief Master.*"

A smug smile crept across his once handsome face. I hated the majority of the war-torn effects from our ongoing battle with the humans. Loathing was an insufficient word to describe how I felt about the rickety table of rotting timbers which replaced the magnificent stone structure that had been the centerpiece of the Summit Room. For starters, the pilfered table—seen as a treasure *only* because it was pillaged from the humans—was *wood*. In the water. Do you have any idea how hard it is to gracefully slide into a chair that is constantly trying to float out from under you? Bothersome objects aside, I hated that the stress of the sieges seemed to age my father another five years every time I saw him. As of late, gray strands decorated his brilliant red hair. War was suckling the life and youth from the once regal king. That said, there was *one* warfare side effect that brought great joy to my twisted little heart: the way it had beaten and ravaged Neleus.

The mermaids of Atlantica no longer chased after him or sighed wistfully behind his back. No, they reserved that for Triton alone—*gag*. When it came to Neleus, they avoided eye contacted and said a silent prayer to Mother Ocean that their families would not *dare* mention a marital union with him. A kinder natured mer than myself would have felt bad for him.

The noble soldier, partnered with his platoon, once shimmied up the side of a ship only to meet the sling of a blade from one temple to the opposite jawline. An angry pink slash, jagged like a thunder bolt, forever sullied his once dashing features. One seafoam green eye, which once held the powerful charisma to charm most any unsuspecting mermaid with a glance, drained to a hollow, milky white. It may have been cruel, but I found it fitting that his outside now more closely resembled the monster lurking within.

Appeased by my apology, Father soothed one hand over the wiry hair of his beard. "Did you see your step-mother to safety?"

"Doralious and his squadron escorted her to her quarters. They will wait there until given further notice." Pulling out my chair, I took a seat at the table. Judging by the snooty looks I received, if the rest of the Council members had their way, those would be the last words I spoke. Unfortunately for them, I had every intention of further ruining their evening.

"Very good." Father leaned back in his chair, one arm draping over his armrest. "Let us begin before the Lemurians bring this castle down on top of us."

Agonizing silence and patience had won me a seat at the table. Since my last birthday, I had secured my place there by biting my tongue on any and all matters discussed. It was a painful endeavor I despised to my very soul. Sure, it often meant sinking my fingernails into my scales to stop myself from lashing out about one inane topic or another, even so I succeeded. Triton endured no such struggle. Every meeting his eyes went glassy, and I could practically see the minnows that powered his simple, little brain swimming round and round.

That day, I had no doubt, would be different. Our kingdom was under attack, the world as we knew it crumbling. I refused to remain silent a moment longer. Biding my time, I listened for the ideal moment to wriggle my way in.

"I will start by saying that there is no prize in engaging the humans now. No bounty to pilfer." Holding one hand out, Calypso—the representative from the Caribbean—adjusted a giant bauble ring situated on her middle finger. "Therefore, I see no benefit in engaging my soldiers. If we hold fast, they will tire and move on."

While the guilt from the attacks on Atlantica and the loss of mer lives sagged Poseidon's once proud shoulders and cast deep shadows beneath his sunken eyes, Calypso seemed immune to the perils of war. The fifty-fifty split she bargained for on the spoils of ships her soldiers pillaged elevated her from a lay-about rock dweller to a mogul dripping in diamonds and pearls.

"*At the cost of how many innocent lives?*" Father slapped his hand to the table, causing the weary oak to groan in protest.

Leaning back in my chair, I folded my hands over my stomach and considered Calypso through narrowed eyes. There was nothing about her I trusted. She was more of a pirate than the men crumbling our walls with their cannon fire. Atlantica floundered, yet she prevailed. If it wasn't so dastardly, I would have appreciated her tactics. Her ploys were blatantly obvious, and she never even bothered to conceal them. Somehow, her slick tongue and clever wordplay convinced the Council she was acting in their best interest. I didn't buy it … but I admired it.

"We can weather this storm and continue on course." Resting her elbows on the table, Calypso steepled her fingers in front of her. Her nails clicked together in rhythmic ticks. "We have come so far and achieved so much! If we let the humans distract us from our goal, they will lord over us forever! As of this moment, they are learning to fear these waters. They sail with leery gazes focused on the sea. Soon, we will rule the oceans while they tremble on the shoreline. We will be masters of our domain that no longer dread those fish-eating Ruffians. Until then, it is the opinion of the Caribbean mer that we bathe in their treasures and send every ship we can to Davy Jones's locker. They stole Poseidon's *first* queen from us; we owe them retribution."

My stare snapped to my father. At the mention of my mother, his pupils fixed and dilated like a Great White smelling blood. Calypso hooked him, using his most painful memory as bait. Adjusting his grip on the trident, he thumped it twice against the ocean floor. If he agreed with her and called the meeting, all would be lost. The moment to act was at hand … and my hands were clammy with nervous sweat.

Scooting back my chair, a puff of sand rose around me. Floating to full height, I met the questioning glances of the Council members with an absolution that was betrayed by my hammering heart. Triton's bulging gaze pleaded for me to keep still. None-too-subtly Father mouthed the words *sit down*. Ignoring the outpouring of family support, I pressed on.

"I believe we can agree that it is in all of our best interest for this war to end in a timely fashion." Hands behind my back, head held high, I swam the perimeter of the room in the self-aware posture of the Indian Sea Mer. "We long to see Atlantica returned to the glory and traditions it prospered in before the humans' *first* attack two long years ago." Pausing behind the representative from the Gulf, I leaned one elbow on the back of his chair, letting the tips of my fingers brush his bare shoulder. Their culture was rooted in the bond between beings, making it no surprise when that simple contact softened his dubious expression. "We want revenge for the loss of my mother. We seek to punish them for every net they have cast." Letting my palm drag over the back of the chair before falling to my side, I flutter-kicked on until I positioned myself at the head of the table opposite of my father. "However, there is one avenue we have completely failed to consider … the request for a peace summit."

The room exploded in uproarious protests which were drowned out only by equally passionate shouts of accord.

To my surprise, Father banged his trident against the table, calling them all to attention. "Whether we agree with her sentiments or not, I believe Princess Vanessa has the floor."

"She's not even a Council member," Calypso sneered, eyeing me with contempt.

Poseidon silenced her with a look stern enough to make the tide rescind. Only when a respectful hush fell over the room did he grant me the nod to continue.

Bolstered by the encouragement of the king, my tone became ironclad conviction. "The humans didn't want this war any more than we did. They rely on our fish for food and our waters for safe travel. They fight us because they fear us—for good reason." Mimicking the zest of the Mediterranean delegate, I tossed her a playful wink. The effort earned me a light-hearted chuckle, and *possibly* another supporter for my cause. Clasping my hands behind my back and jutting my chin out in the regal elegance of the Arctic Mer, I resumed my rotation around the table. "*However*, if we were to send word that we wanted to meet for a peace summit, if our king were to convene with theirs, perhaps we could convince them we seek an alliance … not war." Pausing beside the Atlantic trustee, I bent to whisper against her ear, "Stunning gown!"

Batting the compliment away with a flick of her wrist, a flattered blush warmed her cheeks.

Catching Triton staring, his head listing to the side as if he didn't recognize me, I cleared my throat and swept the room with a trusting smile.

"If we could get them to lay down their weapons," I locked stares with the mer from the Pacific—who expressed his disinterest by twirling his lip piercing with the knuckle of his forefinger — and my voice morphed to unforgiving ice, "they would be completely vulnerable, giving us the perfect opportunity to rally every soldier and strike. By banding together, we could plunge the entire island of Lemuria to the depths."

Genuine appreciation raised the Pacific representative's brows, making the scrolled tattoos along his cheekbones stretch taut.

Lacing my fingers to prevent myself from fidgeting, I faced off with Poseidon to await his judgment of my assessment.

"You spoke out of turn today, Vanessa," he rumbled, twirling the trident between his palms. "That was a bold and risky move for someone seated here as a *guest* alone."

Something within me began to shrivel, a dying flower thirsting for one beam of the sunshine of his acceptance.

"However," he mused, stilling the whirling trident, "your idea shows a great degree of foresight. While risky, if executed properly, it could come with great reward." To the room, he boomed, "All those in favor of the peace treaty distraction leading to an offensive strike?"

One by one, hands raised ... Triton's being the last and most hesitant. Only Calypso kept her hands folded tightly in her lap, scowling miserably that the vote did *not* turn in her favor.

"Congratulations, Vanessa," my father stated, his eyes crinkling in the corner. Was that what pride looked like on his face? Such a thing had never been directed at me before. It held the same blinding effect of staring directly into the sun. "You successfully formulated your first military maneuver. Let us all pray to Mother Ocean that it's an effective one. Neleus, gather my commanding officers. Our strategizing will begin the moment they arrive. Until then, meeting adjourned."

A final bang of his trident dismissed the group. Bubbling with giddiness, I was the first out the door. Eagerness to report back to Alastor with my accomplishment spurred my fins ever faster. I was passing through the Hall of Records, with its row after row of shelves containing chronicled scrolls and tablets, when Triton shouted my name.

Beaming broad enough to make my cheeks ache, I whirred on my brother.

One mighty stroke of his tail and he floated beside me, *not* returning my smile. Instead, the corners of his mouth dipped down in an uncharacteristic frown.

"You played each and every one of them," he accused in place of a greeting. Harsh judgement cast dark shadows over his usually breezy features. "Manipulating them by reflecting some element of their culture back at them. I just want to know why. You have so much more to offer. Why would you lower yourself to cheap stunts like that? Was it *just* so they could see something of themselves in you? It was sneaky and underhanded, Vanessa. Are those the methods Amphrite has taught you?"

Glancing around to see if anyone was lingering or listening, I moved in close enough to bump his chest with mine. "It's *politics*, Triton," I hissed, his accusation smearing my momentary victory. "I did what I had to do for the good of the kingdom."

Towering over me, Triton glared down his nose in disappointment. "There are *other* ways. This one was beneath you."

Cocking one hip, I jabbed my fist to the rise of its curve, a wry huff of laughter seeping from my chest. "We don't all have your endless supply of charm, *brother*." I spat the last word as if it soured on my tongue. "The rest of us make do with what we have, and in this case my flair for theatrics worked *very much* in my favor."

Without another word, I kicked off and left him to chew on that.

# CHAPTER EIGHT

My tail worked side to side without tiring, belly skimming the ground to avoid the resistance of the currents and flying rubble. Through the throne room, where a gaping cavity had been blown through the soaring ceiling, I wheeled around the corner into the hall that led to the sleeping quarters. The aerial strikes had ceased, which I took as a sign that Father and his soldiers had ventured topside for the summit. Bursting through my bedroom privacy curtains with the force of a tropical storm, the flaps of kelp fanned out behind me. Pulling up short, a startled bark of laughter escaped me.

Alastor sat on my bed, back straight, hands in his lap. Floteson draped around his neck, shielding his chin and mouth like a scaly scarf. Jetteson laid across his lap, the cutest little belt I had ever seen. Careful not to disturb my zebra babes, Alastor pivoted his upper body to welcome me.

"Whhh hmmmnd?" he attempted, his voice undistinguishably muffled.

"I'm gonna need you to try that one more time," I giggled.

Floteson and Jetteson's endearing faces popped up the second they heard me. Shoving away from Alastor, they darted across the room and spiraled up my arms. Tenderly, I dotted a kiss to each of their foreheads. Both nuzzled in to my touch.

Shaking off a shudder, Alastor flipped his tail and lifted from the bed. "I said, what happened?"

"They listened to me, Alastor!" Twirling merrily around, I backstroked to the shelf next to my vanity where I kept the alchemy tonics Amphrite taught me to make. Pulling down the halved oyster shell I used as a mixing bowl, I splashed a bit of sun coast surf along the sides then cupped both my hands over it. "The *entire* Council, they listened! I suggested Father approach the humans to seek a peace treaty and he's doing it! Right now! Where's your mother? Is she well?"

Clamping my eyes shut, I attempted to concentrate and slowly drew my hands back. An iridescent bubble swelled from the shell, its surface ebbing and flowing into various shapes and spaces as the spell I infused on it hunted for my father's location.

"The moment the attack ceased she rushed to assess the damage to the castle with the other servants. I was supposed to follow, but … The C-council" Alastor stammered, shoving a stray lock of hair behind his ear, as he struggled to catch up, "took advice from a *nineteen*-year-old princess?"

"*They did!* And not just the Council, my father, too!" Leaving the bubble to continue its search, I spun on Alastor and seized his upper arms. Thankfully, I was able to suppress the urge to shake him in my excitement—but barely. "He *saw* me, Alastor! *Really* saw me! And he was *proud*! It was as plainly written on his face as if it had been scrolled there!"

Alastor's hand rose to his mouth, the tips of his fingers tapping his lips softly. I could see his mind ticking to fill in the blanks of the questions I left unanswered. "All this time, all that's been lost, and you suddenly talked the entire Council into giving up their greed inspired quest and seeking peace?"

Spinning back to my project, I ducked my head to hide the guilty flush filling my cheeks. "In a matter of speaking." Dragging one hand and then the other over the bubble's surface, I tried to steer it to find Poseidon. Still, no luck. "*Blast!* I'm too excited to focus! I can't get this thing to work!"

Reaching around me, Alastor's hand encircled my wrist and turned me to face him. "Peace is not a 'matter of speaking' concept," he stated softly. With his thumb under my chin he gently eased my gaze up to his. "What *exactly* did you say to them?"

Biting my lower lip, my confidence wavered. They were words, only words; what did they matter if I achieved my goal? But they did matter. The intensity of Alastor's tone reminded me of that with the potency of a dagger rammed deep.

My mouth opened, the explanation tumbling out in one long-winded ramble of guilt. "I may have said that the humans would be at their most vulnerable if we declared peace and *then* attacked. However, Father is a reasonable man! I'm sure once he sees how wonderful it is to have peace restored, it will be easy to convince him that there is no need for further attacks!"

Alastor cast his stare to the ground, dragging his tongue over his lips as if choosing his words carefully. When his gaze met mine once more, I found sorrow shading his topaz eyes to a deep russet. "Nessa, in all your life how many things have you been able to *convince* your father of?"

"Counting today?" I swallowed hard, my voice rising a few octaves to a high-pitched whimper, "One."

"And what makes you think this is going to be any different?" he asked, not in accusation, but to tenderly guide me to the outcome I had been too blinded by my own goals and ambitions to see.

Desperation stealing into my heart and oozing through my veins, I caught Alastor's hand and squeezed it tight in both of mine. "It has to be! I … I couldn't think of any other way!"

Our conversation was cut off by a flurry of purple smoke swirling into the room. Amphrite materialized just inside the doorframe, her gills opening and shutting in rapid pants. Nostrils flaring, venom beamed from her glare with me as her target.

"*What … have … you … done?*" The cut of each word was delivered through grinding teeth.

Dropping Alastor's hand as if his touch scorched me, my jaw swung open in search of *some* explanation. "My Queen, I'm sorry! The moment Father returns I will tell him of my true intentions. I will admit that peace in Atlantica was my *only* motivation! There's still time! We may be able to thwart any further attacks!"

Closing the distance between us, she rolled her fingers in the direction of my wayward locating spell. "You silly, *stupid* girl. Meddling in matters you had *no* place in. *You have no idea what you've set into motion!*" Pinching my chin between her thumb and forefinger, she wrenched my head around. Jabbing her index finger toward the bubble, violet sparks of magic flew from her extended digit. "You will watch what you hath wrought. Behold, the destruction of our world, courtesy of your little intervention."

My pulse pounded in my temples, a knot of dread tightening in my gut.

Within the bubble, father's silhouette crested the water line, heavy droplets of salt-water dripping from the end of his beard. Raising one hand, he signaled for a cease fire. Beneath the waves, such a command from the king could not to be contested. Out of the sea, it meant nothing.

Someone shouted in the distance.

A harpoon winged through the air.

My shoulders wretched in a dry-heave as I watched the weapon sink into my father's gut. His limp body curled around the harpoon's momentum. Royal Guardsmen sprang to action. Seizing their king, they whisked him back toward Atlantica as fast as their fins would carry them. Blood gurgled from Poseidon's paling lips, the water in their wake turned black with gushing gore.

Folding me into the security of his embrace, Alastor shushed me softly, his fingers trailing through my hair. Breathing in his scent, my hands curled into tight fists against his chest. With my cheek to his shoulder, I stared into the horrors of the telltale bubble, praying to Mother Ocean that my eyes were deceiving me. Every breath scorched my gills. Every blink irritated lids raw from sobbing. Even then … I couldn't look away.

The soldiers carried Father to his quarters, depositing him gingerly on to his bed. The harpoon shifted with the motion, causing Poseidon's eyes to roll back, an anguished groan tearing from his chest.

Amphrite spun on me, pure hatred radiating from her scowl. "If *anything* happens to him, *this*," she jabbed two fingers from her own chest, to me, and back again, "is *over*. Our partnership will *cease*. I've tolerated your temperamental nonsense and obvious insolence for *too* long. No more. Pray to Mother Ocean that Poseidon lives, *little mermaid*, or you will be dead to me as well."

A flick of her wrist and Amphrite disappeared in a jumble of purple tendrils. A blink and she joined the scene within the bubble, shoving aside a soldier who was wiping blood from Poseidon's face to gain access to her husband. Uncapping a vial she called forth from nothing, she poured a thick, black tonic over his wound which bubbled and foamed within the shredded flesh. Father sucked water through his teeth, his paling face lolling to the side. So distracted was she by the critical situation, that Amphrite's ever present glamour began to waver. Her hair faded to a simple and subtle auburn. Bold, striking features melded into a far more innocent loveliness. A fresh lump of emotion constricted my throat at the realization that her feelings for my father trumped her own need to hide beneath her ever present masks. The tragic poetry of that prompted a fresh onslaught of tears.

Amphrite snapped a command at the soldier across the bed. With a nod, he leaned in and pressed Poseidon to the bed with a firm hand to each of his shoulders. A jerk of his chin cued Amphrite he was ready. Her firm grasp closed around the shaft of the harpoon. Delicate lips pressed into a firm, white line. Face reddening with the strain, she extracted the harpoon with one steady tug.

A pulsating, crimson geyser erupted the instant the spearhead emerged from the lesion. Ears ringing, the world whipped around me in a dizzying whirlwind.

"Close your eyes, Nessa," Alastor murmured against my hair. "You don't need to see him like that."

*Like that.*

Frail, weak … and dying. The all-powerful king reduced to nothing more than the bloody chum we all are in the end. And who sealed his fate? Who played the part of executioner? *Me.* A *human* fired the shot, nonetheless my actions may as well have loaded their weapon. I didn't blame Amphrite for hating me. In that moment I did, too.

Amphrite's hands toiled over Father's wound, manipulating dense vines of multi-hued magic that stitched his flesh back together from the inside out. In a matter of seconds the bleeding stopped. The lingering question being, had it been in time?

Forcibly shoving away from the warmth of Alastor's arms, I crouched beside my vanity and seized the edge of the shell in a white knuckled grasp.

"Open your eyes, Papa." My whispered encouragement into the bubble caused ripples to shimmer over its surface. "*Please,* just … open your eyes."

Every fiber of my being willed his lids to draw back and give me a glimpse of the deep emerald pools beneath.

I was so fixated that Loriana's outraged cries from the hallway barely registered. "Pardon me, but you are approaching *the princess's* quarters! What business have you with her? I demand to know who is in charge here! *Sirs!*"

The methodic claps of mer armor resonating down the hall could not divert my attention, nor could the half dozen soldiers who swam into my room in a tight formation. I wasn't even struck by the usual wave of repulsion at Neleus's presence as he led the charge wearing his animosity like a badge of honor.

"You are in the presence of royalty, sir!" Loriana's lips pinched tight, her indignation visible in the flush rising from her neck to her earlobes.

Hands clasped behind his back, Neleus stared at the wall in front of him as if glancing in her direction was beneath him. "Silence, *servant*, or we will silence you."

I'm sure *that* raised Alastor's hackles. Unfortunately, I was too absorbed to notice.

"Princess Vanessa of Atlantica, you are under arrest for the crime of treason against the crown," Neleus trumpeted, his chest puffed with pride and purpose. "Your plotting put our king in danger and you shall be judged accordingly. Comply or we *will* use force."

A flip of his tail positioned Alastor between the soldiers and myself, his arms pulled away from his sides defensively. "This is absurd! She's just a girl! Blame your Council for listening to *a child!*"

In place of civilized dialogue, Neleus drew his sword. Whirling around, he forcibly introduced the butt of his weapon to Alastor's temple. Loriana shrieked, rushing to her son's side as he crumpled to the ground in a heap. With nothing else treading in their way, the soldiers closed in. Rough hands closed around my upper arms, yanking me upright. My fingers clawed at the vanity top, seizing the edges and holding tight if only for a moment longer. All the while I willed my father to open his eyes. If it was the last thing I saw, I wanted that glimmer of hope to assure me I wasn't the scoundrel I condemned myself to be.

Arching back, Neleus raised his sword a second time. Unforgiving bone cracked against the back of my skull. Thrown forward, black spots danced before my eyes. My chin slammed into the edge of my vanity, prickles of pain exploding through my face. Head rolling to the side, my vision blurred. Eyes suddenly heavy, the siren song of sweet oblivion proved a hypnotic one. Still, what little focus I maintained stayed trained on my father. The last thing I saw — or *thought* I saw — before the descending black veil fell was the faintest flutter of my father's lids.

# CHAPTER NINE

I never considered myself a pampered princess. After the death of my mother, I wasn't bathed in extravagances and doted upon. Poseidon provided adequately for me; however, I always felt that was mostly to keep up pretenses among his people. Nonetheless, it took one night locked in the dungeon, deep within the bowels of the castle, for me to appreciate just how posh my upbringing had been. Expansive quarters and plush bedding were exchanged for rocky, hard-packed ocean floor and oppressive stone walls that seemed to close in with every hour that passed. Unable to move freely at this depth, the water had long since grown stagnate. Gills aching from its burning stench, I kept my breathing shallow to spare them further irritation. Light could not reach that tucked away hollow. The icy nip of the watery abyss cut straight to my marrow. Huddled in the corner, I curled my tail to my chest and hugged it with trembling arms. Chills vibrated my frame — my teeth chattering with a potency that made me worried they would shatter. The one and only upside? My ever present entourage of ghouls couldn't seem to find me down here.

I wasn't the lone resident of that particular pit of despair. Somewhere in the blanket of darkness another prisoner suffered from a deep, rattling cough. Another incessantly begged for Poseidon's mercy ... or death. At a neighboring cell a melodic voice rambled to itself, answering with maniacal giggles. My least favorite of all was the prisoner I dubbed The Screecher. The Screecher would lure us into a false sense of security with his or her silence. Then, without warning, they would open their maw and unleash an ear-piercing caterwaul that would last until the first time their voice cracked. After that they would fall back into a hush, waiting for the urge to strike again. Emotional and physical exhaustion were no match for their vocal stylings. I would drift off, my mind whisking me back to my quarters where I was snuggled beneath cozy layers of handwoven bedding, when that shrill cry would drag me back to the hell imprisoning me.

After yet another symphony of sorrow, my forehead fell against my tail in hopes of claiming a few minutes of rest before the next performance. Stirring water, and the unmistakable flap of a fast-moving tail, snapped my head toward the sound.

"Nessa?" a familiar voice whispered, inching in the direction of my cell.

One flip of my tail rocketed me to the door. My outstretched hands curled around the bars, their rough stone surface scrapping my palms.

"*Alastor?*" I asked the murky blackness, my voice raspy from the polluted water. "Is that you?"

A tender hand closed over mine, providing a nurturing warmth in my prison of ice. "I'm here, I'm right here." I couldn't make out more than the outline of his frame, yet the rush of water from his exhale tickled over my face with each fevered breath. "I came as soon as I could. I had to wait for the changing of the guard so I could sneak in."

Appreciative tears burned behind my eyes. Swallowing hard, I fought to keep my tone steady and neutral. "You can't be here. If they find you, they'll throw you into a cell or ... beach you."

Pulling his hand away far too soon for my liking, I could hear him fumbling with the lock. "*No one* is going to be in a cell, or anything else for that matter. We're going to get you out of here and run far from the reaches of Atlantica."

Grip tightening around the abrasive cell bars, I squeezed my eyes shut. "And where would we go?" I asked, my melancholy audible. "Where could we possibly swim to free ourselves of Poseidon's clutches?"

Silence weighed heavy for a beat. A huff of indifference and the clinks and clanks of him fiddling with the lock resumed. "I don't know where we're going," he rumbled through his teeth, "but we *are* going."

Veiled by darkness my expression softened, my heart swelling to fill my chest. Something had changed between Alastor and me, and I couldn't pinpoint exactly when. More than once, he had seen me at my worst and still hung around to celebrate the moments I was at my best. For that reason, and a slew of others, I would rot in that dungeon before I would let him put himself in harm's way for me.

My moment of contemplative reverie was interrupted by a pair of luminous azure eyes blinking my way from the cell opposite mine. Their limited light allowance set an eerie glow over the wide smile that curled beneath. "If you don't know where you're going, *any* road will get you there."

I had no right to be leery of the mysterious entity. He was a captive there, same as me. Even so, something about that creepy mer set my skin on edge. "Yes, thank you for that," I replied in lieu of a dismissal.

Alastor paused for a brief glance over his shoulder. "Keep him talking, the light helps."

"Keep him talking?" I repeated in a hushed whisper meant for his ears alone. "Before you got here he was blathering on about ravens, writing desks, and something called a Jabberwocky. I think he's crazy."

Across the aisle that smile grew wider still, its stretch bordering on impossible. "I'm not crazy. My reality is just … different from yours."

"I don't care if he's drumming the *Atlantica Pride* anthem on this tailfin," Alastor strained against the persistent lock, "he's helping our cause."

From above came the clap of armor, its drum growing steadily louder. The sound awoke The Screecher, who trumpeted their impending arrival with his/her high-pitched screams.

Reaching through the bars, my hand caught Alastor's and squeezed hard enough for my fingernails to slice my message into his flesh. "This cause is a lost one now. *Go!* Poseidon will show no mercy if he finds you here!"

"You have magic!" Alastor argued, not budging in the least. "Use it to throw open these doors and come with me!"

*"Don't you think I've tried that?"* My nervous gaze flicked from Alastor to the ramp leading to the castle's higher ground — now illuminated with an eerie blue glow, thanks to our looney audience. "Something down here blocks my magic. I can't get out and, more than that, I *cannot* watch another person I care about condemned to

this hole because of me. If you care for me one iota, do *not* ask me endure that anguish again! Go! *Hide!*"

With defeat slicing deep valleys between his brows, Alastor dropped his arms to his sides. Even in that faint light, he met my gaze with a conviction that made my heart ache. "I will hide, but I will *never* leave you. Whatever happens, we go through it together."

"Together," I agreed knowing it was one promise I could never keep. Before he could kick off, my hand shot out to seize his arm. "Alastor, wait! What of my father? How does he fare?"

Leaning in, he breathed the words against my cheek. "He lives. You are many things, Vanessa, but a murderer is *not* among them."

I wanted to hug him. To sing praises to Mother Ocean. To close my eyes and be bathed in the miracle of that news. Instead, I ground my teeth and jerked my head in the opposite direction of the incoming ruckus. "*Go! Hurry!*" I demanded.

Alastor pried himself away, swimming farther into the catacombs of the prison. The moment he disappeared from sight, my head fell against the bars. For an instant, I let bloom the flourish of relief.

You know what squashes a short-lived reprieve in no time flat? A troop of eight soldiers lined up in front of my cell in perfect military precision, their faces devoid of emotion. Hands behind their backs, they dared not look my way, but fixated on the wall behind me.

All except one. Doralious swam point of the crew, any kindness he once showed me replaced by icy indifference. "Princess Vanessa of Atlantica, your trial at The Pit is at hand. Come with us without incident, or we have full authority to beach you," he stated, tensed jawline twitching. "Will you comply?"

His frostiness stabbed icicles into my already battered heart. Pushing back from the bars, I crossed my wrists in front of me and offered them up for the clamp of the cuffs. "Doralious, I didn't mean for any of this to happen. You have to know that."

Slamming open the cell door, he secured the cuffs with more force than was necessary. "Save your excuses for The Pit. You harmed the king, and I am merely here to take out the trash."

A nod to his men and I was hooked by the elbows and dragged toward the spiraling ramp. My tail slapping against the stone, I craned my neck to stare back at the darkness which consumed Alastor. With him on my side and my father's life spared, it seemed fate granted me an ounce of mercy. Mother Ocean was smiling on me. That bolstered my confidence for my trial ahead. After all, I was *still* the beloved Princess of Atlantica. Really, what was the worst that could happen?

The Pit. As the name suggests it was not a place built on sunshine and kisses. Positioned on three sides was coliseum-style seating carved into rock walls. The fourth side of the makeshift arena was a trench so deep it seemed to venture straight to the Earth's core. There were tales of what lay at the bottom of The Pit's chasm. Some said gnarly sea beasts patrolled those waters, grappling over every hardened criminal who was bound and cast to the depths. Others claimed is was a tribe of cannibalistic mer that camped at the bottom. Either way, it was a mystery I had no desire to solve.

Hands shackled and shoved forward by guards, I quickly learned that urban legends weren't required to make The Pit scary. Clamping my lips to stifle a scream, I gaped down at the pitch black abyss beside me. My head spun in a dizzying case of vertigo. In a normal situation, such a trench would be no real threat to a mer. A few flips of the tail and —*voila*—freedom! In the scheme of things, what kind of punishment would that be? Much like a beaching, being cast into The Pit was a death sentence. In both cases the convicted mer's hands were bound, their tail weighed by a rock. In a beaching, it prevented them from lurching and rolling their way back into the water. Death in The Pit was a longer, more brutal punishment. As with all fish, water had to move over our gills for us to breath. Pinned in one spot, the criminal would be able to breathe … for a time. Then, the water would still. No current able to dip that deep. The mer would be surrounded by water, yet unable to claim a breath. If there was a more cruel way to die, I couldn't imagine it.

Poked and prodded to the center of the arena, judgmental stares from Council members and the upper crust of Atlantica glared down at me. Every seat was occupied, the arena filled to capacity by the crowd's morbid curiosity. The moment I swam into view, they erupted in a deafening chorus of sneers and boos.

"You don't seem to have many supporters here, Princess," Doralious scoffed, his cheek muscle contracting in another involuntary spasm. Slamming the heel of his palm into my shoulder blade, he propelled me forward. "Maybe instead of being our next queen, as I once thought, you'll be the first royal tossed into The Pit."

The soldiers flanking him tittered at his pitiless jab.

Pulling my shoulders back, I tipped my chin in their direction. "If not, you boys are being unnecessarily rough and unforgiving to either the future queen or Royal Alchemist. *Both* are positions that can order your beaching. But by all means, shove me again."

"Princess Vanessa of Atlantica!" a shrill voice interrupted with a boom that reverberated through the arena and down The Pit's trench. "You have been brought here for crimes against the crown. The king is unable to proceed over your trial; therefore, he has appointed *me* to act in his stead."

Sagging in defeat, my upper lip curled into a cringe. I knew that voice … but it didn't stop me from praying to Mother Ocean that I was wrong. Let it be a trick of the senses due to the roaring crowd and cavernous space. Let anyone but *him* be positioned on that platform to decide my fate. Heck, at this point I would have opted for Lebo the simple-minded stable hand over … *Neleus.*

Chest puffed with borrowed authority, he hitched the brow over his vacant, cloudy eye. The gesture pulled his scar taut, momentarily straightening its jagged line. "I do believe it is customary for the accused to *bow* before their magistrate."

"You heard him! Bow for your sentencing!" Clapping his hand on my shoulder, Doralious shoved me down with enough force to send me tumbling.

Unable to get my bound hands under me, my face mashed into the ground. Granules of sand ground between my teeth and burned their way up my nostrils. Tail curled under me, I pushed myself up to what humans would consider a kneeling position. Hacking and spitting to clear my airway, my disheveled hair curtained half of my face as I turned to glower at the vindictive Chief Master.

Murmurs rippled through the crowd. Uneasy glances were exchanged between the Council members that had come to know me. Those onlookers that had been shaking their fists and shouting for justice settled into their seats and shifted uncomfortably. Whatever I had done, I was the king's daughter and they were all witnessing my public shaming at the hands of a merman *without* kingly authority. It seemed Neleus didn't have *quite* the support he was hoping for on this endeavor.

Flicking my hair from my eyes, I raised my chin and let the crowd see my grime covered face and nest of hair in complete disarray from a night of sleeping on the floor. Amphrite lingered at Neleus's elbow. Catching her gaze, I held it with an unrelenting intensity. She took her care and doting on my father into consideration when she chose that day's glamour. Her shells, tail, and hair were a brilliantly shimmering white, her eyes an ethereal blue. Appearing a true angel of the sea, she offered me a sympathetic frown. Father's condition must have stabilized, elsewise any empathy she had for me would have expired.

"People of Atlantica," Neleus began, swimming along the perimeter of the first tier seating, "it is with a heavy heart that I state before you the crimes of our troubled princess."

My own nature made me want to throw my head back in a wry huff of laughter and roll my eyes skyward that he would dare refer to me in such a way. The need for the crowd to stay swayed to *my* side forced me to curb that desire. Biting my lip, I dropped my chin to my chest and cloaked myself in a finely braided blanket of melancholy.

"She plotted to lure our king into harm's way," he continued, his claims building in zest and vigor with each word, "convinced the Council through clever wordplay to seek peace with the humans—"

Pausing, he glanced to the crowd, anticipating a rash of boos and hisses. Silence was the only response. Nervous stares of the once eager participants now lingered on the door, as if anticipating Poseidon's arrival and wrath.

Adjusting his posture, Neleus folded his hands in front of him and ventured on. "Driven by her own thirst for the throne, she plotted to send our benevolent king out of the sea where his life was nearly stolen from us!"

Something small, with a sharp bite, struck my shoulder, followed by another and another. Squelching a yelp, I bowed my head and hid beneath the canopy of my own shackled arms. Risking a peek out, I saw the members of the Royal Guard that lined the arena pelting me with rocks, shells, and any other shrapnel they could find.

"Enough of that! We are not heathens!" Neleus bellowed. Fighting to conceal his amusement, his crinkling eyes contradicted his tone. "Princess Vanessa, *treasured* daughter of Poseidon, how do you plead?"

Heaving me upright, the skin of my upper arm was pinched between Doralious's merciless fingers hard enough to bloom in a rash of purple.

Swallowing hard, I met Neleus's icy stare and spoke the truth of my heart. "I *never* meant my father any harm. I love and admire him, more than you know. When I voiced my suggestion to the Council, I thought I was speaking in the best interest of Atlantica. I know now, after this heartbreaking catastrophe, that my words came out of turn. I beg you, people of Atlantica, Council, Queen," my chin dipped in a nod of acknowledgment to each that were present, "and most of all my father, to understand that I held no malicious intent and bear unimaginable guilt for what transpired."

Raising one hand to his jawline, Neleus ran his thumb over the edge of his scar. "Vanessa *is* the first born Princess of Atlantica. That said, others may view her acts as treasonous. To let them go unpunished would be a display of weakness we cannot allow in this time of war."

Movement, in an otherwise still throng, snapped my head to the entrance I'd been dragged through only moments ago. Alastor filled the doorway: shoulders raised, hands balled into tight fists at his sides. His gills opened and shut with each agitated huff. Loriana hovered behind him, apprehension over her son's brewing fury deepening the lines on her face.

"Princess Vanessa spoke out of turn on a pivotal matter that almost cost Atlantica our King," Neleus stated.

The moment of verdict at hand, a hush fell over the vast arena.

"Her penance shall be paid with a period of silence." He continued with an arrogant nonchalance, "Since the princess cannot hold her tongue, Amphrite … *bring it to me.*"

An aghast buzz rippled through the arena. Even those against me were stunned into a slack-jawed silence.

Judging by Neleus's smug sneer, the sound must have filtered to his ears as a thunderous applause.

The fight drained from my body, my vision tunneling in fear. The crowd turned on itself. Some demanded my release, others shouted that the punishment was too lax. Alastor bolted in my direction, raging like a typhoon. Loriana caught his arm, begging him to be still. Vehemently, my head whipped side to side warning him not to risk another stroke in my direction. If he tried to intercede, he would be beached. That I could not allow.

Doralious and his cohorts surrounded me. Unfastening my shackles, they spread my arms out in a wide arc that made my shoulders ache.

"Doralious, please, we were friends once. You can stop this," I pleaded, salting the ocean with my tears.

"That was before I knew you to be the lowest form of bottom-feeder … *a traitor*," he sneered, stepping back as the queen neared. "Consider this our gift to Atlantica."

My magic returned with an electrified jolt the second those binding cuffs fell away. I could have fought on my own behalf, but there was no helping me. The clang of fear ringing in my ears, I flexed my mystical essence and cast it out to one it could benefit— my beloved handmaiden.

Thinking the words, I planted them in Loriana's mind. *"Get him out of here. Don't let him see this."*

I accompanied my order with a delicate touch of magic, one that granted her a physical strength which trumped her son's tenfold. With a sorrowful nod of thanks and understanding, she seized Alastor from behind. Her arms hooked under his pits and clamped onto his shoulders. As Alastor kicked and flailed, she easily forced him and his furious resistance from the arena.

A bittersweet sigh of triumph passing over my gills, I turned my attention to the churning cloud of purple that marked Amphrite's arrival. Considering the last words exchanged between us had been volatile ones, I expected she would relish in this task. Much to my surprise, I found her jaw set tight and her nostrils flared in revulsion. I wanted to be brave, to be the warrior she attempted to mold me into for three years. Instead, to my extreme disappointment, I found myself blinking back tears.

"Leave us!" Amphrite snapped at the soldiers in a tone which left no room for debate.

As if summoned by the potent brew of my fear, my mother materialized behind her. On a normal day, her ghastly manifestation terrified me. In that moment, I sought her gaze. There, in the haunted hollows of her eyes, burned a maternal passion to protect me. Clamping my lids shut, one rogue tear slipped free and was swallowed by the sea.

"*Stop it*," Amphrite hissed with a haughty flip of her cascading locks.

Mother's head slowly turned in Amphrite's direction, revealing a festering cavity in her neck where writhing sea bugs feasted on the decomposing flesh. Her long-stilled gills began to expand and contract. Each superficial inhale swelled her size, her wrath amplifying her to a towering beast of ire only I bore witness to.

Glancing one way, then the other to ensure the soldiers were out of ear shot, Amphrite's face softened. "Do *not* let them see you cry. This is a temporary punishment performed through magical means that has no purpose other than to degrade you. *Don't* give them the satisfaction of stealing your dignity. Rest assured your ability to speak will be restored soon enough, there is no need to mourn that. For now, you need to look Chief Master Neleus in the eye and do *not* look away. Make *him* cast his stare elsewhere if *he* can't take the gruesomeness of his barbaric sentencing."

Understanding washing over her, Mother deflated like a pacified Pufferfish. Bobbing her head in grief-stricken agreement, she vanished without further spectacle.

That was it.

Unless I could find a way to go back in time and take Alastor up on his suggestion to bolt from the kingdom and live out our days as recluses, there was no way out. I thought myself treasured by the merfolk of Atlantica, yet I had sent away the only one who even tried to come to my aid.

"If you want to use your magic to take the pain away, I will —"

"No," I interrupted. Shards of my shattered heart were sawing me in half from the inside out. More than anything, I needed an outlet for that anguish. "I need to feel … *something*."

Equal parts regret and compassion played across Amphrite's features.

Shutting my eyes, I took a cleansing breath to brace myself. Then, with a jerk of my head to let Amphrite know I was ready, I stared up at Neleus with icy detachment … and offered her my tongue.

Violet tendrils poked into the tip of my tongue, holding the wriggling muscle taut. Yet another wisp traced over the meatiest part. Tissue popped. Scorching pain sliced through the tender flesh.

# Rourke

Coppery warmth flooded my mouth and down my throat, choking me. Swaying … wavering, I flexed my resolve to its limits by steeling my spine against the dizzying spots that danced before me. Ruby droplets dripped from my chin, melding into a crimson halo in the water around me. Atlantica's Chief Master averted his eyes.

# CHAPTER TEN

The precession of a princess. Regal pageantry traded for shackles. Showers of lovingly tossed sea flowers substituted for flying stones and insults. The stones stung less.

Blood seeped through my teeth, staining them pink before dribbling down to coat my chin with gore. My puffy eyes were a sliver away from being swollen shut. The pain in my mouth—that dull, pulsating ache—was a constant presence. Still, in that moment, I felt none of it. The agony of it all left me a numb, emotionless lump floating at the insistence of the soldiers escorting me.

"Poor little princess," a mocking voice taunted.

My blank gaze coasted sideways to find a cluster of soldiers that must have scurried from The Pit for the sole purpose of witnessing my further humiliation. *Such chivalry.*

"How will she bark orders at the servants now?" one among them scoffed.

"Maybe she can hum!" a puffy-cheeked soldier, with the beady eyes of a freshwater fish, chortled.

"Nah, she's got her looks, boys." A long and lanky guard shoved his way to the center of the group. Placing his hands behind his head, he gyrated his hips suggestively. "Don't underestimate the importance of *body language.*"

The group erupted in throaty guffaws, the offensive merman being rewarded for his off-color humor with playful shoves and slaps on the back.

Running my pinkie finger under the edge of my cuff, I lifted it away from the spot on my wrist it had rubbed raw.

*"Get out of my way! Move!"*

Tipping my head, stare distant and detached, I watched Triton force his way through the crowd of onlookers. The moment he saw me, his complexion clouded with the tinge of seafoam. Tendons of his neck bulging, he pushed aside those who dared to linger in his path. Docking in front of me, his gills clamped shut in a horrified gasp. He caught my chin between his thumb and forefinger, turning it one way then the other in a cursory inspection.

"Nessa, *no*. What did they do to you?" Features sharpening, his lip curled from his teeth to snarl at the soldiers holding me. "By order of the prince, *let her go!*"

My captors' didn't loosen their hold, yet had the right mind to appear repentant in the presence of the heaving royal.

"A thousand apologies, Your Highness," the taller of the two guards stated. "We are acting under the orders of Chief Master Neleus on behalf of your father. Princess Vanessa is *not* to be released from her shackles, or our care, until she has been safely deposited in her quarters."

Triton lunged in, chest to chest with the brazen guard — who shrank under his scrutiny. "I have been at my father's bedside, holding his hand as he clings to life. I assure you, he has granted authority to *no one*. But if you would like to continue this façade, I will be sure to include your name, *Sergeant Curry,* among those who acted without his consent, which I will present to him the very moment he wakes."

Curry's brow knit tight. His confused gaze ticked over Triton's face, struggling to decipher what was happening.

A click broke the silence, my shackles falling free and floating to the ocean floor.

The guard on my opposite elbow looped the key to the cuffs back onto the whale-skin sheath on his hip, his face the picture of resolve. "Curry obviously needs a moment *I* do not. I turn her over to your care, Prince Triton, with my best wishes to her *and* your father."

"Your compassion will not be forgotten." With the palms of his hands under my forearms, Triton gently raised my hands to assess the wounds on my wrists.

The rush of water from his exhale assaulted the raw and cracked skin, eliciting a wince I couldn't smother.

Triton leveled his stare, his expression broken with sorrow. "I was in that Summit Room. I watched them rally behind you. Then, the minute things turn for the worse, they cast you off like chum in a frenzy."

Pressing one finger to his lips, I hushed him.

From there my hand slid up, cradling his whiskery cheek in my palm. My brother. My sweet boy. Did he even know that with Poseidon's vast indifference to me, I consider *him* my only real family? Life had cut such a deep trench of distance between us, one that I vowed to myself to mend.

Swathing me in a comforting arm, Triton pulled me tight against his torso and protectively shepherded me toward my quarters.

"Fin polisher," Curry grumbled to his cohort behind our backs.

The slight soldier let one shoulder rise and fall in an offhanded shrug. "I'd save my breath if I were you. You'll need it when you're beached for following Neleus."

"*Neleus will answer for what he has done!*" Triton roared, his tone tempering when I shrank away from him. "As will *anyone* that participated in his brutality."

The rest of our brief journey passed in an incoherent blur, my deflated heart surging with renewed hope the moment my curtained doorway came into view.

Hooking the weaved fronds with his hand, Triton pushed them aside and coaxed me forward with his hand on the small of my back. I swam into *my* space … and my heart doubled in size.

Alastor was a vision from the most enticing dream. Diamonds of light played across his skin, casting long shadows over his sculpted features. Floteson and Jetteson circled around the narrow base of his tail, seeking solace in his familiarity.

"I need to get back to Father. I'm worried of what is happening in his absence. Do you mind caring for her?" Triton asked, hovering in the doorway.

"That's why I'm here, to ensure her safety." Alastor's worried stare traveled the length of me, taking in every detail.

I felt the burn of every flaw under the scrutiny of his gaze. The blood that streaked and stained my skin. My hair floating wild and matted. The deep creases of woe that sliced between my brows. Self-consciously, I peered at the shells inlaid in the floor and brushed my tail over their surface.

Turning to leave, Triton paused with his hand on the arch of the doorway. His fingers drummed in two rhythmic successions. Glancing back, he locked stares with Alastor. "Ju-just keep her in here until I get back," he stammered, his voice gruff with emotion. "I've known for some time that the Royal Guard was against her, but I never imagined they would take it this far."

"Atlantica has been ruled by a queen before." Stumbling back from the force of the sharks pushing off of him to torpedo my way, Alastor caught himself with a backstroke. "What problem could they possibly have with her?"

Floteson brushed against my right elbow. Jetteson tickled over my left hip. Hands at my sides, I stretched out my fingertips. The sharks' inky black bodies, freckled with white, curled around me with oil slick fluidity. Closing my eyes, I welcomed their touch of pure devotion.

"I can't fathom the cause." Triton's jaw flexed. "Promise me you will keep her holed away here until royal authority is restored. After today, there's no telling how far the Guard will go."

Leaving those ominous words bobbing in the surf, Triton blew from the room to be the noble prince Atlantica needed.

A hush fell in his wake.

Dropping his chin to his chest, Alastor rubbed a hand over the back of his neck. If there was something he wanted to say, he made great show of keeping silent.

"Sit down," he commanded, a gruff clip stilling into his tone. Crossing the room in a tight barrel roll, he collected a kelp cloth from my vanity.

Easing myself down on the edge of the bed, I swallowed out of reflex. The simple act caused my severed stump to ache. Blinking back a wash of tears, I curled my tail under me and stared at my hands in my lap.

Cloth in hand, Alastor crouched in front of me. With firm but gentle strokes, he scrubbed at the grime covering me, starting with my face. Lifting my chin with his knuckle, he worked his way down in slow-circles, scrubbing my neck and shoulders clean. Job complete, he leaned back to inspect his work. Seemingly satisfied, he cast the cloth aside only to have it float down and settle on Floteson's snout. The drowsy shark blew it away with a snort and flopped to the side with his head on his brother's back.

A flutter-kick of his tail, and Alastor settled onto the bed behind me. Continuing to work in silence, he combed through the tangled mess of hair. His unpracticed fingers divided the strands into three sections and maneuvered an awkward, yet efficient, braid. The stillness of the moment soothed me more than any sentiments of comfort ever could. In the tranquility I could imagine the entire world had been robbed of their voice. That I hadn't been singled out with such brutality.

Masterpiece complete, Alastor dropped his hands. They hovered over my shoulders, the pads of his fingers whispering over my flesh.

"I was furious at you," he murmured to the back of my head. "Then you swam in ..." Drawing in a ragged breath, his exhale crowned me with a wreath of bubbles.

Catching one of his hands, I peered over my shoulder, my expression a question mark.

"Had it been *me* in the arena," head listing to the side, golden embers of truth sparkled in his topaz eyes, "I would have done the same thing if it meant saving *you*."

Opening my mouth, a choked gargle leaked out. My teeth clamped together with a forceful snap, heat rising from my neck to my hairline.

Alastor brushed the thick rope of my waist-length braid over my shoulder. "It's okay, there's no need for you to—"

Green tendrils wafting from my wriggling fingers diverted him from the end of that statement. Magical wisps rolled and dipped before settling in as delicate as a mother's touch to the foreheads of my darling babies. Their heads rose, as if drawn up by invisible marionette strings. Floteson and Jetteson looked to each other before peering up at me. A gasp escaped me. Each now had one eye stained a bright sunrise yellow.

"*The princess knows of the risks you would take for her.*" Floteson lifted from the ground, his tail working side to side in his wide loop around us.

"*And she hopes you never get the opportunity to act upon them,*" Jetteson finished.

My own words were spoken through them in deep, gravelly rasps, providing an outlet that eased my screaming soul.

Alastor's lips screwed to the side, his topaz eyes narrowing. "If you were going to use your magic, why not restore your tongue?"

Jetteson curled around his neck and stared a recoiling Alastor in the face. *"So they can take it from her once more?"*

*"Next time they could make her slice it out* herself!" Floteson snarled, snapping his jaws at nothing.

Shaking off a shiver, Alastor bolted from me as if my skin was coated with Fire Coral. Speed swimming the perimeter of the room, he spun on me with accusation stabbing from his stare. *"Why?* Why do you subject yourself to such treatment? Because of your claim to the throne and the *chance* that you *might* rule someday? These people," shaking his head, he peered out my window, which had a charming view of those milling in the courtyard below, "to them you're a symbol. They don't … care about you."

One corner of my mouth dimpled in, my expression one of open understanding. Floteson and Jetteson twined around me, awaiting their next cue. This time I fed them no lines. Alastor needed to work through this matter on his own.

After a moment of his gills frantically expanding and contracting, he deflated. His strapping shoulders sagged. "No matter where we go, no matter what we do, you could never outswim Atlantica's reaches."

Gazing up from under my lashes, my chin dipped in a brief nod.

Bolstered by a fresh—yet significantly less potent—outrage, he wagged a finger in my direction. "And you know what else? This little talking shark thing? It's creepy. I think if you were going to give them voices it should have been something whimsical and non-threatening."

Stifling a yawn from the crippling exhaustion setting in, I gave my boys an offhanded nudge.

Floteson snaked around Alastor's shoulders, grazing against his ear. *"Do we disturb you?"*

Jetteson took the more direct approach, streaking straight for his face. *"Perhaps you'd fancy a snuggle?"* he ventured in his grating timbre.

Alastor batted them away. Fixating on my face, the intensity of his stare made my cheeks bloom in a brilliant fuchsia flush. With a flick of his fin he closed the gap between us. As he situated himself on the bed beside me, his tail brushed mine. Shoving my frond pillow behind his back, he fluffed, readjusted, then relaxed into it with a sigh. Lapsing back into a comforting silence, he laid a light touch to my shoulder and guided my head down onto his lap. The moment I settled in, he started at my temple and traced his fingers down my jawline.

"Sleep now, my Princess," he soothed. "You are undoubtedly tired. It was cruel of me to monopolize your time. Allow yourself the slumber you have rightfully earned."

My long blinks couldn't contest that. The demands of the day weighed heavy, my mouth incessantly throbbing. Clinging to the refuge of his touch, I watched the brightly colored fish waltz across the stage of my window until the current of sleep fell on their performance.

# CHAPTER ELEVEN

A gentle hand on my shoulder shook me awake. "Princess Vanessa? You need to wake up, Your Highness. It's urgent."

I woke with a jerk, staring up into kindly face of Loriana ... whose son I was currently drooling on. The sun was setting over Atlantica, cloaking the palace in a radiant lilac. Bolting upright, I wiped at the corner of mouth and nudged Alastor. He'd fallen asleep sitting up, his necked craned to the side at an angle sure to cramp.

"It's not what it looks like!" he snorted, coming to with a start. Eyes bugging, he leapt from my bed, spilling me unceremoniously to the floor. "Mother! I—"

"We will discuss the inappropriateness of your presence here, later." Pursing her lips, Loriana silenced him with a sideways glance, and she helped me up. "Right now, our girl needs all the love and compassion we have to offer."

Something lurked behind her eyes that made my stomach knot with dread. Forehead pinched, I urged her with a dip of my head to speak on what was plaguing her.

Gnawing on her lower lip, she laced her wringing hands together. "It's your father, Princess." Sorrow foamed and capped each word. "He has taken a turn for the worse. Your presence has been requested. There are murmurs that it is to say your final good-bye."

Tail failing me, I slumped back against the edge of the bed. Iron-clad dread sank in my gut, anchoring me in that spot. I should have been racing to my father's side, cradling his hand in both of mine. Yet if I swam from that room, I was entertaining a truth my fragile heart could not comprehend.

Blinking back tears, I tapped my throat with my fingertips.

"I'm sorry, Princess," Loriana shifted uncomfortable, "I have heard of no orders to return your voice as of yet. Tragic as it is, it seems your visit will be a muted one."

Unable to fathom such cruelty, I drifted from my bed and floated for the door. Those ever present, chilling eyes watched from every dim corner, yet no phantoms materialized. Their presence wasn't need. *I* was the ghost in the room; a shadow of the strong and self-assured girl I had worked so hard to become.

"Vanessa," Alastor reached for me, the tips of his fingers brushing the small of my back, "do you want me to go with you? I can wait outside."

I didn't look back, but tilted my chin in his direction and shook my head. If I clung to him now, I would never let go.

Working my tail side to side down the hall, I braced myself for what was to come. There was a high likelihood Father would be covered in healing tonics to ward off infection. The urgency to which I had been summoned warned that such measures were ineffective. Which bode the unsettling question: what would the majestic king look like drained of his valor? Digging my fingernails into the scales along my hips, I prayed to Mother Ocean that the jolt of pain would wake me from this nightmarish existence.

The same merfolk and soldiers who jeered at me mere hours ago paused in their tasks to look my way with pity. The story they had already written for me was scrawled across their faces. To them, I was the poor little princess, moments from being an orphan. Lifting my chin, I ignored their manufactured sympathy. The welts dotting my arms from their thrown rocks made the sentiment ring hollow.

The hallway of the sleeping quarters ended at the royal chambers. A golden arch surrounded Poseidon's doorway, the pillars situated on either side were elaborate totems of crowns, tridents, and hefty mer tails. On either side of them, two Royal Guardsmen floated at attention, prepared to defend their ailing ruler from any external threat he may face.

Amphrite lounged against the pillar on the right, picking at her nails in somber, black regalia. The moment she saw me, she pushed off the wall. She borrowed that day's façade from the Pacific Sea mer, down to the lacework tattoos highlighting her cheekbones and the shark-tooth choker decorating her dainty neck. An onyx rope braid hung to her rump, swaying across her back as she swished to meet me.

Her shoulder brushed mine, yet she kept her superior gaze trained straight ahead. "Remember what I said, Vanessa. I would *hate* to see you cast aside as a lonesome mermaid with no one to guide her through these treacherous seas."

It seemed safe to say our truce during my trail was a temporary one.

A flip of her tail and she disappeared, towed out by an undercurrent of animosity.

Father's weaved frond curtain rustled, pushed aside by my trembling hand. A hesitant flick of my tail propelled me into his quarters where one glimpse of him stole a gasp from my parted lips. Poseidon, a daunting presence in every memory of him, had shriveled under the press of his ailments. Yellow-rimmed eyes sunk into sallow cheeks. Laboring gills sputtered to claim weak, wheezing breaths. One ashen hand lay limp beside him, the other draped over his heart. Even in his weakened state he was at the ready to return the salute of his guardsmen.

Swallowing my trepidation, I inched to his bedside. My fingers laced with his, the icy chill of his flesh sending shivers coursing through me. Biting the inside of my cheek, I surveyed his condition with the critical eye of an alchemist. His wound had festered, the skin around it red and oozing. The sickly sweet smell of infection permeated off of him. Even so, these conditions seemed *easily* treatable by anyone capable of swimming the line between science and magic. Much like the queen, and seasoned alchemist, who—barely a blink ago—had threatened me and sashayed off.

Unless … it wasn't a threat at all. Amphrite schooled me on magic, she knew the extent of my capabilities. More importantly, she never did *anything* without carefully plotted reasoning. Why then would she entrust me with her husband's life instead of handling the matter herself? What was in it for her?

"*I get the ear of the queen when you take the throne.*"

Amphrite spoke those words when first asked her motivation for seeking to mentor me.

I was the long shot in the battle for the throne.

Everyone knew that.

But … if I were to save Poseidon from the brink of death, what then?

A slow smiled spread across my face.

That plotting, scheming queen was a diabolic genius.

Turning one palm skyward, I conjured a ball of jade energy that snapped and crackled with bolts of light.

Father's head lolled my way, his heavy lids fighting to open. "Vanessa?" he croaked in a feeble whisper.

"*Uhhh!*" I grunted, squeezing his hand to make my presence known.

"I tried so hard all these years," cloudy eyes unable to focus peered right through me, "and still I failed."

Leaning closer, I shook my head in hopes he could fix his gaze long enough to see I *never* thought of him that way. Feeding off my emotions, the ball of healing energy swelled, casting an emerald glow through the room.

Finally, he found me. To my surprise, the eyes staring back at me were completely devoid of emotion. "I tried to love you … yet never could."

The words gutted me. Reeling back, my ball of energy dissipated.

Water stirred on the opposite side of the bed, my mother emerging from nothingness. For a beat I gaped at the fresh-faced beauty that had been restored to her—if only for a moment. Once more her flesh held the soft luminescence of a polished pearl, her hair a glossy Orca black.

Amethyst eyes, perfectly matching mine, pleaded for understanding. "*Vanessa, my love, go now. What you'll learn here will only bring pain.*"

Oblivious to our newcomer, Father pushed on in his strained hush, "I knew your mother loved another when we met. Titonis was forthcoming with that truth. Even so, our marriage was arranged and could not be contested. To *her* I was a dear friend. To *me* she was everything—the very epitome of beauty. I convinced myself, as all foolish men do, that it was enough. That with time she may actually grow to feel as I did. I would have granted her anything … as I proved the night before our wedding when she told me she was pregnant with another merman's child. Had I canceled the wedding, I would have bestowed a legacy of shame on her. She would have been banished from Atlantica. Unable to imagine my life without her, I agreed to proceed with the wedding and raise the baby as my own."

A sequence of syllables, meaningless if separated, but string them together and they held the power to thrash and demolish my world while I stood impotent to prevent it.

"*Vanessa, please* …" Mother beseeched me, her full lips clamping together.

Head listing to the side, I tried to fathom what she could *possibly* be hiding if *that* wasn't the worst of it.

"Titonis was so grateful for my kindness, she vowed to devote herself to me. I like to think that for a while, she actually did." A fit of hacking coughs interrupted his conscious clearing exposé. Only after they passed did he settle back onto his pillow, face red and eyes watering. "It was after Triton's birth that a cavernous distance formed between us. Outsiders thought us to be the perfect family. In private, my queen struggled with the demands of life as a royal. She grew distant ... withdrawn. I will admit to my share of jealousy."

"Jealousy?" Mother's ruby lips curled from her teeth in a spiteful snarl. "*You were a vicious beast and you know it!*"

One weak hand rose, Father wiping away the spittle that formed in the corners of his lips before continuing on. "My greatest fear was of losing her to the pull of her heart, which *never* belonged to me. Nagging curiosity bested me one day, and I … I followed her. She swam from the kingdom without hesitation, straight into shallow waters. Words cannot describe what I saw that day. It defied the meaning of the term impossible. The current swirled around her gleaming body. I remember shielding my eyes with my arm. When I dared to look back, I found *my queen* had replaced her gorgeous tail with *revolting human legs!*"

Mother's shoulders rose, her hands squeezed into white knuckled fists at her sides. "*Vanessa! Not all truths should be revealed! For your own sake, turn around and leave these quarters now!*"

I couldn't have moved it I wanted to. The most I could muster was a meager shake of my head.

"Before you were even born, as you swelled in your mother's belly, I trumpeted to all that would listen that *I* was your father." Even as his blinks grew long with exhaustion, his face instinctively contorted in disgust. "I learned the truth that day, watching her run from the sea into the arms of that *human* … and I resented you for even *being*."

Jaw swinging slack, my eyes burned with unshed tears. Reality, in its most abhorrent form, wriggled through my mind. Its shadowy tentacles lashed out, destroying the rose-colored world I thought I knew.

Rounding Father's lavish shell bed, Mother plowed in my direction; her hands raised, curling into claws. I had no doubt, had she possessed a corporal form, she would have seized my arms and dragged me out. *"Get out, girl! Every word he spits is poison! Swim! Swim far from the borders of Atlantica and never look back!"*

A nervous laugh bubbled from my throat, morphing into a choked sob. One trembling hand pushed a rogue strand of hair behind my ear. My blurring gaze searched her face for some clue of what other horrible truth lay in wait.

"I toiled with the decision to inform the Council of your mother's betrayal." Poseidon's head fell to the side, sinking farther into the plush of his pillow.

*"Vanessa!"*

"It was harder still to announce the verdict against her …"

In a blink Mother's exquisite charms melted away, dripping from her form in heavy globules that exposed the true revulsion beneath. Skin cracked, taking on the blue hue of death. Hair fell out in clumps. Jaws widened and stretched outward into the vicious snout of a barracuda. The stench of rot assaulted my senses.

Swelling in size, she glowered down at me, and moving at a speed that would impress a marlin, she darted in.

*"Get out!"* she bellowed in a beastly roar.

It was too late. In the light of the king's nightmarish spewings, I saw her spectacle for the meager attempted distraction it was.

Our eyes locked, holding each other in the only way we could to ride out the storm of Poseidon's confession.

"My brother, Hades, hated that I made him carry out her sentencing. As he clamped on the shackles to bind her powers, he swore he would leave Atlantica and never return. Which, of course, he ultimately did. Unfortunately, not before doing as he was ordered by rolling her onto the beach and leaving her to die … at *my* command."

Ears ringing in the aftermath of my exploded world, my head pivoted from my mother to Poseidon. One was a horrifying spectacle, the other an exalted king. One meant to protect me, the other begrudged every breath I took.

The dark aspects of my tortured mind, which I feared from the moment they manifested, acted in my favor. Yet another certainty I based my young and resolute life on was flipped over with the ease of a human child's toy boat against white-capped waves crashing against the shoreline.

Another onslaught of hacking coughs racked Poseidon's frame, bloody bubbles of phlegm burst on his pallid lips in ruby speckles. When the fit passed, he flopped back down. Each breath wheezed passed his laboring gills in a high-pitched whistle.

"Don't think it has gone unnoticed how hard you have worked in your pursuit to rule." He gasped, his eyes rimmed with pink-tinged tears. "You must know that can never be. You are a *half-breed*, Vanessa. Your kind has no place on the throne. The most you aspire to … is to serve your brother well."

"*Child, are you well?*" Mother reached for me in concern. Catching sight of her own grisly hand, she curled the offending appendage into a fist and let it drop back to her side.

How could I answer such a question when I couldn't imagine *anything* ever being well with me again?

I watched with detached interest as my own hand rose seemingly under its own accord, the emerald orb flickering to life in my palm once more. Its tingling warmth traveled up my arm, radiating through me.

Cradling the orb, I dipped my head and brushed it to my chin. A whispered touch restored my tongue, the swell of it feeling foreign after its absence.

"I have the capabilities to heal you." Trauma left my throat raw, yet the coarse, scratchiness of my voice could not squelch the conviction of my tone.

"I want nothing from you." Poseidon's head slumped my way, his gaze betraying him by lingering longingly over my magical display.

"All I have ever wanted was to make you proud. Please," I beseeched him, extending the sparking orb in his direction, "may I show you?"

Letting the pull of exhaustion draw the curtain of his heavy lids, he jerked his chin in a brief nod.

*"Vanessa, what are you doing?"* An edge of unmistakable concern tainted Mother's tone.

I was making a ghoul nervous—there's a claim not everyone can make.

Hoping to calm her with the assurance of my resolve, I lowered the orb to Father's wound. The skin began to stitch together from the inside out, the black veins of infection retracting. "Did you ever stop to think that the meeting you witnessed on the beach was my mother informing her human love that he was my true father? She may have been driven by the desire to find an acceptance for me you never offered."

Poseidon snorted, provoking another fit of chest rattling coughs.

Continuing my task, I waited for his rash to ease before pushing on with my point. "Even if that was the case, that man played no part in my upbringing. *You* did. You are the *only* father figure I have ever known. I have learned much from you, my King. Namely, how to maintain a cold disinterest toward those we are *supposed* to care for."

Without warning, I drew the orb back, yanking out every bit of the healing energy I had bestowed.

The mighty king's eyes, faintly returning to their emerald sparkle, snapped open. His face creased in question. As fast as my magic worked, the absence of it reversed the effects in double time. The wound I tended to began to weep. Spidering black veins of disease flared and spread over the span of his chest. Each strangled breath rattled from failing gills.

Mother pulled back, her hand fluttering to her lips. *"You don't need to do this, Vanessa. For if you do, there will be no coming back from it. Not completely. Not once it has blackened your soul."*

*"Shhhh,"* I soothed them both simultaneously. "My mother did not die by *your* hand, nor shall you die by mine."

An element of relief stole through Poseidon's pained grimace. Mother murmured praise of thanks to Mother Ocean.

Lost in the entrancing lightshow within the orb, I raised it to shoulder height. "Unfortunately, you *could* have prevented it, yet failed to act. Now, to end the debate in your mind and prove once and for all that I truly *am* my father's daughter, I shall do the same."

Rolling my fingers into a fist, I crushed the orb into dissipating tufts.

# Rourke

His gaze fixed on the dying embers of his last hope, the King of Atlantica drew his final breath.

And I felt … *nothing*.

# CHAPTER TWELVE

Conch shells trumpeted their sorrowful blasts. The black shroud of mourning draped from the highest window of the tallest tower of the castle. Atlantica hung its head, the sea swallowing the collective tears of all those who grieved their fallen king.

Things moved at a head-spinning pace—the period of mourning being rushed by the urgent need to restore rule. The Caribbean mer became increasingly vocal in their *insistence* for retaliation against the humans for Poseidon's death. They wanted action, and they wanted it *now*. With their numbers and plentiful bounty, the Council felt it was *mandatory* to hurry the Choosing Ceremony. A successor needed to be named *before* the Caribbeans could rally and pose a threat of political mutiny.

Pouring over historical scrolls since youth, I anticipated the pomp and circumstance of such an event. *I hadn't* prepared myself for the trauma of living it. Poseidon's body rested at the foot of the cathedra in the throne room. Wrapped from the crown of his head to the tip of his tail in ropes of seaweed, careful attention was paid to bind him to a plank comprised from loose logs plucked from the surface. Two guards held either end of his gurney, keeping their departed king in place until signaled.

Triton and I hovered shoulder to shoulder, not speaking. Knuckles brushing against each other's offered a closeness we both thirsted for. All eyes were on us. Every culture of mer was represented in the melting pot that filtered into the space, shuffling to find their own space to view history unfolding. All the bodies mashed in together was rapidly morphing the situation into a confining, claustrophobic one. To distract myself, I scoured the sea of faces in search of Alastor. Somehow, I felt my constricted gills would loosen if I could see his face.

Mid-sweep, my glance fell on the vision of sorrow veiled in black a beat before she lunged. "Amphr— *Ughhh!*"

Fingernails clawed at my throat, gouging chunks from my flesh. Teeth set in a deadly snarl, she spat her accusations in my face, "*I trusted you!* It was an easy spell and I trusted you! You would've been the exalted one, bound for the thrown! Instead, you *let him die!* Traitor! Defector! *Insurgent!*"

"*Guards!*" Triton bellowed. Prying Amphrite's hands free, he shoved me protectively behind him. "The queen is a bit overcome. Escort her to her quarters *at once.*"

Ushered out by two stationed guards that hooked her under her arms, Amphrite held my stare, challenging me to be the first to look away. "*This isn't over! You and I … we* will *finish this, Princess!*"

"Don't let her get to you." Triton kept himself positioned between Amphrite and me until she was safely out of sight. "She's overwhelmed, just like the rest of us."

"She will never forgive me," I muttered, more to myself than him, my hands smoothing over my ruffled ponytail.

"It's okay, we've got each other." Rocking forward, Triton bumped his elbow to mine, his ocean blue eyes pleading for validation. "Whatever happens here today … we're in this together."

For a beat all I could do was stare, my tongue caught as if torn out once more. Triton, my *half*-brother. Would he still cling to our sibling bond if he knew of my human ancestry? Or, worse yet, that I let Poseidon die? How could I open my heart to him when I knew that one slipped phrase could shatter our family's fragile existence?

Forcing a tight smile, I linked my forefinger with his pinkie. "Together … to the end."

"*People of Atlantica!*" the crowd parted at Neleus's boom, my skin crawling at that loathsome sight of him.

Drawing back to the outlining walls, they revealed an opalescent pedestal in the center of the room. Only two items rested upon it: a golden trident glistening in the waving diamonds of the late day sun, and a small, spiral shell that looked so out of place there its presence seemed accidental. In moments one would belong to me. Casting a sideways glance to the body of the king, my drumming heart reminded me with absolution which way *he* would cast his vote if able.

"As the eldest," hands clasped behind his back, Neleus swam slow circles around the pedestal. Devilish delight crinkled his eyes at the corners. "Princess Vanessa will swim forward. Placing her hand over the plinth, either the trident or the Ursela shell will choose *her*. Then," a pause for dramatic effect, "with that act, Atlantica's next ruler shall be decided."

The assemblage erupted in a thunderous applause, only to be hushed by Neleus's raised hands.

"Come, Princess," Neleus invited me forward with a sweeping wave of his arm. "Destiny awaits."

Time slowed with the first flick of my tail.

Triton gave my finger a pulse of comfort before letting his grasp slip from mine.

The melding faces of the crowd stared without blinking.

Alastor swam in without a moment to spare, tossing me a quick wink of encouragement.

Puffing my cheeks, a rush of water moved over my gills.

Pulse drumming a steady chorus, I approached the pedestal.

One trembling hand reached for the trident.

A slight twitch.

A faint shimmy.

Rapidly blinking disbelieving eyes, I gawked at the golden artifact that lifted, ever so slightly, from its perch.

*"Everything you want is mere moments away, my darling girl."*

The desiccated rasp of my mother's voice whipped my head up.

One decayed hand, unseen by anyone except me, rested under the center point of the trident, guiding it up.

The opposite forefinger pressed against fetid lips. *"Shhhh."*

Under her guidance, the trident lurched farther in its ascent.

Every dream I had ever had was within my grasp … and I shook my head.

"No," I whispered, "not like this."

Before she could argue otherwise, I offered my palm to the ursela shell.

It leapt from its roost without hesitation and settled easily into my grip.

Poseidon's words echoed through the farthest reaches of my mind.

*Serve your brother well.*

Time caught up in a dizzying blur. Triton kicked his way beside me and extended his hand. The trident drew to him with a magnetic force. Cheers and applause rose from the crowd. The signal was given, and Poseidon's body was released. He floated up in an offering to Mother Ocean, the hope being she would bless the heir that succeeded him. One by one, spectators clamped their fists over their hearts, hailing the newly crowned *King* Triton for the very first time.

"The Alchemist power granted by the shell is real. *He* will be little more than a symbol to the kingdom," Alastor murmured after slinking through the crowd to edge up beside me. Extracting the shell from my hand, he nudged my shoulder for me to lift my hair.

Silently watching my brother's spectacle, I obeyed.

"Today, your destiny claimed you. That is a rare fortune few are granted." As he spoke, Alastor positioned the shell between my collar bones and tied the reeds behind my neck.

He meant to comfort me.

There was no way he could have known.

The shell granted enchantment to those *without* magic. With my given attributes its pull was hypnotic. My skin warmed the second contact was made. Every cell of my body sang out in an electrified rush. A monsoon of bolstered power coursed from head to tailfin.

One cynical brow raised in the direction of my mother, who scowled her disapproval in a ghoulish display that once would've haunted my nightmares. I thought it, and she vanished in a whirl of eddying wisps.

Closing my hand around the shell, a smile tugged at the corners of my mouth. Armed with my new treasure, I felt a long lost piece of myself had been restored ... *and that piece craved chaos.*

# CHAPTER THIRTEEN

## TWO MOON CYCLES LATER ...

I long to be thinner. Ca-can you do that?"

Offering the adorably plump mermaid a winning smile, I tossed my head back, my curtain of hair brushing over the small of my back. "Darling, helping downtrodden merfolk, like yourself, is my very *reason* for getting out of bed each morning!"

My patron's shoulders rose. Beaming in my direction, a deep dimple sank into her left cheek. "It seems rumors of your kindness left out your limitless generosity ... uh ... Princess? Alchemist? My apologies, I'm unsure which title is most fitting."

"Please, calling me Vanessa is *more* than adequate." Floating to my cabinet of potions and ingredients, I snatched one vial of a chalky white concoction from a line of others identical to it. For the fun of showy spectacle, I returned to the table in a half-turn, back-flip and handed her the vial. "Here, drink this twice a day and have a sensible dinner."

"Thank you, Vanessa," she exclaimed, hugging the vial to her chest, "You have no idea what this means to me!"

At that same moment, Triton filled the doorway. His mighty hands clamped on either side, he leaned. "*Vanessa!*"

Instantly, my patient dipped in a formal bow, her cheeks reddening in surprise.

"Your Majesty! I ... she ... *I called the princess Vanessa!*" she blurted in an awkward confessional.

Glancing over her shoulder, her eyes widened in hopes I would come to her rescue.

Forehead pinched tight, I stared back as if she were mad.

The moment her panicked head whirled back to Triton, I shot him a wink to let the poor mer off the hook she found herself wriggling from.

"That *is* her name." Triton's forced scowl lost a bit of its potency with the contradictory humor twinkling in the pools of his eyes. "I would wager she has been called far worse. Now, if you would pardon the intrusion, I need a moment with my Royal Alchemist."

"Yes! Of course, my King!" she said, backing out the door in a series of bows. "And thank you again for the potion my … Vanessa."

Clamping her lips shut on the high-pitched whimper of embarrassment that *eek*ed out, she darted out without another glance back.

"Another satisfied customer!" I giggled, throwing my arms out wide. My heart swelled with pride to *finally* be doing something to help the people of Atlantica, even if it didn't look as I pictured it would.

Responding with a noncommittal huff of laughter, Triton swam farther into my parlor. His wandering gaze scoured every wall, investigated every nook, mostly like in search of outwards signs of the misery he felt *sure* I wrestled with.

"The elixir that maiden left with, is that similar to the tonic I have seen a slew of others toting about in the town square?" he asked in that same tone mothers use when they are trying to catch their young in a fib.

"One and the same." Plopping down in my carved-coral chair, I draped an arm over the back of it and flopped my tail onto the matching desk. "Why? Have there been complaints?"

Taking the seat opposite me, Triton rested his elbows on my porous desktop. "Not as of yet. Amphrite never maintained set hours to tend to them. *For now*, they're just thrilled you're seeing them."

Biting the inside of my cheek to fend off a smirk, I dutifully took the bait. "For now?"

Lips screwing to the side, one brow lifted expectantly. "All of those merfolks receiving the *exact* same tonic? I *know* you're disappointed, Nessa, but word will spread."

Flipping my tail under the desk, I leaned in, mirroring his attentive posture. "That's why you think I prescribed that? Disappointment at my new station in life?"

Triton's kingly masked cracked, revealing my sweet-natured brother beneath. "I can't remember a time you *weren't* working tirelessly to prepare for the throne. Then, fate swayed another way. *Anyone* would be disappointed by that."

Rubbing my chin with the palm of my hand, I tried to keep the sardonic edge from my tone. "And that's the *only* reason I would give them all that same tonic? Because of my own discontent? Did you ever think that *maybe* I gave them the same elixir, of water lilies and plankton, to placate them because there is nothing wrong with *any* of them? That all they actually needed was someone to listen to them? Take my friend that just left. She feels she needs to be thinner to find love. The truth, that she is absolutely perfect the way she is, totally evades her. You tell me, my dear brother, what harm is there in handing her a vial of confidence? One, without side effects, she can gulp down and see herself for the vision she truly is."

His gills expanding, Triton deflated in a gush of water and bubbles, concern still clouding his features.

"As to your claim of my disappointment, let me let you in on a secret, *little brother*." Dropping my voice to an urgent whisper, I rolled on with my exposing outburst, "Never before have I been so free. Free from my endless pursuit to win Poseidon's good favor— Mother Ocean rest his soul. Free from my quest for a throne I never stopped to ask myself if I even *wanted*. And free from the spirits that plagued me each and every time I delved into magic."

*The rub of everything that unfolded? I was being completely honest. Every day I awoke feeling a leaden anchor had been lifted from my shoulders. People hear my name now, and think of me as eternally hungry for power. That wasn't the case. Shortly after the coronation, Triton gifted me with my own little parlor at the bottom of a dune shadowed by the castle. There, I performed my civil duties as the Royal Alchemist. The space was cramped, the storage lackluster, the furniture outdated; and I loved every alcove and cranny. I didn't have to fight for it, didn't have to prove myself worthy. I need only to be, because it was the path fate had chosen for me. Plus—and this is just between us—everyday that Triton was king that boy aged another five years. I was certain another three or four more moon cycles and his blond hair would be completely platinum. I did not envy him that.*

Triton's expression—a swirling menagerie of horror and confusion—reminded me there was a key point to my tale I had forgotten to clue him in on.

"Oh, yeah. Haunted since I was three. Saw our decomposing mother. Did I forget to tell you that?"

Triton leaned back as far as the limits of his chair would allow, his eyebrows disappearing into his hairline. "We are clearly going to have to have a longer conversation about *that* at some point. Right now, however, my focus is the plethora of fresh power you were bestowed with. If you aren't using it to benefit Atlanticans, what *have* you been doing with it?"

A beaming smile dawned on my face, my cheeks aching at the strain. "Oh, I've found ways to keep busy."

Raising one hand, I snapped my fingers over my head.

Floteson and Jetteson appeared from the shadows in an instant, slicing through the water with their mismatched gazes locked on target—namely, their mama. Jetteson curled over my shoulders, Floteson twining up my arm.

"When I first granted them voice, they were little more than puppets, spewing my own thoughts back at me," I explained, giving each of my sweet boys a scratch under the chin. "Since then I have found a way to bring forth their personalities and allow them to speak their minds."

"He's an inadequate king!" Jetteson hissed, baring his fangs. "Overthrow him and claim the throne that should rightfully be yours!"

Feigning shock, I pinched his beak-like mouth shut with two fingers.

"*Oh my*! Children *do* say the darnedest things! You'll have to excuse him, he's a bit of a cheeky one." Out of the corner of my mouth, yet plainly for Triton to hear, I muttered, "None of that treasonous talk, sweetness. I would prefer *not* to see you served on a platter at the next royal banquet."

"The princess *will* prove herself with her surplus of skill," Floteson countered, peering up at me with adoration. "The people will learn to love and trust her, while her brother's inadequacies will become glaringly obvious."

After Floteson wriggled off, I folded my arms over my chest and pressed my lips into a firm line. My fingers drummed against my triceps. "Well … this is awkward."

Triton's massive shoulders quaked with a chuckle. "How many fish died so you could teach them to give those responses on cue?"

"Numbers can't determine value," I countered, returning his grin.

"Believe it or not," Triton muttered, dragging his fingers through his beard, "I didn't come all the way out here for a performance of your predatory marionettes."

Lower lip jutting out, I pretended to console two zebra sharks that were completely indifferent on the matter. "Don't take it personally, boys. Truly unique art is seldom appreciated." Shaking off the guise, I tilted my head in Triton's direction. "So tell me, *my King*, what did bring the ruler of Atlantica out here to my quaint establishment?"

"I hate it when you call me that." Triton's nose crinkled. "Especially when you know all I really wanted was to be King of the—"

"Manatees, I remember."

Triton glanced nervously over his shoulder, as if to confirm no one was listening—a hard thing to be sure of when some of his subjects had sonar hearing. "It's Calypso and the Caribbean merfolk," he said in a barely audible whisper that made lip reading mandatory. "There are rumors their army of soldiers are headed here to Atlantica. They feel my failure to launch a counter attack against the humans after Father's death is evidence I'm not fit to rule."

Gliding my knuckle back and forth over the ursela shell's smooth surface, I mulled over the threat this presented. "What reason are they giving for providing such a strong military force here in the capitol?"

"Right now, it's all hearsay. My guess? They're going to try to use the power and station they've acquired to overthrow me." Nostrils flaring, Triton shook his head in disgust. His crown wobbled with the motion, as if even it was unsure it belonged there.

The fingernail of my index finger clicked against the center swirl of the shell. "The Pacific merfaction won't stand for such treachery. We could be looking at civil unease in the bloodiest fashion. What *exactly* is it you think I can do to help?"

Shoving his chair back, Triton sprang up to swim the length of the room. "I need to know what the humans are doing. If I had intel to bring before the council I could rally them back to the proper cause with *all* merfactions united. We would need to know what kind of numbers they have, the weaponry we are up against, and where their armies are stationed. The question becomes how we would go about acquiring such intel?"

"Listen to you sounding like a proper king." Catching a lock of onyx hair that wafted beside my cheek, I rubbed the end of it between my thumb and forefinger. My voice trailed off as I contemplated the situation. "What we need is a bird's eye view of what we are up against ..."

Triton spun on me. His eyes bulged, and jaw swung slack at what I guessed to be the first idea he had ever experienced. "Want me to recruit a seagull? I know a guy!"

Blinking, I stared at him. "The manatees would've been lucky to have you."

"Your Majesty! King Triton!" Doralious called from outside. A beat later he leaned against the stone arch of my doorway, his gills rising and falling in fevered pants. Simply the sight of him set my teeth on edge. "The delegate from the Gulf claims to have further information into our ..." his icy glance sliced right through me, "... *sensitive matter*. Your presence is required immediately."

"Thank you. I'll be right out." After a curt nod dismissing his man, Triton cast me one final, beseeching look. "Please, Nessa? Anything at all that you can find out could be of use. And we both know you have ... *ways*."

Blood bubbling in my veins, I glowered at the space Doralious had vacated.

"*Doralious* is still in service to the crown?" I spat the accusation at my brother, not even attempting to mask the loathing in my tone.

"This is a sensitive time." Triton's wide shoulders sagged, his stare pleading for understanding. "I need all the help I can get, and Doralious has the benefit of years of experience. Once we restore the necessary order, I will see to it that he answers for what he did."

"*What he did was taunt me while I was having my tongue be ripped out!*" Slapping my palm against the table, I exploded to full height. Floteson and Jetteson coiled around my waist, hissing their own protest.

"And I had Neleus *beached* for that, lest you forget!" Triton shot back, easily matching my intensity. "As the newly appointed king I *cannot* afford to make enemies in the infancy of my reign! Not until my authority is asserted and recognized in *all* seven seas."

"I seem to remember you vowing to punish *all* that were party to my victimization. Has my protective younger brother been silenced by political posturing?"

Triton's shoulders sagged. "That's an over simplification of a —"

"*I detest him!*" I interjected.

"I know."

"He's *not* to be trusted!"

"On that I agree."

"If he crosses me in any way I *will* turn him into a sea slug!"

"I expect nothing less."

Irritation slowing to a simmer under Triton's stoic calm, I relented with a sigh. "At least promise me you'll watch your back on all matters pertaining him, *little brother.*"

One corner of Triton's mouth tugged back in an almost grin. "Does that mean you're agreeing to offer your aid?"

"Get out of my parlor." In place of a confirmation, I jerked my chin toward the door. "Go be a king. I'll let you know if I come up with anything."

Following him out, I leaned my shoulder against one side of the arch and watched him shrink into the distance.

"Floteson, Jetteson," at the mention of their names, two little heads popped into my periphery vision, anxiously awaiting orders, "keep an eye on my brother. Report back with *any* potential threats against his rule."

"Yes, Princess," they chorused, dutifully dipping their heads.

Side-by-side they swam off to honor my command, their bodies braiding together with sleek fluidity.

# CHAPTER FOURTEEN

fter searching the palace kitchen, stables, and courtyard, I found Alastor in his sleeping quarters. Never having ventured into his space before, I stopped short at the narrow archway. The servant's quarters were modest: a burrow in the soft sea sand for a bed, one boulder carved into a bench seat, and whatever personal effects they chose to decorate with. Even so, that wasn't what made me pause before ducking inside. It was the hypnotic beat that resonated from his room.

Tail flipping in a slow and steady tread, I placed my shoulder against the wall to settle in and listen. Mahogany hair was knotted at the nape of his neck, one loose strand falling forward to brush his cheek. With serene focus, he thumped a rhythmic cadence on three hollowed turtle shells. Swaying with the tempo, the muscles of his torso flexed with each motion. Only when the music released him from its spell did Alastor glance my way. A slow smile curled across delectable lips. "Didn't know I had an audience. I would have rose for the ovation. How long have you been there?"

"Long enough to have a new favorite song." Stooping under the archway, I caught sight of a tightly rolled knapsack in the crater of his bed. "Going somewhere?"

Moving the turtle shells aside, he floated to full height.

"I am, actually." The steadiness of his tone was countered by the nervous pinch of his brow. "Your brother wants me to be his right hand and head of his personal security. Not at all surprising, he doesn't have much trust in those currently in place. To do that, however, I have to leave my position at the castle and begin basic training with the Royal Guard."

Pursing my lips, I nodded with fictional understanding. "In case you didn't notice, we're at war. I know because someone *harpooned my dad.*"

*Don't give me that look, you judgmental little polyps. I am well aware my comment was crass. In my defense, the man I thought was my father died, my lifelong dream was squashed, and twisted family secrets came with startlingly revelations of my linage. All things considered, a little teenage sass was justified, if not expected. And you're basically foliage, so back off.*

If Alastor was offend by my attempted snark, his magnetic smile didn't let on.

"Lucky for you, I'm a complete coward with every intention of flipping away as fast as my fins can carry me at the first sign of danger. It's basic training, Nessa, not the front line. Three full moon cycles and I will be back here with a new station and my same charismatic charm." When I didn't answer right away, he playfully swatted at my tailfin with his. "Before Triton offered me this opportunity, my only prospect for the future involved following in my mother's footsteps and remaining a servant to the throne. I admire my mother, I do. But I don't want her life. You can't fault me that."

"When do you leave?" I asked after a beat, chewing at the inside of my cheek.

Eyes, the inviting shade of an early twilight, searched my face for … something. "You've got me for two more days."

"That doesn't give us much time," I mused, drumming my forefinger against the point of my chin.

"Time for what?" he asked, his eyes darkening.

My gaze swept over him, taking in every inch of his lanky frame. "For us to do something *monumentally* stupid."

Swishing in close enough for the warm current of his breath to tickle over my cheek, his voice dropped to a husky whisper, "I like where this going. What did you have in mind?"

Raising my shoulders to my ears, I chirped in a giddy titter, "*I want to walk on land!*"

Punctured by my non-amorous intent, he shrunk back.

"That's … not where I thought this was headed," Alastor muttered to himself, before feigning enthusiasm for my benefit. "Can your magic do that?"

"I don't know … yes? Maybe? My mother could do it. I'm hoping it's hereditary. Let's find out." I knew I was rambling, yet couldn't seem to stop.

Linking my fingers with his, I didn't give him a chance to argue. One thought of shallow, turquoise waters and the ursela shell warmed against my chest. Holding tight to Alastor, the two of us dissipated in a rolling emerald cloud.

"*Beluga, sevruga, come winds of the Caspian Sea!*" Arms thrown out wide, I tipped my head back and bellowed each word toward the sky.

"*Is that necessary?*" Alastor's head snapped one way then the other, anticipating some sort of magical strike.

Arms slapping to my sides, my shoulders sagged.

No magic manifested in glowing tendrils that licked and coiled around me.

No sparks brightened the sea to a radiant turquois.

Nothing. *Again.*

"Apparently not." Running out of ideas, my lips screwed to the side. I tried every spell, tonic, and glamour Amphrite taught me. Still, no success. I couldn't form one human toe, much less a set of legs.

"It's okay," Alastor assured me, his knuckle dragging up and down my arm, "you tried your best. Maybe it just can't—"

"*Mother!*"

Pulling his chin back, Alastor's forehead puckered. "As nicknames go, that one is not my favorite."

"Not you ... I'm trying to ... never mind." Batting the conversation away with a flick of my wrist, I gave a tap to the magical wall in my mind that had kept all my disturbing visions at bay. It crumbled with ease. The rubble built itself back up, bit by bit, into the form of my mother.

Arms crossed, putrefied lips pinched, and fin tapping, she glared my way in annoyance. "*Well, well, well, look who has finally decided she needs her mother.*"

Filling my gills, I exhaled in an exasperated sigh. "I'm sorry, but you have to admit your presence is a bit off-putting."

"*What?*" Alastor cried, his hands raised, palms out.

"Not you," I clarified.

"You can see my confusion, us being alone and all."

"We're not, my mother is here." I gestured to where she hovered, which to him was a space occupied by three fluttering minnows. "She's going to help me make the spell work."

"*Oh, am I?*" Mother mocked, flipping her patchy hair. "*Is that why I've been summoned like a lowly handmaiden?*"

Chin falling to my chest, I shook my head before forcing a smile into place and trying again, "You weren't summoned. I asked you here because of your vast wisdom and talent."

One shoulder, rotted clear to the bone, lifted coquettishly. "*I do like the sound of that. What spell are you attempting?*"

"I want human legs, to allow me to walk on land like you did."

One eyebrow hitched as if finding the matter beneath her. "*That's simple enough, how did you get rid of me?*"

"For the love of Mother Ocean!" I exclaimed, throwing my hands up in exasperation. "I said I was sorry! Harping on it isn't helping anyone!"

Forefinger pressed to his lips, Alastor contemplated me through narrowed eyes. "It was smart to wait until I was emotionally invested before letting me see this side of your crazy."

"*No, Vanessa, think,*" Mother corrected, in her ghoulish rasp. "*How did you make me vanish?*"

"I ... simply willed it."

"*There you go.*" A sly smile creeping across her face, Mother vanished. This time, of her own accord.

"It *can't* be that easy," I scoffed, looking to Alastor as if he had even the *slightest* clue what was happening.

"Mm-hmm," he offered, quite literally at a loss for words in the face of my madness.

"However, it is the only option I *haven't* tried ..."

"I feel like little more than a prop in this scene," Alastor mused, fingers drumming against his chin.

Taking a brief pause to offer him a sympathetic grimace, I then closed my eyes and gave asserting my will a half-hearted try.

Trusting instinct over training proved to be the key ingredient. Quick as a blink, a wall of green grew from ocean floor to encompass me. The magical cocoon of my creation severed my comforting tie to Alastor. In stifling solitude my body was ravaged. Convulsions rocked through me, their bone rattling force causing my teeth to sink into my tongue. Gagging at the rush of coppery warmth that spurted in my mouth, I tried to relax my body in the face of a change never meant for it. Scales peeled away, revealing tender flesh beneath that took to the ocean's chill like a million tiny daggers ground deep. Jaw swinging slack, a muffled scream of bubbles tore from my chest. A rough, spastic roll of my hips split my tail into two. Newly formed human legs kicked and flailed, instilling a fresh rash of panic at my inability to keep myself afloat.

Job complete, the curtain of magic parted, allowing Alastor his first glimpse of my transformation. I had hoped to treat myself to an eyeful of his shocked reaction. Unfortunately, I gulped down a lungful of water and, for the first time, felt it burn down my esophagus. Eyes bulging, I grabbed my throat in desperation and need of air.

"Oh, this is brilliant," Alastor grumbled with a shake of his head and darted for me. Hooking one arm around my waist, he flapped for the surface with all the speed his tail allowed.

Vision blurring, I gazed up at the daylight that shimmered through the water, taunting me with the promise of salvation.

"While we have a second," Alastor's frustration became evident in the firm set of his jaw, "maybe the next time you attempt this spell, you do it *closer to shore!*"

Coughing and gagging, I took in another lungful of water. Black dots danced before my eyes, the dark abyss of unconsciousness threatening to consume me.

*Now, if memory serves, not all of you were merfolk before joining the ranks of my little garden. I believe there to be one or two pirate scoundrels within your midst. For those of you that don't know, mer breathe primarily through the gills along our rib cages. However, our kind do enjoy lounging on rocks to bask in the sun from time to time. Tiny little lung sacs allow for these little jaunts. They only grant about ten minutes of air time, but this little biology lesson is crucial for what came next. Are we all caught up? Fantastic. Now where was I?*

Just as I began the descent into darkness's sweet embrace, Alastor pressed his lips to mine and breathed a lungful of air into my mouth. My first kiss. *His* kiss, breathing life into me. Eagerly gulping it in, I weaved my fingers into his hair and clung to my own exquisite lifeline. The hard-drawn line of our friendship had finally been crossed in the most enticing of ways. Melting into him, I lost all desire to *ever* revert back to what we had been. Inhaling my way to a clear head, I reveled in his touch combined with the soft caress of the sun's rays as we ventured higher.

Breaking the surface in a dramatic spray, Alastor pulled away long enough for a brief inspection. Assured I was at least conscious, he pressed his forehead to mine. His hands lingered at my hips to keep me afloat.

"Are you okay?" he asked, sinking farther in to the sea to allow water to move over his gills.

Eyes tearing, I coughed up mouthfuls of ocean in a series of unattractive heaves.

"The term shallow water …" I panted, "… means something very different … for humans and mer."

Bobbing with the surf, Alastor cast his gaze to the ships barricading the shoreline. "Just beyond that fleet is the *actual* shallow water. I should thank you for not transporting us there. One glimpse of my tail and they would have had me on skewers over a spit."

"What a barbaric visual." I cringed, curling my hands around his forearms for added support.

"Those are the people you are about to walk amongst. You need to know what to expect." Droplets of water decorated his impossibly long lashes, falling away with each blink. "We know you can't swim over there, evidence of that can't be contested. Fortunately, you have the nifty little talent to poof yourself over there. Get yourself within walking distance and you can stroll from the sea like you belong there."

"A quick stroll on unsteady legs. What's the worst that can happen?" My attempt at a cavalier laugh came out closer to an uneasy cackle.

"Nessa ..." Voice dropping to throaty murmur, Alastor snaked one arm around my waist. Pinning me to him, his free hand caught my chin and tipped my face to his. "I hate that I can't go with you. There are so many unknowns regarding this fool's errand. The most crucial of which is how long you can *maintain* this glamour. Please, is there *any* way I can talk you out of this?"

A mermaid, intricately carved into the hull of the largest in the line of the ships, caught my gaze. The irony of it wasn't wasted on me. The humans appreciated our beauty enough for decoration, yet sought to destroy our kind. "If you were here with Triton, you could have distracted him with a shiny object or barking seal pup. It seems for your desired objective you're traveling with the wrong royal."

"If I was traveling with Triton, I would've dragged him to the surface by the scruff of his neck instead of pressing my lips to his," he crooned against my ear.

"Are you sure?" I spoke the words merely as a distraction from the pit of fear burrowing into my gut. "You'd be the envy of practically every mermaid in Atlantica with him on your arm."

"Don't do this," Alastor pled, refusing to play along.

Turning my face to his, I dove into the molasses pools of his concerned gaze. The tips of my fingers swept over his cheeks, my palms settling over the stubble of his jawline. "I'll be back before you can miss me."

Bolstered by the risk of death, I lurched forward to brush an awkward kiss to his lower lip. Before he could react, I was gone in a cloud of smoke.

# CHAPTER FIFTEEN

Water dripped from the modest garment I conjured for myself: a simple sheath dress that brushed the tops of my newly acquired *feet* with each step. Everything was so *heavy* in the human world! It was as if the air itself pushed back with a stifling hand in my venture from the sea.

"*Avast*! Movement! *We've got movement*!" a voice from one of the ships shouted.

Swords hissed from sheaths.

Rifles cocked.

Cannons swung my way.

Fingers wriggling in preparation of the barrage of energy balls I was prepared to unleash, my efforts were defused by a collective groan from the cluster of sailors above.

"Are ya daft, girl?" a gruff voice bellowed. "There are bein's in these waters that would wear your skin for garters! Git ye'self tah shore!"

Ducking my head, in fear they would see the guilty blush filling my cheeks, I forced my leaden legs forward and splashed from the comforts of the sea. Panting at the effort, I stood dripping on the sandy shore. Casting my stare down one side of the beach and then the other, I studied this glimpse of a part of my ancestry I never before considered. Humans were so … *busy*. A cluster of chattering women scrubbed clothes on the shore bank. Men covered in a sheen of sweat pulled in nets full of flapping fish. Chubby-faced children ran and played in the sand.

Shimmering red fabric, softer and more supple than anything I had ever had the pleasure to touch, snapped and twirled around me. "The pretty lady needs a pretty new dress!" a man with giant teeth, and equally sizable gums said in a singsong voice.

"No, thank you," I answered … and took my first steps on dry land.

Wet sand squished between my toes, tickling the tender flesh. Shoulders raising to my ears, I tittered a nervous giggle.

Finding their world blindingly bright, I shielded my eyes with the crook of my arm and squinted at the jarringly crisp colors. The white sand beach drew up a steep embankment. Atop its peak sat giant, stone structures that soared skyward, reaching heights which seemed to brush the puffy, white clouds drifting above. Each and every home on that hilltop appeared as regal as a castle. Did they *all* think themselves royalty?

Inhaling deeply, I filled my lungs with the fragrant scent of flowers wafting in on the breeze.

A soft tugging at the hem of my drab gray skirt drew my gaze down. A child gazed up at me with moon eyes and the face of an angel. Extending one chubby hand, she offered me a white-pedaled flower with a brilliant yellow center.

"To put in your hair," she explained, tilting her head to display a matching flower tucked into her own flaxen waves.

"Th-thank you," I stammered. At her expectant stare, I hesitantly obliged and situated the stem behind my ear.

Beaming up at me, deep dimples dipped into both her round little cheeks.

"Flora! Come now, darling!" a lovely woman, who appeared to be an older version of my new friend, called out. She welcomed the child to her side with a smile and loving hug.

I expected to find monsters trudging on these shores. Or soldiers patrolling the beach with weapons poised and ready. Instead, I found families, caring and love. Despite my better judgment, I allowed my gaze to flick over the faces of the men milling about, searching each one for some sign of similarity. If my birth father wandered past, would I even know?

Shaking myself from that frustrating riddle, I meandered farther down the beach. A short walk—during which a hardy breeze dried my hair—later, and the crowds died away. The only sounds to be heard were cawing seagulls and thunderous waves crashing against the shoreline.

Suddenly, a realization made my heart lurch in an eager stutter-beat.

Casting my stare over my shoulder, hair lashed against my face. There were *no* soldiers on shore. Not even one passed on patrol. Chewing on my lower lip, I calculated the implications of such news. Slowly, a smile curled across my face. The people of Lemuria armed themselves against us by guarding the water well. Beyond that ... they were exposed and vulnerable.

# CHAPTER SIXTEEN

Tail working side to side in a blur, my hair tossed out wild behind me. "We can use this! *I* can use this! I don't know how yet ... I'm too excited to focus on the details! Even so, I *know* we have something here!"

Alastor kept pace with me, silent as the dead—to everyone *without* my curse. The moment I returned from topside he sought to inspect me tip to tail. I batted him away and swam off, blathering on about my findings. Now, in typical merlad fashion, he was pouting.

My excitement couldn't be tarnished by his sulking, not with the castle's silhouette cresting on the horizon. "I *have* the magic. We saw that. I just have to find a way to amplify it. It would be fantastic if I could ask Amphrite for help, but she's still in her phase of cursing my name and spitting on my fins whenever I'm within range. Is there anything such as a *'sorry you blame me for the death of your husband'* token of apolog— *Whoa!*"

My relentless blathering was cut off when Alastor snagged my elbow and whirled me to an abrupt stop. Slamming my back against the side of the industrial tower that marked the edge of the Indian Sea District of the square, he silenced me with one finger pressed to his lips.

"Caribbean mer," he whispered in warning, and jerked his head for me to look.

Hands gripping the edge of the tower's stone fascia, I peered around the corner.

Upon sweeping glance, everything *appeared* normal. Closer inspection revealed that the residents of Atlantica's normally blended, intermingling society had schooled to the safety of their represented sea zones surrounding the square. All bustled about, pretending to be busy, while watching Caribbean soldiers floating through the square in tight military patrols. Weaving through them — her head held high and amber gaze fixed on the castle — swam Calypso. Even at that distance I could feel the raw determination radiating off of her.

Parents scooped up their children and ushered them inside. Pacific mer planted themselves in defensive positions that dared an attack. Their numbers swelled by the minute, more of their ink and self-mutilated kind swimming in eager anticipation of the promise of violence. Members of the Royal Guard, stationed at the castle entrance, tightened their formation and readjusted their grips on their weapons. Curtain doors fluttered shut. Stone shutters slammed. Atlantica battened down the hatches for the brewing storm sizzling in the air. Civil unease threatened to blow down what was left of our crumbling kingdom.

"We need to get to Triton, *now*," I stated through clenched teeth, "His throne is in jeopardy, and I just might be the weapon to save it."

"*Guards!*" Doralious thundered, descending the pillar-lined incline that led to palace entrance. "The castle is under lockdown. *Do not* allow them, or anyone else, access!"

"M-more than we already are?" the soldier directly in front of me stammered, shifting under the weight of my glare.

"The fate of our kingdom lies in *their* hands," I muttered to Alastor out of the corner of my mouth. "All of Atlantica should be nervous."

"Military was mobilized without authorization from the king," Doralious explained. Swimming behind his blockade, he positioned himself at the head of the line to lord over his men. "We have no choice but to consider it a potential threat. One *anyone* could be linked to. Until further notice, no one gets passed."

"But ... she's the princess," a hulking Guardsman with a surprisingly high-pitched voice chirped.

"*And* the Royal Alchemist," another soldier added.

I could have argued. Asserted the authority of my station. Time being of the essence, I expedited the issue with a flip of my wrist and a magical nudge. An emerald tendril cuffed Doralious in the back of the head, snapping his skull forward to *thunk* against the temple of the next guy, and so on, and so on, right down the line. In the end, the lot of them were slumped on the seafloor in a tangle of fins and limbs.

"*Alchemist.*" Floating over the pack, I tossed the word down at them. "He *just* said it. Means I'm magically inclined. The fact that *none* of you saw this coming concerns me for the Atlantica schools."

Frantically glancing in one direction and the other, Alastor ushered me toward the castle with a hand on the small of my back. "Daylight, I'll miss it when we're rotting in the dungeon."

We found Triton in the Throne Room with the delegates that *weren't* staging a passive aggressive coup against him.

Chest puffed, golden crown gleaming in the shimmering sunbeams, Triton swam slow circles around his huddled Council. "Who knew about this? An act this brazen couldn't have been constructed in utter silence. *Someone* must have heard something."

"There were whispers, sire," the Indian Sea delegate stated in his typical no-nonsense tone. "No one believed they would be foolish enough to attempt such a thing."

"We can force them out." The Pacific Sea delegate rolled his shoulders, making his pecs dance. Since the last time I saw him, he had embedded Great White teeth along his spine to fashion a deadly fin. "Their numbers are no match for our brute force."

"As of yet, all they have done is congregate at the capitol. There is no law against that. If you strike first, it will appear unprovoked." The Arctic representative could be counted on to deliver frosty indifference.

"What then?" Triton spun on her, his outstretched arms falling to his sides with a slap. "I do nothing and appear weak?"

The Mediterranean mer closed the distance between her and Triton, swimming shell bra first. Catching one rippling lock of his golden hair, she twirled it around her forefinger and gave a gentle tug. Her other hand rested delicately against his chest. "What you need is a bold act to assert yourself as the *passionate*, capable ruler that you are. Send a message without saying a word to that assembly of thugs."

"I like that ... idea." Gently as he could, Triton pushed her wandering hands away and kicked backwards to force a little distance between them. "We just have to choose the *right* demonstration."

"If I may interject," flipping my hair over my shoulder, I propelled myself to the center of their cluster, *demanding* their attention, "today, I walked on land."

The declaration was met with a chorus of shocked gasps accompanied by a slathering of disgusted *tsks*.

Chin jutting forward, I pressed on. "Utilizing a spell perfected by my mother, I ventured into the domicile of our enemy. There, I found their weakness."

And ... silence.

Fighting off a victorious smirk, I rubbed the pad of my thumb against the soft curve of the ursela shell. "They protect the water, but no farther. My spell allowed me to breech their defenses. If I could harness that ability and bestow it on our soldiers, we could assert our dominance over the humans once and for all. We could finally put an end to this war and destroy the Caribbean's strong hold simultaneously!"

For a moment, their dubious stares acted as their only response.

"Can you *do* that?" the newly elected Gulf mer ventured with dumbfounded astonishment.

"No ... not yet," I admitted. Watching their interest drift off on the current, I rushed to tag on, "The idea *just* came to me. I need time to formulate the spell and perfect it! Given time, I'm certain I can!"

*Okay, that might have been a bit of puffed up bravado. But that's salesmanship, folks! To get that yes!*

"Work on that." Triton's head bobbed, his jaw grinding as he mulled over the matter.

I fought off the impulse to wriggle in glee — *barely*.

"See if that's something we can use. In the meantime, we need a strategy to enforce my reign, particularly to the Caribbean merfolk."

"*Ugh!*" Miss Atlantic Sea's shoulders sagged as if the topic caused her physical pain. Her hands rose protectively to fiddle with what appeared to be mini-tridents dangling from her ears. "I already hate myself for saying this … *however*, the Caribbean asserted their station from the human artifacts they acquired. Remove those, and what do they have?"

"Those items are nothing but a painful reminder of those human beasts that stole my father from his kingdom," Triton declared, slumping into his throne.

It was with a conflicting blend of pride and sorrow that I realized my happy-go-lucky brother, who I once convinced to lick a jellyfish tentacle, was gone. In his place sat a merman of impeccable strength and drive.

He looked like a king.

He looked like … *Poseidon*.

Stamping his trident against the ocean floor, he bellowed, "There is a trove past the Atlantic District, outside the borders of Atlantica. I want *every* human artifact under the sea gathered up and deposited there. From this day forward, any trace of the *human* way of life is banished from the kingdom! Failure to comply will result in a trip to The Pit or … beaching."

*Baby brother's first bold proclamation. If only it came gifted with the foresight of how deep the knife of that ruling would cut. Or … that it was my belly it would be thrust in to.*

# CHAPTER SEVENTEEN

Tensions ran high through the kingdom. As expected, the Caribbean mer took to relinquishing their human treasures with the sulky resistance of children handing over their favorite toys. The courtyard was emptied. The bartering marketplace closed. All of Atlantica seemed to be holding their breath, as if afraid one wrong ripple would set off the typhoon we could all feel brewing.

My method of coping was to throw myself into honing the human spell. After days of working tirelessly, I found myself at a magical cross-stream. I had to find the precise blend of science and the supernatural. To achieve that, I needed a mystical boost. Fortunately, I knew where to find such an enhancer …

Nervously fiddling with the ursela shell, I concentrated on keeping my posture cavalier as I cut through the Hall of Records to the Temple of Kings. Despite the swell of nerves lodged in my throat, I managed a tight smile and nod to the castle staff I passed along the way. Stopping at the foot of the Thetis statue, I stared up at the stone beauty with her flowing locks cascading to the rise of her tail. The Olympus Pearl sat beside her, calling to me with its promise of power. Since the day — so many years ago — when I first touched it, I felt its pulsating allure whenever I neared.

Fear, like thousands of tiny sea bugs, skittered up my spine. If I got caught, even Triton couldn't protect me. I would be beached without trial or questioning, my lifeless body left to rot in the sun for the hungry seagulls' delight — clearly, they would have to clamp those magic blocking shackles on me first. What fun would my public execution be if I diverted it by growing legs and sauntering off?

Heart pounding an ominous reprise against my ribs, I glanced over my shoulder to ensure I was free from prying eyes. My fingers fanned over the pearl. First the right hand, then the left. In a swirl of green, it vanished—whisked away to the confines of my Alchemy parlor. A replica filled its space just as quick, settling into the same spot without so much as disturbing the dusting of sand around it.

"And where do you think you're going with that?" a stern voice boomed, echoing all around me.

Spinning with a frightened gasp on my lips, my hands clamped instinctively around the ursela shell.

No one was there.

I was the temple's lone visitor.

Before relief could set in, the voice returned, bouncing off each of the cavernous walls. "Did you think you could take something of such valuable without anyone noticing? I hate to break it to you, but you aren't *that* stealthy."

Whirling in search of my accuser, bile scorched up the back of my throat. Gruesome images of my own horrifying death flashed behind my lids.

"Those stone tablets belong in the Hall of Records. Where *exactly* do you think you're taking them?" Underlining threat weaved through the tone like an elaborate tapestry.

Motivated by self-preservation, I flutter-kicked to the wall. Realizing the ruckus was resonating from the next room did nothing to ease my trepidation. Back pressed to the sandstone wall, I inched toward the archway. Hiding behind one hand-carved pillar in the shape of King Neptune, I peeked around his massive tail into the Hall of Records.

Amphrite's head steward, Samuel, floated in between two rows of shelves where the tablets containing Atlantica's political history were stored. He held a stack of them to his chest, scrawny arms trembling under their weight. Six Caribbean soldiers surrounded him, circling predators sniffing out chum. Samuel's terrified gaze flicked over each of their faces, as if anticipating the first strike.

"We're in a time of war, *boy*," one monstrous soldier growled, his top lip curling back to reveal yellow stained teeth and blackened gums, "and it looks to me like you're trying to make off with information our enemies would pay a hefty sum for."

"N-no!" Samuel stammered, his eyes bulging with panic. "Queen Amphrite asked me to the fetch them! I'm only honoring her request!"

A bald soldier with black scales tattooed across the back of his head glowered at the quaking merlad. "She's no longer queen, or hadn't you heard? Her commands are as useless as *you.*"

"Huh, I don't remember getting that *particular* message." Somehow Doralious managed to match Neleus's gruff tremor which had been as soothing a sound as rubbing rocks together. He truly seemed the second coming of the sadistic guard. Standing at the hall entrance, Doralious was flanked by a crew that matched the Caribbean's in threat and number. Stabbing the tip of his sword into the sand, his hands casually folded over the hilt. "Perhaps we should ask King Triton to clarify such a bold statement."

Honorable soldiers would have respected rank and backed down, conceding to the demands of the Royal Guard without question. Perhaps it was the solitude offered by the otherwise vacant hall, but the Caribbean soldiers tightened their formation, their beefy shoulders slamming together to form a solid wall of muscle and rebellion.

"Humans sail above us and could attack at *any* moment," the tattooed soldier snarled. "We are doing Triton a favor by keeping the valued tablets of Atlantica safe and secure ... despite him taking away the booty we *earned.*"

"And you think the tablets to be safe with *you* standing this close to them?" Doralious snickered to his men over his shoulder. "It seems a counterproductive task if you ask me."

"What are you implying?" the beastly mer huffed, his chest rising and falling with each heaving breath.

Keeping the tip to the ground, Doralious's fingers closed around the hilt of his sword in a clear warning. "I *imply* nothing. I'm *stating* that your kind pillages and plunders more than the cannon fodder meat-sacks that walk above. Who then are the *real* pirates?"

"Big accusations from someone hiding behind a sword, who only earned his position after a superior warrior was put to death," Tattoo-head countered, snapping his jaws in a menacing punctuation.

"Hiding behind it? No. I would happily hand it over ..." Flipping his sword over the back of his hand, Doralious caught it in his palm and pointed the tip toward his accuser. "… embedded deep in your gullet."

"Drop the sword," Gigantor-mer spat, "or have it fed to you."

Weapons hissed free on both sides. Samuel backed away whimpering, his shoulder slamming into the row of shelves behind him.

I couldn't say who lunged first, yet in a blink, bone weaponry was meeting in vicious claps. Heaving soldiers danced around each other in a deadly waltz, their swinging swords hungry for an ounce of flesh.

Doralious and Tattoo-head locked blades, pressing back against each other hard enough to redden their faces with the strain. Tattoo-head bared his teeth, leaning for Doralious's face with ravage intent. Eager to keep his features intact, Doralious shoved the larger mer with every ounce of strength that he had. Reeling back, Tattoo-head spun around, his sword sinking into Samuel's gut with the ease of cutting water. The two men locked stares over the fatal penetration. The masks of shock they wore perfectly matched. A small line of blood trickled over Samuel's lower lip as he tipped his head to quizzically inspect the sword rammed through his core.

A blanket of silence snuffed out the battle. One by one the soldiers acknowledged their egregious error by dropping their weapons.

"Well, *now* look at the mess you made." The recognizable commanding cadence whipped all their heads around.

Retracting her black veil of mourning, Amphrite floated to the center of the cluster with her back urchin quill straight. She acknowledged Samuel with a sympathetic tilt of her head, cringing at the crimson foam bubbling down his chin. Inspecting the extent of his injury, she shot a glare, which could have reduced them all to guppies, at the guilty parties.

"Do you know who I am?" she asked the Caribbean soldiers, black eyes flicking from one to the next.

The beastly mer snapped to attention, his hands clasped behind his back. "Of course, Your Majesty," he muttered with a nod of respect.

"*Majesty*, that's right." Sizing him up, Amphrite's mouth twitched into a disgusted pucker. "The bereaved queen of the late and honorable Poseidon. That's the title most associate me with.

Fortunately, I'm also one of the most powerful alchemists Atlantica has ever seen."

A blanket of silence fell as men that relied on brawn over brain struggled to piece together what she was getting at. If she wanted them to catch up, she probably should have drawn a map.

Beside her Samuel fell to his knees, whimpering while the life gushed from his pulsing gash.

"Really, Samuel, that's enough of that." A wave of Amphrite's slender hand and the steward's lips were sewn shut with a thread thin reed.

The other men winced at the callous display, their stares nervously flicking to the exit.

"Oh, I'm sorry. Did that seem crass? Should I let his whimpers draw more onlookers in to this grisly little spectacle?"

Glancing to the floor, the shelves, or each other, they each shook their heads whilst adamantly avoiding eye contact with her piercing stare.

"Right. Then let us instead discuss the opportunity before us." Crossing her arms over her chest, Amphrite drummed her fingernails against her upper arms. "I *could* wave my hand and fix your little mistake. His wound hasn't festered, no poisons were involved, and it was made with mer artifacts versus human. These elements combined would make the healing a simple one. After I did this, I would want my steward to deliver to me the files I requested—undisturbed and without question. *Or,* we can all stay here, watch him bleed to death, and cross our fingers that this little slip-up doesn't lead to a kingdom wide civil war. Thoughts? Feel free to discuss amongst yourselves."

Tattoo-head nodded his agreement first, his demanding gaze flicking to his brethren and the guardsmen in encouragement for them to follow suit. Even Samuel bobbed his head in favor of his own mercy.

"Then it seems we have an accord." Dangerous intent dripped from the upturned corners of Amphrite's triumphant smirk. A flap of her tail and she hovered in front of Samuel. He stilled as her hand raised, eager for the relief she promised. Instead, she halted and spun back around as if remembering she'd left her cauldron bubbling. "Oh, there is *one* more thing. We haven't discussed the subject of payment yet. You can't get something for nothing, you know."

The last of his energy exhausted, Samuel slumped to the ground, his wavering gaze struggling to focus on his hesitating savior.

"*Anything*! Name it!" Doralious barked.

"I may ask Samuel to run errands like this for me from time to time." After a casual circular motion with her forefinger, she then pressed it to her cheek. "If that happens, I don't want any of you interfering. Both he and I are left to our own devices, and no one will have to know about the nearly fatal consequences of your little display of testosterone."

"Yes, my Queen," they chorused one after the other. Each punctuated the declaration by clapping their closed fist over their heart.

"There now, resolution without bloodshed. It can be done. Tell your friends." A theatrical wave of her hand formed vining wisps of purple haze that rolled around Samuel, retracting the blade from his gut and knitting his flesh back together. By the time they dissipated, not a mark remained, and his lips were unraveled to freedom.

Falling forward, Samuel latched onto his queen in an exuberant squeeze of heartfelt appreciation. "Thank you, my Queen! I knew you would save me. I never doubted you for even a moment. I trusted your wisdom, and—"

"Lips can be restitched, Samuel." She grimaced, pulling away after a quick pat to his back.

"No, ma'am," he peeped, clamping his lips together in a firm line … for barely a beat. "Whatever you desire, I will happily meet your request. All you have to do is speak the—"

A snap of her fingers and Samuel disappeared in a swirl of smoke.

"That's enough from the help," Amphrite scoffed in his absence with a roll of her dramatically lined eyes. Pulling her shoulders back, she dazzled the soldiers with the full wattage of her elusive smile. "Now, gentlemen, if you'll excuse me."

Tossing her hair back in an ebony current, Amphrite swam from the hall with her usual regal elegance.

The men exchanged somber nods, acknowledging the secret each would take to their grave, before swimming off without looking back.

Expelling a breath I hadn't realized I was holding, I spun to find myself face-to-face with Amphrite.

"Oh my riptide!" I gushed in a hushed whisper. "That was *insane*! Are you okay? I mean, of course you're okay, you're *amazing*! But—"

Amphrite stabbed one finger in my direction to halt my ramblings, white lines appearing around her tightly pinched lips. "No small talk. I'm no longer interested in *anything* you have to say. Now or ever. I am only speaking with you to let you know I am well aware of the spell you're working on, Vanessa."

"W-wha— How?" I eloquently stammered.

One eyebrow arched in an elegant dismissal. "I have eyes all over this kingdom, girl. You would do well to remember that." Violet wisps snaked around her, brushing over her form that began to fade before me. "As to the spell—*get it done*. Save us all. Or these men will tear this city down stone by stone."

Then, she was gone.

# CHAPTER EIGHTEEN

There are people in life we look to for social clues as to how to behave—those seemingly unflappable few that seemed to possess a boundless grace in the face of the most dire of circumstances. The sight of one of these pillar individuals in a ruffled state sets our world askew with a rush of overwhelming alarm. That is exactly the effect Amphrite's foreboding message had on me.

*"Princess, was your outing successful?"* Jetteson asked the moment I burst into my Alchemist chambers.

"Can't talk! Panicking!" Kicking to my storage cubby for all I was worth, I shoved the kelp curtain and exhaled a ragged breath. There sat the pearl. Exactly where I sent it.

*"You did it!"* Floteson murmured in awe.

Jetteson draped over my shoulder, breathing against my ear, *"You'll be unstoppable."*

I couldn't form the words to respond. Crouching beside the pearl, the desire to drag my fingertips over its alluring iridescent surface coursed through me. My gills quivered, a throaty sigh escaping my parted lips.

Giving in to that urge, my palms cradled the silky smooth curve of the artifact. The very moment of contact, jolts of electricity crackled through me in euphoric waves. Every cell of my body sang out in a blissfully symphony. Head falling back, my body rode the current of pleasure. So lost was I in my private indulgence that I failed to see a downside … until I tumbled straight back. My skull cracked against a rock on the sea floor, and I sank into the darkness.

"Princess?" the concerned voice called to me from down a long tunnel, beckoning me back to a harsh world. "Vanessa? Can you hear me?"

My heavy lids fluttered open, Loriana's compassionate frown blurring into focus.

"What happened?" I asked, my throat arid and raw.

Over Loriana's shoulders Floteson and Jetteson's heads appeared, their eyes brightening at the sound of my voice.

"Of that, I'm not sure," with one hand on my shoulder and the other grasping my arm, Loriana eased me to sitting, "but I *do* know I have been looking everywhere for you! Are you well? Can you swim?"

My boys circled around my midsection—my own writhing, scaly belt.

"Looking for me?" Clamping my eyes shut, I swallowed hard and prayed to Mother Ocean that the sea would stop spinning around me. "I just came back from the Hall of Records. There was a spell ..."

Hooking one arm around my back, Loriana's soft scent of sandalwood soothed me. "Yes, I remember you telling me you were headed there. That was *two days ago*. Are you telling me you have been here this entire time?"

Brow furrowing, I scanned my parlor for clues of what had happened. Bumping into a wall with the wash of each current was a crystal clear sphere ... exactly the same size of the pearl I pilfered. I remembered touching it, and then ...

Could it be?

Had all its energy been siphoned into me?

It seemed I would have some sort of solid evidence of that.

Raising one hand in front of me, I turned it over, searching for some sign of a change.

Nothing.

How could that be?

I wasted so much time, risked so much, and had *nothing* to show for it.

Another thought instantly snapped me from my disappointed musings. "*Alastor*! He's leaving for basic training! I need to say good-bye!"

Loriana's head listed to the side, the corners of her mouth sinking into a sympathetic frown. "My sweet girl, he already left. He hated leaving without saying goodbye. However, when he couldn't find you, there was no other choice. We will send word to him that you are here and safe."

"*No*! We're at war! He could be called into action at any moment! I *have* to see him!"

Grasping my upper arms, my loving hand maiden pivoted me to face her. "You can and you will, I *promise* you that. Right now, though, I need you to focus and be here with me. The Caribbean mer have surrounded your brother in the throne room. He's barricaded in so tightly that even the Royal Guard can't reach him. The Pacific mer are storming in for a counterattack and they won't care who gets in their way. I *know* what you can do, Vanessa. The whole kingdom does. We have no choice but to call on you to save King Triton ... *to save Atlantica*."

# CHAPTER NINETEEN

Growing up inquisitive in the castle, there wasn't one corner or nook I didn't know like the fan of my fin. Thanks to lively, day-long games of hide-and-seek with Triton and Alastor, I knew that directly behind the throne there was a crack I could peek through which would keep me hidden from sight. That was where I solidified, doing my best to keep the tendrils of my smoky magic contained.

Squinting, I peered into the center of the throne room, biting the inside of my cheek in disdain at the inquisition unfolding. Triton floated in the center of the room, the base of his trident stabbed between the mosaic shell tilework. Around him hovered a wall of Caribbean mer in an impassable fortress. Every door was blocked, every window obstructed. Chest puffed, Triton looked every bit the noble king. Only my familiarity with his quirks and foibles revealed his true anxiety to me in the reflexive twitch at his jawline.

Dragging a stone-carved stool across the floor with a deafening screech, Calypso positioned her seat directly in front of Triton and flopped it down with the casual air of defiance.

"The humans, who killed your father, go unchecked. Yet you steal from your own merfolk to prove a point." Her sandstone gaze dragged down the length of him, outwardly finding him wanting. "That seems the desperate act of a juvenile king, if you ask me."

Tipping his head back, Triton glared down the bridge of his nose at her. "Fortunately, with you acting against Council rules, no one had to."

One of the soldiers behind him growled, baring yellowed teeth with blackened gums.

"*Shh, shh, shh,*" Calypso soothed, as naturally as a mother pacifying her fussy infant. "By failing to act, he will prove himself as unfit to rule as we know him to be."

"What makes you think I will fail to take action?" Triton glowered. "I have a few decrees I'd like to put into place *right now.*"

Tossing her head back in an easy laugh, Calypso's rope braids tickled the rise of her tail. "Because," she merrily stated, "rumor has it the humans are soon to launch another attack. We're going to keep you here, silent and inept, while your kingdom crumbles. Then, when all of Atlantica feels you have failed them, my soldiers and I will bring the thunders of Olympus crashing down on the humans once and for all. Who, then, do you think they will regard as their true leader and salvation, *Your Majesty?*"

Arcing back, Triton spit on her tailfin. "*You treacherous wretch!* Mer will die! Their blood will be on your hands!"

Calypso didn't even bother to look annoyed as she flicked the spittle from her scales. Why would she when so much was stacked in her favor? "And from their sacrifice, a new age will be born throughout the Seven Seas. One free from the oppression of a patriarch. I, for one, will appreciate their martyrdom."

The other soldiers displayed their lively support in the form of huffs of laughter and a series of masculine shoves to their cohorts.

Waiting for their show of camaraderie to still, Calypso batted her eyes coquettishly at my stewing brother. "Have a seat on your throne while we wait, *my King,*" she spurted his title as if doing so was an insult on her ancestry, "for it shall be your *very* last ride."

A motion of Calypso's hand and two soldier's seized Triton's arms with more force than necessary to deposit him ceremonially onto his regal cathedra. The throne back separating us seemed to radiate the heat of Triton's seething fury. So many guards trained to protect him, and *all* had found themselves shut out of this demonstration. I had rage all my own on that matter.

Needing his attention, without alerting the Caribbean soldiers, I mentally ticked through my options:

Poke him in the side? No, he's ticklish and would squeal like a girl.

Conjure the figment of manatee pup and lead him to me? No, once he saw it he wouldn't be able to focus.

Whisper his name? No, he wouldn't be casual, whipping one way and the other in search of me.

*Triton, for the love of Mother Ocean, turn around!* I thought in frustration.

Through the crack I watched Triton's spine straighten. *Vanessa?*

No soldiers moved. No echo resonated off the soaring architecture. It was almost as if …

*Triton, are you in my head?*

*No! You're in mine! How are you doing this?! Where are you?*

*I'm behind you.* Seeing his weight shift, I hurried to add. *Don't turn around!*

Hesitantly, he settled back into his seat. *This is more than alchemy, Nessa. This borders on sea witch territory.*

My mouth swung open in offense. Clamping it shut, I stabbed my thoughts at him as hard as I could. *That is a filthy, offensive term! I came here to help you, you blow-hole! And … I touched the Olympus Pearl, which I think is to blame for this. But still, insulting implication!*

*I'm sorry. I love you for being here, really, I do. That said, you have to leave. It's not safe,* he warned.

*For* anyone *in Atlantica,* I countered. *I'm not leaving you here. Once they no longer have a need for you …*

I trailed off, not daring to think the unimaginable.

*You have to!* Triton demanded. *Only you can sneak away undetected! The Caribbeans have done something which will cause the humans to retaliate. I'm sure of it. You must align our soldiers for the attack! Thwart Calypso's plotting. Orchestrate a military maneuver that will prostrate the humans and Caribbeans before us!*

*Oh, is that all?* I thought with a sardonic tilt of my head. *How could I possibly do that?*

A heavy silence fell, one in which the only sounds to be heard were the murmured conversation of the Caribbean mer and a muffled thumps and booming reverberations in the distance. It was broken by two words that instantly clamped my gills shut and knotted my stomach.

*Your spell.*

Swallowing hard, I adamantly shook my head. *I-I can't! I'm sorry, brother, but it's not ready. I haven't practiced. There's too much at stake and too many elements that could go wrong!*

Reaching one hand behind him, as if scratching his back, Triton pressed his fingertips to the gouge in the throne—the only show of support he could muster between our two trapped souls.

*I would ask something of this magnitude of no one else.*

*Then do not expect it of me!*

I watched as the swirled pads of his fingerprints brushed over the rough edge of the broken stone. *You can do this. You're more powerful than you allow yourself to imagine.*

I could manage no response, strangled by my own ineptitude.

*Vanessa,* his thoughts become firm and unyielding, forcing their way into my tumultuous mind, *I hate to do this. Even so, for the good of our people, for the good of Atlantica, I order you to invoke that spell.*

And there it was.

A kingly decree I couldn't contest.

Tears burned behind my eyes that I refused to let fall. Clapping my hands to my sides, I bent in a formal bow in a show of respect he would never see.

*As you wish ... my King,* I stabbed the thought at him, then disappeared in a puff.

"Stand down, or we will put you down!" Doralious bellowed to the troop of Pacific mer charging the castle in a tight formation. At his shout his men released the battering ram they fashioned to pound free the giant boulder that denied them access to their king, and drew their weapons.

Political correctness aside, it was the Pacific delegate himself that ran point on the mission. His tensed jaw stretched his facial tattoos into sharp slashes of war paint. His hand curled around the most vicious weapon I ever laid eyes. At its base was the jagged snout of a sawfish, its ferociousness amplified by a rope of shark's teeth twined around it. "Your incompetence knows no bounds," the delegate hissed through teeth sharpened to razor-sharp points. "Move aside. Let *true* warriors protect and serve the rightful king."

Lucky me, I solidified right in the middle of that awkward exchange. All swords and brutal armaments whipped my way. Swallowing hard, I forced a croak through my constricted throat. "You're all busy. I see that. I just thought you might like to know your king is alive and in good health from someone who has spoken to him, and knows of his commands."

"*Lower your weapons!*" Despite his order, Doralious's own sword held steady. "We have orders from our king!"

The Pacific mer didn't so much as blink. "*That* is a princess with a clever tongue and magic. We take orders only from the king himself. For the moment she is as much of an obstacle as the rest of you."

Edging in closer to Doralious, I dropped my voice to a whisper. "Did Triton tell you of the spell I was working on?"

Pulling back, he shoved me aside with his elbow to line the point of his sword with the delegates throat. "How dare you waste our time on such trivial fantasies. Men, strike down any Pacific mer that moves towards this door!"

The delegate's head tipped, his pupils dilating with bloodlust. "Are you keeping us out, or the king in? Perhaps *you* are in on this mutiny."

Civilians, young and old, were drawn in by the ruckus. The weight of the situation not enough to squelch their curiosity.

"*By royal command, return to your homes!*" I shouted, my pulse pounding in my ears.

A few turned away, some wavered, yet none made the commitment to *actually* remove themselves or loved ones from the escalating situation.

"*You* are the traitors by challenging the Royal Guard," Doralious sneered, chest puffed in full bravado of his station. "Stand down! I will not ask you again!"

The delegate floated eye level with him, heaving chest bumping heaving chest in challenge. "We bow only to the king. *Lower your weapon.*"

"*Go, now!*" I screamed at the onlookers at the same moment the thundercloud of war cracked open to unleash its hellish fury.

Who struck first, I couldn't say. A cyclone of violence swelled around me, tainting the water with the coppery stench of blood and the claps of connecting swords.

A child shrieked.

Bodies slumped.

Atlantica turned on itself, the water clouded by spilled blood.

Freeing my own weapon, forever strung at my hip, I threw myself in the skirmish. Blocking an incoming strike from above, I spun in a low crouch to scoop up the sawfish blade of a fallen Pacific. I popped up between Doralious and the delegate just as both lunged for a savage collision. Doralious's sword lodged between spikes of my sawfish rapier. The seething delegate's downward blow sufficiently blocked by my well-placed foil.

For a beat, I held them there, locking eyes with one before flicking my stern gaze to the other. "Doralious, there was a time I valued you to be more than a narrow-minded, algae sucker. For that reason alone, consider this my courtesy visit. At sunset I *will* invoke my spell. You and your men want to live? Get as close to the shoreline as possible before then. The swim to shore is a *killer* without a tail."

Biting the inside of my cheek to fight off tears of frustration, I dove backwards in an elaborate flip, and evaporated into a cloud of magic. All the while praying to Mother Ocean that these head strong men wouldn't destroy what was left of my home while I was rushing to save it.

# CHAPTER TWENTY

The ribcages of whale sharks, tarped with quilted canvases of sea fronds, made up the training barracks for the Royal Guard. They slept on mats, two to a tent, on a wide sandbar used for combat drills.

"At attention, men! We have a visitor; the Royal Alchemist, Princess Vanessa!" the pudgy faced guard with droopy eyes bellowed loud enough to make a Trumpet Fish envious.

Inwardly, I cringed. These young men were learning to be selfless warriors. What had anyone in my family done except marry well? Forcing a tight-lipped smile in the face of the awkward situation, I laced my fingers in front of me as the men rushed into their line-up. Some were still chewing, others wiping their mouths on the back of their hands. I was the haughty royalty that interrupted their meal time. *Fabulous.*

"Princess!" The commanding officer, recognizable by the two sand dollar medallions strung to his shark-hide belt, threw his arms out wide and welcomed me with an easy smile. "To what do we owe this honor?"

Word of what was happening at the castle had yet to reach them. *Finally,* something seemed to work in my favor.

Alastor picked that moment to duck out from the mess hall, knotting his wavy curtain of hair at the nape of his neck. My gaze wandered over him, warmth swelling in my chest.

The scruffy line of his jaw.

The tiny scar above his lip.

The carved perfection of his chest.

The V of his hip bones right before they plunged into his sunset orange tail …

Becoming painfully aware of my audience, I cleared my throat and addressed the commander while blood filled my cheeks. "My apologies for the interruption. We've had a bit of a royal emergency that requires I request a moment of Recruit Alastor's time."

The commander's spine stiffened at the unorthodox request. Anyone else would have been turned away; however, the blood coursing through my veins made me a hard girl to say no to. Or such was his skewed outlook. If he knew the truth, that I was a half-breed mutt, he would've ordered them to kill me on the spot.

"I suppose for a moment or two …" He trailed off, faltering under the watchful eyes of his recruits.

"Atlantica and your king, thank you," I said with my most beguiling smile I could muster and skirted around him. "This is a private conversation. I trust you and your men can grant us a moment."

"Yes, Your Highness, of course." The commander begrudgingly bowed. Judging by his reddening neck and cheeks, the recruits would soon be swimming laps in his effort to reassert his authority.

Pulling back the flap of his tent, Alastor welcomed me into his cramped abode with a formal wave of his arm. Sunlight shimmered through the water, casting golden diamonds over his torso. Edging past him, I avoided contact, as if his skin was a scorching toxin … which it very well may have been if I let myself indulge. The moment the flap fell shut behind us, he clasped his hands behind his back and forced his troubled gaze to meet mine.

"You didn't care enough to say good-bye," Alastor sniped, audible hurt adding an unforgiving slice to his tone. "What then would prompt a spontaneous visit?"

Raising one finger to halt his accusation, I clarified, "In my defense, I had every intention in partaking in the long standing tradition of the tearful good-bye. Unfortunately, I touched the Olympus Pearl and spent two days unconscious in the closet of my shop."

Shoulders shaking with a snort of laughter, Alastor's expression softened. "Only you."

"We can marvel at the wonder of the anomaly that is me later, right now a larger matter looms."

"It always does," he sighed.

Lowering my voice to a conspiratorial whisper, I closed the distance between us. "The Caribbean mer are holding Triton captive in the castle. The guardsmen couldn't get to him and the Pacific mer have intervened. Things got bad, and *fast*. But, as we both know, I have ways of sneaking in undetected ..."

"You used magic."

"I used magic." For a moment I fixated on a freckle just alongside the bridge of Alastor's nose. Under different circumstances I would have liked nothing more than to brush my lips against it, to feel the warm current of his breath teasing over my face. He had a magic all his own, and it made coherent thought nearly impossible.

"Triton?" he prompted, one corner of his mouth pulling back in a knowing half-grin.

"*He kicked me out!*" I erupted, focus on my mission returning. "He's insisting I invoke the spell to grant our soldiers," glancing over his shoulder, I made sure no one was peeking in the tent, then mouthed the offensive word, "*legs*. If I succeed, the power in his reign will be carved in stone with a force *no one* can ever question again."

A valley of concern furrowed his brows. "Are you ready for such a lofty endeavor?"

"Those holding him could decide at any moment his life no longer has value to them." Blinking hard, I fought back the wash of tears burning behind my eyes. "I can't lose him, Alastor. He's the only family I have left."

His thumb skimmed over my jawline, gently tipping my face to his. "That wasn't an answer. *Are you ready for this?*"

Laying my hand over his, I offered him the only assurance I had to give, "I have to be."

Reaching behind my head, Alastor plucked the driftwood stick carved into a whale's tail from my hair. His scent, salty sea water and sandalwood, inebriated my senses. Casting the stick aside, he weaved his fingers into my hair and shook the locks free from their tightly wrapped bun. Cascading over my shoulders, they brushed the small of my back in their descent.

When his gaze met mine once more, his face was an open locket of sincerity. "My mother once told me of a flower on land called the wild orchid. Its enchanting bloom is an exotic beauty that rivals all other flowers. Even so, that's not what makes it special. A breed of it can be found in almost any climate, its radiance conquering the most unforgiving conditions." Both his hands gently cradled my face, his lips breathing the words into me. "*You* are my wild orchid, and I cannot wait to be there when the world gets to watch and be dazzled by the strength and elegance of your bloom."

I wanted nothing more than to get lost there, in the sweet surrender of his touch. Thankfully, my desire to keep him alive interjected the painful reminder that time *wasn't* on our side.

Pressing my fingertip to his lips, I backed to a more breathable distance. "You're one of the soldiers now. They'll put you on the front lines. You saw what happened to me, and you know what to expect when I invoke the spell. When you are given the call to formation, and it *will* come, position yourself in the shallowest waters you can stand. When it happens, kick for the surface and don't stop until you break through."

Dropping his chin to his chest, he blinked up at me from under impossibly long lashes. "I love that, in spite of everything, you're worried about *me*."

"Is that *all* that you love of me?" I asked, feigning insult.

Catching my driftwood hair accessory as it floated past, Alastor clamped it between his teeth long enough to gather my hair and twist it into a loose knot. His topaz stare melded with mine as he used the stick to secure the strands back in place. "From your wit to your demanding ambition, there isn't one element I don't love," he admitted in a throaty rasp. "The second I return I fully intend to offer you my heart ... forever. You see, I have no choice. It already belongs to you."

Again those pesky tears welled in my eyes. This time, one slipped from my lid unchecked. Pushing away, I swam to the exit, knowing if I didn't leave then I never would. With the tent flap hooked on my arm, I glanced back, memorizing every subtle nuance of his face. "Hurry back to me, Alastor ... and bring forever with you."

# CHAPTER TWENTY ONE

I never thought I would miss my mother's ghoulish presence. Yet there I was, wishing her melted face would appear to impart a bit more wisdom about the spell *she* created. Cutting through town square, my mind ticked through the plethora of questions I would ask her ... if she would only materialize. Flutter kicking between the castle and the housing for the Arctic members of court, which resembled jutting icebergs, I took the shortcut to my parlor. Pushing back my curtain door, I pulled up short at the presence already filling the space.

Cocking one hip, I jabbed my fist to it. "Huh, I suppose when I wished upon a starfish for my mother I should have been a *tad* more specific."

She turned at the sound of my voice, a vision in white. Harsh black hair had been traded for chestnut waves that swept past her shoulders, the sides tied back with delicate ivory sea flowers. Her tail was the color of a snowflake falling into the raging sea. A vest of the tiniest seashells imaginable was slung over her shoulders, secured at her breastbone by a flourish of pearls.

"Amphrite!" Swimming into the parlor, I swept over my bottles of tonics and potions with a glance to ensure all was in place. "Welcome to my *private* parlor where you have obviously made yourself at home. If you came to kill me, may I suggest you wait a day? Then you can take part in the spectacle after my failure. You know: hand out rocks to be thrown, whisper insult suggestions to the angry masses ..."

Folding her hands in front of her, she tipped her head in a convincing mask of pity. "Honestly, Vanessa, not *everyone* is your enemy. I don't know *why* you believe that to be the case."

"Uh," I muttered with a wry chuckle, "maybe it's low self-esteem. *Or*, when it comes to you, maybe it's because you *specifically said it*. So, you know, no real stretch there."

Pale pink lips pursed in a subtle pout. "I was grieving. Surely you can understand that?"

"And now?"

Something dark flashed in her eyes, disappearing in a blink before I could tag an emotion to it. "Now, I want only to help you." With the snap of her fingers, my cauldron began to bubble and roil. Vials and ingredients leapt from shelves, floating over to add themselves to the mix. "All that power lying beneath the surface, untapped. Yet, if I had to wager, I would guess you have no idea where to begin."

Filling my gills to capacity, I exhaled a rush of bubbles and fast moving current. "There's numerous places I could begin. It's what comes after that I'm hung up on—more on that topic in a moment. First, you haven't spoken more than a dozen words to me since my father died. Why, in the name of Mother Ocean, would you offer to help me *now*?"

"Without help," leaning over the cauldron she wafted the scent of its brew to her nose with one hand—lips drooping with disappointment, she summoned a vial of rainbow trout ribs to her waiting hand and sprinkled them into the brew, "Poseidon's entire family could be cast from the castle that is rightfully ours. That is a matter that affects *me* as well, considering I am *very* comfortable in the life to which I have become accustomed."

"You're suggesting we team up to keep Triton on the throne so *you* don't have to move?" Eyes narrowed, I waited for a punchline or taunting hook I was sure would follow.

"What can I say?" Lifting one shoulder in a coy shrug, the shells of her vest clicked a soft applause. "Royal living suits me. Now, what are you hung up on in the spell?"

In retrospect I should have protested further, delved deeper into her seemingly materialistic motives. Feeling stiflingly overwhelmed proved to be my downfall. Seizing the opportunity with the vigor of a human grasping to the last buoy in a stormy sea, my mouth opened and the paradox I had been juggling tumbled out. "If I focus the spell on them one at a time, it will drain my energy too fast. Which would be fine, *if* I could hit them all with the same potency of magic at once. Unfortunately, even with the boost from the Olympus Pearl, I'm doubtful I can expand my reach that far."

"That's an easy enough fix." She batted my words away as if they were bothersome sea gnats. "We simply need two channels. You harness the power and pass it through me; I'll syphon it out to all the soldiers. Think of me as your own personal conch shell, giving your magical *'voice'* a little amplification."

"You know if I hit you with that much concentrated magic and you *don't* disperse it, the force could kill you?" I reminded her, still hunting for the trap in the offer.

"And I will have no one but myself to blame. What say you, my dear? The brew is complete. The stage set. Every prop in place. All we need now … is our *star*. Take the lead, my sweet child." With a warm smile, she offered me her hand over the cauldron's frothy foam. "*Seize* your destiny."

Heart pounding in my ears, I expelled the apprehensive breath lodged in my gills. Energy crackled between us the moment I laced my fingers with hers, Amphrite's pupils dilating in anticipation.

Bowing my head, I swallowed hard and spoke the words which would alter the course of my existence forever:

"*Prometheus, Athena,*
*Bring the winds of the Pacific Sea.*"

Luminescent emerald wisps snaked from the cauldron, lighting the cavern with an eerie glow.

"*Fermoris, bronchioles,*
*Et Max Sartorius,*
*Mutate to thee!*"

Eyes bulging from their sockets, I watched the silhouette of a merman rise from the angry brew.

"Again! Quickly!" Amphrite prompted, squeezing my fingers in a vise-like grip.

Once more, I recited the incantation. The floating image changed, wriggling and writhing as if in pain. Its tail tore in two, kicking and flailing until it solidified into human legs. A blink and it was gone, mutated into a vicious claw of magically-infused tendrils. Shooting out from the confines of the cauldron, it punched into Amphrite's chest.

Her body convulsed, head wrenching back at sharp angle. Her fingernails gouged my flesh in her struggle to hold on. Jaw falling slack, smoke belched from her mouth in an erupting geyser, darting off like a monstrous beast with an intent all its own.

At a loss for any other aid to offer, I held her as tight as I could until the very last puff of smoke hiccupped from her lips.

Red-rimmed eyes snapping open, Amphrite's body sagged against the cauldron.

"Next time, *you* be the syphon," she wheezed.

"Noted," I mumbled, barely listening ... but for *very* good reason.

On my worktable beside us, the now crystalized Olympus Pearl came alive. Within it the ravenous storm cloud of my creation descended on the waiting soldiers, hell bent on devouring them all. I lost the ability to think ... to breathe. All that existed in my world was the occasional glimpse of thrashing limbs and sporadic, garbled shrieks of terror. Mermen splashed, kicked, and fought their way to the surface — the struggle complicated by their inexperience with their new legs. One by one, they burst from the water gasping for air. Those that could stand pulled in their flailing brothers, gifting them a foothold in an unknown world. Panting in equal parts adrenaline and fear, the soldiers pulled their weapons and charged the shore. The battle cry of one spread to the lot of many in a mighty roar. The people of Lemuria had no time to prepare. The walls of their defense had already been breached. Soon, every bit of life as they knew it would be claimed by the sea ... by *us*.

"Vanessa, dear, you're drifting." Amphrite nudged me softly, rousing me from a much needed slumber.

I came to with a snort, forcing my anchor-heavy lids open wide. *"Is everything okay? Did anything falter?"*

We learned mere moments into the battle that the spell could only be maintained through a constant vigil. Clasping hands, uttering the spell for the umpteenth time, tossing fresh ingredients into the cauldron, all were required at regular intervals to prevent the magic from wavering. Minutes turned to hours, hours to days, and the battle raged on. We found we could only doze in shifts, waking each other if our subconscious drifted too far into sleep's warm embrace. There laid the pivotal threshold where the thread to maintain the spell could be severed. Exhaustion had long since set in, bringing with it a dull ache deep in my bones.

"For now, everything is as it should be. We should probably recite the incantation again soon, give it a bit of a refresher." Gazing into the cauldron, Amphrite flicked her wrist in an off-handed gesture to the table. "Your pets brought us a satchel of food from the palace kitchen. I have no idea how they managed it. The way they dote on you is truly endearing."

Floteson's head raised at her mention, only to flop back down over his sleeping brother's back.

"They're my boys." Rolling my jaw one way and then the other, I tried to work out the kink from having fallen asleep on the side of the cauldron.

The late day sun hung heavy in the sky, casting a golden amber halo over the ocean and everything she contained. The third day of battle was drawing to a close.

"The west wing of the Lemuria castle crumbled into the sea. Flames engulf the heart of the city. Our victory is within reach," Amphrite stated, her tone cold and emotionless.

An ominous chill tiptoed up my spine, setting my nerves on edge. "As promising as that sounds, we must sustain the vigil until the *very* end ... for the sake of our soldiers."

Floating away with a lazy stroke of her tail, Amphrite hovered in front to the pearl, gazing at the perils of war playing out with an almost wistful expression. "You really are quite strong, Vanessa. I firmly believe you could have invoked this spell without me."

"Your faith in me trumps my own." Something about her posture, this sudden feeling of detachment, set off trumpets of warning in my mind. "I'm convinced I'd still be staring into the cauldron hoping for a blinding epiphany."

Amphrite's forefinger brushed the crystal surface of the pearl, tracing the outline of a rampaging soldier. "So many lives saved because of you ..."

"*Us*," I corrected, rising up to full height.

Gradually her head turned my way, daggers of accusation stabbing from her murderous glare. "Yet you couldn't be bothered to save your own father."

And there it was, the hook I feared the moment I saw her in my parlor.

"I told you, it was too late; there was *nothing* I could do!"

Squeezing her eyes shut, she held up one finger to silence me. "*Nothing* is such a subjective word, wouldn't you agree? There were options you could have dabbled with. You just chose not to utilize any because you no longer had a *need* for your father."

The bubbles in the cauldron were beginning to fade, a sign the magic needed to be renewed. Unfortunately, Amphrite didn't seem in the mood for the necessary hand holding and I doubted my ability to go it alone. "That's *not* true. I went in there to save him."

*What happened afterward was another matter …*

"But you failed!" she snapped, spinning on me. "And in doing so you stole Poseidon from us *all*." She punctuated her statement by parting her vest and laying a protective hand to the swollen pooch of her mid-section.

My gills clamped shut, momentarily forgetting how to function. "You're … *pregnant*."

"Her name will be Morgana," she declared, rubbing her belly in a small, circular motion, "and I foresee her spending much of her life fighting to get out from under the evil stigma associated with her dear, *departed*, older sister."

"Think of all of our men, Amphrite," I urged, struggling to keep my tone calm and steady. "If you kill me now, every one of them will die."

"Oh, *I'm* not going to kill you," she purred with a deadly smile. "But, my dear, sweet child, you will *wish* I had."

With those as her parting words, she vanished in a cloud of lavender smoke, riding the current out.

Beside me, the cauldron gave one final glug and the last bubble of the remaining brew burst.

"*Amphrite, no!*" I screamed my throat raw at the void she left.

With a nauseating knot of terror twisting my gut, I reluctantly turned to the pearl.

As the sunset on the third day, the first soldier seized in pain.

Legs failing him, he shrank to the ground. His tail returned before he settled in the sand. The human he was fighting wasted no time taking advantage of this development. Arching back, he let the metal of his sword wing through the air, landing with a sickening *thunk* as it freed the merman's head from his shoulders.

One by one more mer fell. Some were able to scoot themselves back to Mother Ocean's soothing swaddle. More found themselves at the mercy of an enemy without an ounce to spare. Carnage and horror burning into my eyes, I had to do *something*. Sweeping all the remaining ingredients from the shelf, I dumped them all in to the simmering cauldron. Crouched down beside it, I tried to focus my depleted magical energy for just a … little … longer. Hoping even a few more men would make it back to the water.

In the distance, water churned with the unmistakable sound of a school of bodies swimming my way.

*"Princess Vanessa, what's happening?"*

*"How could you do this to them?"*

*"They're dying! Have mercy, you witch!"*

Within the pearl more men fell, their purple faces and clawing hands scrapping across the ground with the promise to haunt me forever. Somewhere amongst them was Alastor, possibly struggling just as they did. Swallowing hard, I closed my eyes and did the unthinkable. Retracting the fingers of my spell, I used the pearl to riffle through the essences on that beach for that one particular voice. I found him in a sweeping cyclone of magic, his legs about to be stolen from him, bruises and scrapes decorating every inch of his flesh. A horde of humans, with their weapons drawn, eagerly awaited his vulnerable moment.

As the angry mob stormed my parlor, I drew my strength into my core. With one final, exhausted push, I gifted Alastor every magical charm I had left. My only hope being it would be adequate enough to get him home.

# Chapter Twenty Two

"This way, my Princess!" Floteson hissed in an urgent whisper, leading me to a crack in the wall at the back of my cavern I had never noticed. Leave it to puny sharks to have a second way out of *any* situation. While he led the way, Jetteson nudged the small of my back for me to follow.

Angry voices tore through the water in a deadly rip current. The venom in their collective tone screamed for me to flee. Still, there was another part of me that hesitated before wriggling through the crack in the walls.

"I need to know … all those people …" I whimpered in a choked sob.

Jetteson coiled around my wrist, persistently yanking me onward. "Answers will come, my liege, *after* we get you safely from here."

Reluctantly, I let them pull me, the cold stone scraping over my skin as it thrust me headlong into freedom. My boys shepherded me along, swimming behind me to urge me on whenever my speed or motivation faded. The water grew darker the farther from the hub of Atlantica that we swam, the chorus of voices fading to a haunting echo. On a constant swivel, my head turned to all I was leaving behind. My heart cracked and crumbled a little more with every flap of my tail.

"We must head to the dark regions. The area off of Bermuda that no one dares to travel." Jetteson ground his teeth, his tail swishing side to side as he mulled it over.

Floteson shot him a disapproving glare. "The insane asylum for lost fish and mer? That's no place for a precious treasure like our princess."

Tears streamed down my face, each swallowed up by Mother Ocean. Maybe the area dubbed the Isle of Misfits was *exactly* where I belonged. Each blink brought back the image of all the falling soldiers. Only in this vision, their clawing hands, once reaching for the sea, closed around my throat and squeezed in an unrelenting grip. Unable to think ... to breathe, I stopped short. My gills rising and falling in a raspy wheeze.

"I-I have to go back." I forced the words through my constricted throat.

Floteson darted behind me as if to block my retreat in the expansive sea. "My Princess, no! You can't!" Swimming in close, he snaked around my neck to line himself eye-to-eye with me. "They view you as a villain. They won't care to hear any arguments to the contrary."

"But ... Amphrite," I stammered, the argument sounding weak to my own ears.

"*No one* except the three of us even saw her in your shop," Floteson interjected, the grating voice of reason. "They will think you seek to shift the blame. For now, at least, Atlantica is off limits to us."

Slowly nodding my understanding, I straightened my spine and raised my chin with the regal air taught by a haughty upbringing and countless hours of etiquette training. "You're right. Atlantica *is* off limits. Fortunately, that's not where we're going."

Exchanging matching looks of confusion, Floteson and Jetteson twisted in a swirl of scales and teeth. "Where, Your Majesty?"

"To Lemuria, or what's left of it." Combing my fingers through my knotted hair, I twisted it back into a loose knot, my resolve building with every thump of my battered heart. "There are people writhing on the shores of that burning town screaming for help. And I am the *only* one able — and willing — to provide it."

Without waiting for their response, I turned in a tight back flip and kicked in the direction of those that called to me. I expected my boys to argue. To my surprise, they swam to catch up without a word. Their protruding jaws clenched tight, they matched me stroke for stroke.

Our destination?

Not the beachfront, where the cluster of Atlanticans huddled in search of their loved ones. The targeted destination was the rocky shoreline I strolled along, away from bustling nucleus of the town.

There I would grant myself legs.

There I would earn back a bit of salvation for my tortured soul … if it wasn't too late.

The earth trembled beneath my cracked and bleeding feet. The south tower of Lemuria's most extravagant castle broke away from the structure and crumbled into the ocean. Its splash rained over the shoreline. Smoke-filled air scorched my temporary lungs, burning down my throat. Tears blurred my vision, the cause equal parts pain from the soot-filled air and misery at the ugliness surrounding me. When I first stepped foot on the sands of Lemuria, I found it a lovely, enchanted land that possessed the mysticism of a world conjured in a dream. Now, its beauty lay crushed under the savage boot of violence. A flash of white drew my gaze to the embankment. There, alongside the blood-splattered walking path, smoldered a bushel of the same white flowers the human child tucked into my hair. Their petals wilted to russet ash before blowing away on a passing gust. Dark thoughts turned to that sweet lass. Would I find *her* amongst the lumps of burning flesh and fin that riddled the beach? That innocent soul had done *nothing* to deserve such a tragic fate. Then again, who amongst the fallen masses had?

Inching across the rocky shoreline, I made my way to the heart of the once regal city. At the rise of the final hill, my quaking hand rose to my mouth. Before me lay a macabre mosaic of death. No supple white sand could be seen. Bodies, both human and mer alike, covered every inch. Many having fallen in haphazard stacks two and three deep. Gagging at the stench, I shielded my nose and mouth with the crook of my elbow. Lifting the bottom hem of my skirt, I stepped over bodies with as much care and respect as the situation allowed.

"Alastor!" I shouted, the word morphing into a coughing fit that wretched from my aching lungs.

Silence and crackles from the burning village acted as my only response.

No one called out.

No weak hands raised in search of salvation.

I was too late.

There was no hero to the dead.

Tears cut zigzag paths through the soot that covered my face. I sought closure and resigned myself to the most desperate method possible to claim it. Squelching dry heaves, I nudged fallen men and rolled over those that landed face down in search of the one mer I *prayed* I wouldn't find. Hands slick with blood, at each corpse I felt the same sense of dread that I would find myself staring into Alastor's lifeless eyes.

Hooking one hand under a sinewy arm, I eased yet another body over and emitted a surprised gasp.

"*You!*" I marveled in confusion.

Yellow-slitted eyes blinked up at me, a wide, maniacal smile stretching over his face.

"You may have noticed, I'm not all here myself," he chortled, then winced in pain despite not having a visible mark on him.

Gaze traveling the length of the stranger, I gasped to find mer fins at the end of very human legs. Somehow, he had gotten stuck mid-transformation.

"You were in the cell across from me in the castle dungeon." Brow puckered in confusion, I eyed the odd little man whose luck hadn't improved much since our last encounter. "How can you be here … like that? It defies logic … makes *no* sense."

"Sense?" he giggled, his bulbous eyes rolling skyward as if such a concept bored him. "That's nothing more than a somber illusion created to squash imagination."

"You seem to have the fever riddles … if that's a thing." Standing up, I stretched my back and gauged the distance to the sea. "I could drag you to the water from here. The entirety of your tail may be restored once you've returned to Mother Ocean."

"My tail comes and goes." He shrugged. Rolling on to one elbow, he pushed himself up to sitting. As he sat up, a leather-bound book thumped to the ground, which he quickly hid under his arm. "I'm much more comfortable here for now, thank you."

Catching myself staring at his wild grin, I physically shook myself from its captivating spell. "If you require no aid, I must press on. I'm looking for someone very dear to me, who I fear was not gifted the luxury of time *you* have been."

Folding his hands in his lap like a proper gentleman—who just happened to be scantily clad in nothing except a strategically placed clump of seaweed—he tipped his head and beamed up at me. "Oh, you mean Alastor? The son of a servant, turned warrior? He was here. Don't know where he's gotten off to now. Things got a bit … wonky at the end."

Attention snapping back to him as if tugged by a hook and line, I dropped to a squat beside him. *"You know Alastor? How? Who are you?"*

Where others may have shied away from my intrusion, he moved in closer with a fluid roll of his neck.

"The name is Sterling," he purred with a playful wiggle of his eyebrows.

"It's a pleasure to formally meet you." I tried, and failed, to keep the demanding undercurrents from my tone. *"What can you tell me of Alastor?"*

Smile vanishing, Sterling blinked up at me. His face erased of emotion, like sands rescinding with the tide. "Who?"

*"Alastor!* The son of a servant? You *just* spoke of him!" I snapped, thin patience waning.

"Ah, yes!" That manic smile returned, never quite reaching his crazed eyes. "We swam together, then we ran together, then …" His voice trailed off, distracted by a smoldering leaf riding the smoke-filled breeze.

*"Then what?"*

His head jerked my way, staring as if seeing me for the first time. *"Others were falling – one, two, three –*
*soon it would be me.*
*I found another option,*
*thought I'd take a friend.*
*Deciding on your boy, I hoped he hadn't met his end.*
*I found him, mid-battle,*
*sliced and battered like worthless chattel.*
*He took a step, then two, then three.*
*Finding freedom without leaving the key.*
*Where he is now, I cannot say.*
*Somehow the boy found a way.*
*Wherever he is, wherever he may go …*
*every adventure requires a first step, you know."*

My chin fell to my chest, hope dragged to the depths by the rants of an imbecile. "That makes ... no sense. He only needed to get to the water ..."

"Common sense won't really work here." Sterling cringed, sucking air through his teeth.

"So, Alastor is just ... *gone?*" Tipping my head, tears spilled from my lashes.

One arm folding over his mid-section, Sterling rested on the opposite elbow. One finger drummed again his bottom lip in contemplation. "Or ... was he ever really here at all?"

My hands slapped my knees, teeth grinding to the point of pain. "*You said he was!*"

The blank face returned. "Who?"

"*Alastor!*"

"Oh, yes. Quite right. He was *just* here. I'm afraid you missed him. Don't really know where he's gotten off to now ..."

Shoulders slumped in defeat, I rose to standing.

Whether that lunatic had actually seen him or not would remain a mystery. Even so, one thing was becoming clear: Alastor was gone. My hope, my heart, my future vanished without a trace. Under the sea, or on land, there was nothing left for me. I could run, but to what point? Triton was all I had left. He would be furious—justifiably so. And, surely, I would face punishment. Still, my brother's love was the only buoy I could cling to.

Accepting that fate, I strode toward the sea. I would own my blame ... face judgment ... and pray it was enough.

# CHAPTER TWENTY THREE

Reeds, stained black with squid ink, waved in the surf as far as the eye could see. I had thought swimming in from behind the castle, through the residential dwellings of the commoners, would be the safer alternative than blazing through town square. I realized that for the egregious error it was at first glimpse of those telltale reeds. Every home found a place for their flag to commemorate the fallen soldiers.

My mere presence spread through the town like a plague. One by one, mer paused in their tasks to stare. The sudden oppressive silence drew more from their homes, adding to the glaring masses. This was one growing cluster that needed little more than a drop of blood to whirl into a full-blown frenzy.

"Boys," I spoke softly to my sweet babies that followed in my wake, keeping my focus fixed on the steady building crowd, "go to the cave where I first found you and stay there, hidden from sight, until I send for you."

Darting in front of me, Floteson and Jetteson strung their bodies together, blocking me from proceeding one flap farther without them.

"No!" Jetteson's jaws snapped his disdain.

Floteson's head whipped side to side in adamant refusal. "We will *not* leave without you!"

"My darlings," I cooed, cradling their cheeks in my palms, "it's sweet that you thought that to be a question. Care for each other, and take heart knowing we shall be reunited soon."

A flick of two fingers and my outraged sharks vanished in a puff.

What fate awaited me would be mine. I took what solace I could knowing I had at least protected my boys.

Head held high, pulse drumming an anxious reprise through my veins, I kicked into the boundaries of the village.

Merfolk lined the narrow swim path that weaved between the modest dwellings. The heat of their stares bore holes into my flesh as I passed.

From somewhere in the crowd came a word, *"Murderer!"*

It fed to another, *"Witch!"*

And another still, *"Monster!"*

More bodies joined the band, adding their palpable hatred to the inferno growing against me.

A rock pelted my shoulder blade, jarring me forward.

Someone spat on my tail.

The shower of hatred intensified the farther I ventured.

Up ahead, the back entrance of the castle came into view. On either side of the door, two of Triton's personal guards watched with interest. There was a distant age — yesterday, to be specific — when they would have laid down their lives to prevent an assault on their princess. In that moment, judging by the contempt dripping from their sneers, they would have liked nothing more than to join the crowd by palming a stone and hurling it my way.

I once hoped to rule these same mer as their beloved queen. Instead, my shoulders sagged under their blanket of hate.

"He trusted you," a familiar voice accused, the crowd parting to allow her slight form passage. "My boy *loved* you. And where is he now?"

A face that had only ever looked to me with love, pierced my heart with a mask of loathing.

"Loriana," I sobbed, my chin quivering, "I failed him. I am so sorry."

*"You are not a princess!"* Her forefinger, which had separated my hair into countless braids, stabbed in my direction. *"You're nothing more than a siren luring men to their deaths! All that time I cared for you as if you were my own."* Shoulders shaking with an anguished howl, Loriana fell into me. Clinging to each other, we rode out her purge of anger. *"And how do you repay me? By stealing the only thing I ever cared about. I rue the day you were born, Vanessa! May you be beached for your sins!"*

"I feel that particular wish will be answered sooner than you think," I muttered, mashing a kiss into her hair as my tears flowed in torrents.

Blinking hard, as if waking from a dream, Loriana pulled back to an arm's distance. Her gentle eyes widened with shock and appellation at her own words. "Oh … *oh no.* Princess, my humblest apologies. I spoke out of emotion, foul things you have to know I didn't mean—"

Catching her hand, I gave it a quick pulse of comfort.

"*Shhh* … none of that," I soothed. "A lifetime of love cannot be erased by one moment of ugly honesty."

Our fingers remained linked as long as possible until the castle's pull forced me on and broke our hold.

Rounding the bend, I had an eye line on the servant's entrance, and Amphrite's ripening form filling the doorway. Sky blue hair rippled around her shoulders. Her gown, luminescent curls of marsh grass, flowed around her like the bobbing tentacles of a jellyfish. One hand to her chest, she curled her shoulders in and feigned concern.

"Guards!" she breathlessly called, making great show out of protectively rubbing her belly. "With *everything* that has happened, I don't feel safe with the princess being inside the palace. Not in my *fragile state* when I have *so much* to lose."

Needing no further provocation, the two merman positioned themselves between Amphrite and me, fingers tapping the hilts of their swords in an open threat.

Over their well-muscled shoulders, I watched a malicious grin curl across Amphrite's cobalt lips.

My vision tunneled.

The slow and steady thump of my pulse hammered in my temples.

Against my breast bone, the ursela shell blazed red hot.

In a blink, I hovered nose to nose with my enemy. Emerald vines licked around me as my hand clamped to her belly.

"Your child will be born, strong and beautiful," my voice tore from my throat in an unrecognizable growl, "but as the sun sets on her *third* day of life, your tail will be replaced by human legs. You will be torn from your child and cursed to walk the human realm *forever*!"

The guards spun into action. Seizing my shoulders, they pinned me to the ground.

"*This spell shall be unbreakable!*" I screamed, unaffected by their manhandling in throes of my face-off with *true* evil.

Twisting my arms behind my back, they slapped on a pair of magic-stifling shackles. "Princess Vanessa, Alchemist to the Kingdom of Atlantica, you are under arrest for the crime of treason and genocide of your own people, as well as assault on the queen."

"*You will lose all that you love,* just *as I have!*" I vehemently promised my smug step-mother, the tendons bulging in my neck.

Hauling me upright, the guards hooked my elbows to drag me away.

"*I know the truth about you, Amphrite!*" I craned my neck to shout, "I know who the *real* sea witch is … *Your Majesty!*"

# CHAPTER TWENTY FOUR

"*B each her!*"
"*Slice off her fins!*"
"*Toss her in the chasm!*"

My reception to The Pit, for a second time, was not a warm one. Not that I blamed any of them.

"*Enough!*" Triton—my salvation—swam into the room, a gruff tremor reverberating from his broad chest.

"*All Hail the King of Atlantica!*" Doralious bellowed from beside me, where he held my elbow in an unforgiving grasp.

Every mer in the stadium rose in respectful tribute to their ruler, their closed fists clamping over their hearts. The number of guardsmen had noticeably shrunk, as had the presence of any Pacific mer.

Holding up one appreciative hand, Triton lowered it slowly to ease them to their seats. When his gaze fell to me, it radiated with an anger I didn't know my mild-mannered brother capable of.

Moving as one mindlessly obedient body, the onlookers took their seats.

When silence fell, the new king tore his attention from me. Filling his gills, he sent his voice booming to the depths of the chasm. "Today, my fellow Atlanticans, the way we have been living our lives came under attack. Hundreds of our soldiers lost their lives because of the evil and dastardly humans. A terrible sadness has befallen every heart under the sea. How, then, do we respond? Do we let fear and unyielding anger drive us to further attacks? No!" Stamping his trident to the ground, he punctuated his declaration. "Enough blood has been shed. Enough lives have been lost. It is time for us to band together, to take solace in a simpler way of life where we rely on our cultures and traditions instead of human trinkets, and pray fervently to Mother Ocean to ease our troubled souls as she does the stormiest of seas."

Growing restless, Doralious shoved me forward with a rough bump to my shoulder blade. "And *the prisoner*, my King?"

Lips screwing up to the side, I raised one eyebrow and cast a sideways glance in his direction. "So eager to see me punished that you would interrupt the crowned ruler of the Seven Seas?" I *tsk*ed, and pointedly peered up at Triton from under my brow. "One *might* question your up-bringing."

Our long standing private joke cracked Triton's kingly façade. Unfortunately, not in the way I hoped. Combing his fingers through his growing beard, his shoulders sagged. Deep lines of sorrow slicing between his brows.

"I haven't forgotten," he muttered, forcing himself to meet my demanding stare. An intense storm of torment clouded his eyes to a deep sea blue. "That said, the *prisoner* in question is my sister —"

Doralious launched off the ground. His arms pulled from his body, posed for battle. *"Your Majesty, her crimes* cannot *go unpunished! Why kind of message does that send to the families of all that perished?"*

All emotion drained from Triton's features, the lethal result sending chills shivering through me. "I remember you once took great joy in the princess having *her tongue* removed, Doralious. Interrupt me again, and I will see to it that you get to experience that *same* penance."

Doralious snapped back as if struck. Jaw clenched, he begrudgingly swallowed his anger, and bowed his head. "Humblest apologies, my King."

"As I was saying," Triton raised his voice to reach the farthest corners of the arena, "Vanessa is my sister. My love for her makes it impossible for me to be impartial in her sentencing. Therefore, it is with a heavy heart, that I turn that task over to the Council to ensure a just punishment is delivered."

And just like that, any hope for mercy I was clinging to washed away with the rapid turning tide.

# CHAPTER TWENTY FIVE

Triton did not relinquish his position, but allowed the elected representatives from five of the Seven Seas—the Caribbean being excluded for obvious reasons, and the Pacific's absence still a question mark—to join him at his stately platform. Each delegate's expression appeared more stoic and pinched than the next.

"Princess Vanessa, Royal Alchemist of Atlantica, you are accused of treason and genocide of your own people—a crime of the highest magnitude. Is it true it was *your* spell that allowed our soldiers to walk on land?" Triton asked with a frosty detachment that made the tips of my fins curl.

Craving the warmth of his smile and the sunshine in his laughter, memories from a simpler time flashed through my mind.

*Triton falling back in a blissful swan-dive. "Vanessa can be Queen of Atlantica! I'll be King of the Mana-minis!"*

Doralious rammed his elbow into my ribs, forcing the water from my gills in a pained huff.

"Yes, Your Majesty," I confirmed, pressing my bound armed against my throbbing side. "It was."

"And is it true that once they were there and vulnerable, you withdrew your magic, leaving them to *suffocate and die?*" Spine straight as a Pipefish, Triton glared down with an anger that morphed his face from red to purple.

*A young and unsure Triton, self-consciously calling out, "Vanessa? Would you ... I mean, I know our schedules are insane, but I ... miss you. Do you think we could dine together tonight? Maybe catch up a bit?"*

Lunging forward, I flung myself to the restrictive limits of the shackles. My shoulder blades, stretched to their breaking point, screamed in pain that my brewing fury denied. "How can you ask me that? *Alastor was out there!* Do you honestly believe I would *ever* intentionally bring him *any* harm?"

I expected my brother to rage back at me. Instead, he squeezed his eyes shut and dropped his chin to his chest. Even at this distance I could see the ragged breaths dragging through his quivering gills. When his head rose once more, he wore a somber mask that stung more that the harshest of words.

"Answer the question," he rumbled.

*Triton, still round with baby fat, curling up on the floor beside my bed. Holding my hand through the torturous effects of the Fire Coral.*

"No! I didn't *withdraw* anything! My power," admitting the truth out loud hurt more than any swordfish blade ever could, "wasn't strong enough. I maintained the spell as long as I possibly could."

The sharp-featured representative from the Arctic Sea, turned both hands palms out in a frosty shrug. "Why or how you revoked the magic is of little consequence. It was *your* spell that enchanted them. A spell you *claimed* you could control. Which we now know to be a falsehood of the most lethal kind. To put this in the simplest possible terms, it doesn't make our soldiers any less dead."

"*Organa!*" the raven-haired seductress from the Mediterranean scolded. "A bit of compassion for those in mourning, if you please!"

"My apologies," hands folded in front of her, one snow white brow raised at the bothersome triviality, "I forget that warm water mer need to be coddled."

Ignoring them both, I targeted my stare on Triton. My tail flipped back and forth beneath me, ready for battle. "I never wanted to *do* the spell! *You* insisted! I relented for *you*! To save you from the Caribbeans that I was *sure* would kill you as soon as your value to them was exhausted, and to save Atlantica from civil war!"

Seizing the coral bannister in front of him in a white knuckle grip, Triton boomed, "*Am I in their clutches now? Do our factions battle still?* The *second* you invoked your spell their soldiers grew legs along with ours! *All* were forced to kick to the surface or perish! The merman put their own issues aside to focus on our common enemy, and Calypso was dragged to the dungeon to await sentencing. From that moment on, if you couldn't maintain the spell you could have eased it off. Something! *Anything,* to buy them a few minutes more!" Suddenly remembering his audience, Triton pulled back and gestured the delegates forward with a jerk of his chin. "Enough of this. Let's get on with it."

"Of course, Your Majesty," the Gulf mer soothed, her face the very definition of empathy. "However, you may need a moment to brace yourself for what is to come."

Triton pulled back, eyes narrowing in disbelief. "You can't possibly mean ..." Purposely, he trailed off to avoid uttering the words that mer of all distinctions dare not speak.

The Arctic mer bobbed her head in a brief nod, "She betrayed the throne at the expense of hundreds of lives. Only one punishment fits a crime of this magnitude ... *the Kiss of the Kraken.*"

The crowd erupted in shrieks and gasps.

Ears ringing at deafening vibrato, my tail failed me, sending me crumbling to the ocean floor.

"*No!*" the most unlikely voice shouted in my defense. Head snapping to the side, I gaped up at my protector ... Doralious. Had my former friend finally regained his sense? "We don't know what it will do to her!"

"Yes, we do," Triton somberly mumbled. "It will kill her."

"Or worse!" Doralious raved, floating from the ground on puffed up purpose. "We can all attest she has a caliber of power and magic few have ever seen! Add to that the ursela shell and the rumor that she touched the Olympus Pearl, and there's no telling what will happen! A beaching in magic-defusing shackles is a far less risky, and more merciful option!"

As protectors went, he wasn't the best. Still, his argument held weight.

"For *centuries* this punishment has been reserved for those who commit the vilest atrocities against their own kind ... for good reason." The delegate from the Atlantic, who wore her hair the bright blue and yellow combination of a blue tang fish, seemed to loathe the very taste of the words rolling from her tongue. "These laws are in place to protect us from others rising up in a similar fashion. We cannot show her favoritism, no matter her station within the kingdom."

"Perhaps we could enslave her the remainder of her days!" Doralious offered hopefully. "Think of the asset she could be to Atlantica if properly controlled!"

"Triton, please ..." Struggling to reclaim the water that had been knocked from my gills, I beseeched the *one* person with the power to undo the verdict.

Hope died with a shake of his head, murdered by a brutal, stabbing betrayal.

"No," he muttered. "The punishment meets the crime. It is just."

A red haze tinged the edges of my vision.

The crowd around us vanished.

All I could see was Triton and all that we had meant to each other for so as long as I could remember.

"*There was no crime,*" I sneered through my teeth, forcing myself off the ground. "You *know* that. Everything I did, every so-called crime I'm accused of, was to save *you*. Or, have you forgotten?"

"I have forgotten *nothing*," Triton countered, his chest swelling with his own venomous rage.

Stretching to full height, my fingernails dug into the palms of my tightly balled fists. "The spell wasn't ready! I *told* you that! You *insisted* I rush it!"

"*Not at this cost!*" Triton thundered, his face contorted with rage. "*I never wanted this!*"

"*They were going to kill you!*" I screamed, matching his intensity. "*What should I have done, Triton? You tell me!*"

"*You should have let me die for my people!*" Perched at the edge of his pedestal, a pulsating vein throbbed at Triton's temple. "*That is my place! That is my duty! All those lives that were lost, do you not realize I would lay down my life here and now to bring them back? You robbed me of that choice. Denied me the right to honor my people in the noblest way a king ever could!*"

"*How could I do that? You are my brother and I love you!*"

"*I am your king!*" he roared, silencing the room.

The drumming of my own heart in my ears was the only sound to be heard.

"Tomorrow," wetting his lips, Triton leaned back against his trident, "as the sun sets over Atlantica, you will be bound in the courtyard for all to see. The Kraken will be summoned. Its venom extracted and injected into your veins."

"We were family," I managed in a barely audible whisper.

Mourning reflected back from Triton's regal front, as if already peering at my cold carcass. "May Mother Ocean have mercy on your soul."

# CHAPTER TWENTY SIX

A dark, dank cell acted as my suite the night before my execution. Others probably would have spent the sleepless night replaying the highlights of their life on an endless loop. Not me. Hours passed with my face pressed against those algae-covered stalagmite bars. During my previous stay in the dungeon, Alastor appeared from the darkness. His only goal being to save me … to protect me. If he was anywhere close by, and free to venture of his own accord, he would come for me again. I knew that without a shadow of doubt. Every splash I heard, every push of moving water, I scoured my limited sight line for his amber eyes.

Certain, this time, that I heard someone coming, I leaned into the bars and searched the shadows once more.

"*Alastor!*" I whispered, my heart launching in a stutter-beat when a face, indeed, emerged.

The guard who swam forward snorted in contempt.

"Not quite, *Princess*." He sneered and overturned my food tray in the hall.

As I watched the remnants of my dinner settle to the ocean floor out of my reach, he clanged Calypso's tray down in the cell opposite me and kicked off without another word.

Stomach rumbling in protest, I rested my forehead to the bars and filled my gills to capacity.

"*Psstt.*" The noise from across the aisle brought my gaze up.

Calypso's arm was extended from her cell bars, half a seaweed wrap balanced in her palm.

"Thank you," I mumbled, and reached for her kind offering.

"A bit of advice with this gift," the *other* accused traitor to Atlantica ventured, retracting her hand slightly. "Whoever it is you're waiting for, remember … once you've given your heart, it's a hard treasure to reclaim."

With a gentle toss, she landed the wrap in my hand.

Appetite suddenly lost, I stared down at my last meal and let the impact of her words bob in the water between us.

Blinking hard, I let my eyes adjust from the pitch black cell to the glowing amber diamonds dancing through the water from the late day sun. Two guards, resembling beluga whales in personality and stature, held me by each arm. Their none-too-gentle grips bruised purple bands around my biceps.

Mer from every district filled the courtyard; a melting pot of cultures brought together to see history be made. This time, there was no booing. No one threw anything. Their sorrow-filled silence welcomed me to my fate. In the center of the square, two gigantic rib bones from a whale shark had been planted into the ground. Directly across from it sat a pedestaled throne for Triton. My brother lorded over the event, Doralious hovering behind him like a lowly remora clinging to the side of a predator.

As the guards stretched my arms out wide, securing each wrist to a section of bone with ropes of braided reed, I let my gaze skim over the last faces I would ever see. Most passed in a melded blur, until one in particular demanded my focus. Calypso. Alongside the courtyard, she was bound to a bone spike all her own. Our eyes met. The defeat I felt reflected back from the black pools of her irises. Whatever happened, whomever we had been, we were now equals.

Wincing as the tightening reeds pinched my skin, I forced myself to look Triton's way. He was a beacon of emotional neutrality. Cold and unfeeling as stone—at least on the surface. I envied his stoicism. Emotion had me leaking out every orifice of my face.

Tipping his scruffy-bearded chin to his loathsome servant, Triton muttered, "Let us begin."

Reaching behind the throne, Doralious extracted a flounder-sized conk shell.

One.

Two.

Three trumpeted blasts.

Each emotionally filleted me and spread my sins out wide for all to see.

The steady beat of my heart stalled as the water in the square began to churn. It ebbed and flowed in a vacuum rush. Raven hair blew out in a curtain behind me, then tossed forward to lash my cheeks. The ocean floor trembled. An ominous rumble, reminiscent of thunder, reverberated from the depths. A massive shadow formed in the distance, the sheer size of it making my jaw swing slack. Swelling and retracting, it neared, growing larger with each inbound stroke. Children screamed and hid behind their mothers. Mermaids clung to the strong arms of their men. The thinned down Royal Guardsmen tightened their grips on their swords. The irony of all their reactions wasn't lost on me. *They* were safe. The beast had been summoned for me.

Tentacles, long enough to envelop Atlantica whilst offhandedly sinking a passing ship, swam into focus. Quivering suction cups made brief appearances in between each rolling stroke. A bulbous head, ridged and pocked, emerged like a nightmare from the dusky water.

Rising from his throne, Triton stamped his trident down in an order for the beast to bow before him. Recoiling at the sound, the Kraken's tentacles shrank back in writhing squiggles. It floated in retreat with a jerk, then a hop. Again, Triton stamped. The tips of the Kraken's independently moving limbs sunk into the sand as if something *that* monstrous could possibly burrow out of sight. The one glassy, auburn eye visible to me—twice the size of my head—fixated on my bound frame. Head listing to the side, I tried to decipher the emotion emanating from that bulging eye. Was that … compassion?

"Beast! Bow before your king!" Triton demanded, his face reddening in a blend of rage and embarrassment.

The eye of the Kraken seemed to beseech me, begging my understanding.

Remembering back to Triton and me in the throne room, I thought to give the Olympus Pearl another go—if any of its magic remained. Focusing on the very beast called to kill me, I allowed the fingers of my mind to reach out to his.

*Easy, friend*, my mind soothed his. *Be at peace. No one here means you harm.*

. That large pupil fixed and dilated, pain and anguish radiating from its stare.

*It is I that have been called to harm.* His thoughts resounded through me with a force that made my bones rattle. *That is what they do. Rulers for centuries have used me to do their vile bidding. I do not wish to hurt you, little mermaid. Yet I fear I have no choice.*

*The trumped up merman with the stick is my brother, and I assure you that you most definitely do not have a choice.* At this declaration, the Kraken bounded back once again.

"Guards!" Triton bellowed. "Ready your weapons. This monster shall submit one way or another!"

*Steady, now*, I soothed, tipping my head to meet his eye, *and I shall tell you a secret.*

The Kraken paused, hovering in his constant wiggling state.

*I am like no other you have infected before*, I explained, the confident façade I forced remains my best performance to date. *I have powers you couldn't begin to fathom. Hence our ability for this brief conversation. If anyone could survive your venom, it would be me. With that in mind, I make you a promise. If I do, I shall rise up over all of Atlantica, and we shall seek our vengeance.*

Two revolutions of those freakishly large tentacles and the Kraken positioned himself alongside Triton's throne. In a gesture that appeared to everyone else as him succumbing to the command of his king, he bowed his gelatinous heap of a body before me. *Yes … My Queen.*

With a satisfied nod, Triton stamped his trident down hard enough to crack a chunk off his coral pedestal. My new friend responded to the cue by peeling back its tentacles to expose the beak on his soft under belly.

Sliding his sword from its holster, Doralious kicked to the beast with a determined posture. The Kraken's beak creaked open, allowing the Chief Master to scrape the edge of his pointed tongue with the tip of his blade. Pulling back, Doralious held the weapon high. Face set in mask of dutiful resolve, tar-like goo dripping down the sword.

Closing the distance between us, Doralious balanced the middle of his blade on the back of his wrist to protect the poisonous cargo.

"No," I gasped, despite my deep longing to stay strong.

The soldiers bookending me grabbed my shoulders to hold me steady. Clamping my lips down hard on a threatening whimper, my bulging eyes watched the edge of Doralious's sword drag across my tricep, slicing the flesh in a bloom of crimson. Sucking water through my teeth, I winced at the white hot rush of pain radiating through my limb as the wound was slathered with the Kraken's toxic sludge. With each drum of my pulse, the venom snaked through my veins, slithering closer to my heart where it would soon encircle in a lethal embrace.

Returning his sword to its sheath, Doralious mournful bowed his head. "I am truly sorry, Princess."

A nod to his men and the three backed to a safe distance, eyeing me as if the venom could seep through my pores.

I don't remember the details of all that followed, only the haunting sensations:

A sharp pain in my right side, contorting my body at an unnatural angle.

Joints popped in a chorus of sickening crunches.

The coppery taste of blood filled my mouth, gagging me.

My body swelled, straining the limits of my flesh before muscle and tissue began to shred.

A cloud of black tinged the edges of my vision, my consciousness waning.

Arms locked akimbo, my head whipped back.

Every muscle tensed to the point of pain.

A deafening rip was drowned out by the anguished cry that tore from my chest.

Head lulling to the side with exhaustion, a choked sob lodged in my throat.

I could feel nothing from the waist down, and one glance led me to the gruesome discovery of why.

My tail had exploded in a spray of mutilated scales and dangling hunks of meat.

Every bone below my pelvis shattered into unrepairable shards.

"Is this normal?" Triton's quandary could barely be heard over the incessant roar of my mind.

Parents shielded their children's eyes.

Merfolk heaved at the gruesome display.

Calypso rose from behind the bone to which she was bound.

"Beastly venom laced with magic," she marveled, equal parts awe and reverence drenching her tone. "Peer into the face of your creation and *tremble* before her."

Death's door flung open, luring me inside. The only thing that prevented me from crossing its tempting threshold was the ursela shell pulsating against my breast bone. Emerald tendrils crept from the shell, enveloping me in a loving cocoon. Two ambitious wisps vined out, targeting the Kraken. They brushed against his tubular cheeks, each caress asking an unspoken question. The Kraken relented, his tentacles falling slack as he bowed down once more. The globe of his eye never shifted from me as the wisps entered through his iris.

The surge was sudden and jarring.

Body sizzling with syphoned energy, my only goal became not to die.

Lips moving in a silent prayer to Mother Ocean, I felt my organs shift in preparation for … *something.*

The Kraken sagged, the eye visible to me rolling skyward.

I wanted to cut the tie, to spare my only ally — and friend — in that square.

Unfortunately, that decision was not mine.

Energy, pirated from the Kraken, transformed what was left of my mutilated tail into eight black tentacles which curled and coiled around me.

Purple suction cups sprouted forth from freshly formed gelatinous flesh.

*Pop, pop, pop, pop, pop.*

The Kraken waned, his monstrous head slumping into the sand.

Meanwhile, I coursed with untapped energy the likes of which I had never felt before. Breaking free my bound arms was now as easy as snapping a rogue thread.

Trapped in a foreign body, I slumped to the ground in a drained heap. All the while, those outlandish tentacles writhed around me.

I wanted to cry.

Wanted to scream.

Wanted to lash out at anyone and everyone.

Triton's voice, resonating through the square, interrupted my building bloodlust. "Doralious, confirm death and retrieve the ursela shell."

The shell throbbed against my chest in protest. Protectively, my hand closed around it.

They had taken so much.

Tortured me.

Mutilated me.

Robbed me of my identity.

Now … it was *my* turn.

# CHAPTER TWENTY-SEVEN

The water around me stirred. Two tentative soldiers followed their king's orders and approached my slumped form. One used the tip of his sword to sweep my hair aside. The fingers of the other brushed over the back of my neck in his awkward fumbles to untie my shell. My upper body remained still as stone, luring the nameless soldiers into a false sense of security. Those simple-minded fools were oblivious to my tentacles slipping up behind them until the wandering appendages twisted around their throats and squeezed tight.

A slow smile curling over my lips, I pushed off the ocean floor with one unified stroke of my free tentacles.

"Easy, boys," I purred to my captives. "Get a lady's consent before you start the manhandling."

A quick pulse and I could have shattered both of their tracheas with ease. As intoxicating a thrill as that would have been, I settled for the slightly more subdued gratification of knocking their skulls together with a dull *thunk*. Each settled into the sand in a listless heap.

"Vanessa," Triton called, trumped up on his own authority, "my many thanks to Mother Ocean for sparing your life. Be her mercy as it may, you must know that the remainder of your sentence can only be banishment from the kingdom ... forever. Without further incident, I need you to hand over the shell and leave the kingdom at once."

I'm not even going to pretend I heard a word that prattled from his lips. Raising my head, my attention was diverted by the Kraken who laid utterly still, his large pupil fixed and dilated. He knowingly saved me ... and paid with his life.

"*Ursela.*"

That grating tremor found my ears like the sweet serenade of an angelic choir. Eagerly welcoming her long-missed ghastliness, I scoured the crowd for my mother. Upon first glance, all I saw was the same useless wretches who floated helplessly by as I was tortured and dismembered.

Then, a blink.

A retrained focus, and the truth was revealed.

I found her in the sea of faces, putrid and repugnant as ever, beaming up at me with visible pride. Best of all? She hadn't come alone. Mommy brought an army. Mixed through the throng of mer was every soldier that died on the island of Lemuria. One by one, they clapped their fists over their hearts and bowed before me.

"Vanessa?" Triton attempted.

Again, Mother spoke one word in a breathy sigh, "*Ursela.*"

The shell pulsed against my chest in an appreciative surge.

The other apparitions raised their voices with hers in an otherworldly chant:

"*Ursela.*"

"*Urselaaaaaa.*"

"*Ursssssela.*"

By all lines of reasoning, their blood stained *my* hands. Still, not one of them moved to condemn or harm me. Instead, they honored the part of me others wished to vanquish.

"*Vanessa!*" Triton stamped his trident against his crumbling pedestal, grinding his teeth in agitation. "*You* will *answer me!*"

Gradually, I tipped my head in his direction, glaring up at him with sinister intent. "*Vanessa* is dead. You can call me ... *Ursela.*"

The guards surrounding Triton and the perimeter drew their weapons, each assuming a defensive stance.

Hitching one eyebrow, I admired their adorably pointless posturing.

"Call yourself what you will," Triton declared, white knuckling the staff of his trident in his struggle to maintain control, "the directive remains the same. *Hand over the shell at once.*"

Ignoring the fact that he had spoken at all, I let my leisurely gaze sweep over the testosterone exuding soldiers. Phantom images only I could see dodged and weaved between them, the dead offering up each merman's weak point that would bring them down with one strike. A broken rib here. A torn tailfin there. A frequently dislocated shoulder that required little more than a carefully placed tap. The knowledge was a heady tonic of bliss.

"I *despise* men who are threatened by a strong woman," I murmured, biting my lower lip seductively.

Raising one hand with an elegant roll of my wrist, I simply snapped my fingers. Every soldiers' sword leapt from their grip, slicing through water in my direction. Four I caught in my tentacles. The others turned on their owners, arching around me in an ominous threat.

"Vane—"

One sword wielding tentacle stabbed Triton's way, its intent *strongly* implied.

"Ah, ah, ah," I warned, with a wag of my forefinger.

Pressing his lips in a firm white line, the young king swallowed hard. "*Ursela,*" he corrected. "This spectacle isn't necessary. This situation can still have a peaceful resolve."

Curling one shoulder in, I threw my head back in a loud guffaw. "*Peaceful*? Is that what you view this evening's spectacle as? I saw it as a girl being brutalized while an entire kingdom watched. However, it was deemed okay, because she was a *villain.*"

Triton rose from his throne, his broad chest swelling. "No one said what happened here was *okay*, Vanessa."

One sword winged through the air, end over end. My magic caught it a mere hair from Triton's throat.

"*My name,*" I snarled through my teeth, "is *Ursela*. I suggest you remember that."

The live soldiers closed in all around me, preparing to take me on in hand-to-tentacle combat. I could see them all without turning, from their raised fists to each waving lock that swayed around their heads. They sought to protect their king. Who would protect *them*, I wondered.

"Ursela," Triton begrudgingly corrected, his Adam's apple bobbing under the blade's deadly point, "stand down. No one needs to get hurt. This isn't you."

"*Isn't me?*" a ragged scream tore from my throat, hoarse with emotion. "No. It's who *you* made me! *Your* hand sculpted my fate. My apologies if you find your handiwork unsettling."

Triton didn't argue further. Settling back into his throne, he cast a cursory glance to his Chief Master. "Take her down ... by any means necessary."

"As you command, Majesty," Doralious snarled. With a mighty battle cry ripping from his chest, he led a swarm of soldiers in their charge. *None* of them were armed with more than a monsoon of raw adrenaline.

I let them come. Welcomed them with my arms thrown out wide and a gracious dip of my head.

"*Lose yourself in the darkness,*" my mother whispered against my ear, the funk of her breath assaulting my senses.

My smile widened at the return of her much treasured guidance.

"What a *wondrous* idea." Expelling a potent dose of ink, I retreated into the murky water. Thanking the Kraken trait that allowed me to see without issue, I watched with giddy interest as the soldiers blindly combed the water in search of me.

Not wanting them to stumble onto their weapons, I whisked those pesky items off to my alchemist parlor with little more than a passing thought. Then, I set to my *deliciously* fun task. Weaving between the soldiers, I brushed an arm here, grazed a cheek there. I *was* the unseen ghost whose presence prickled down their spines. This brilliantly maniacal waltz ended when I found myself nose to nose with Doralious. Unlike the others, he didn't yelp or start in surprise.

"We were friends once." Lips pulling from his teeth in disdain, Doralious's hands balled into fists at his sides. "Do you forget that, witch?"

One stroke of my tentacles and I swirled around him, causing him to spin to keep up. "We *were* friends," I agreed. "Then, you turned on me when I needed an ally the most. Your priority became asserting yourself as the premiere henchmen to the throne by withering my spirit whenever we shared a space."

"If I could affect your sensitive soul so easily, you were never equipped for the throne to begin with, you mongrel half-breed!" Shoulders hunched, chin drawn to his chest, he blazed straight for me. One fist pulled back as he swam, committed to the strike.

I *may* have stroked his ego a smidgeon by letting him get close. That made it all the more fun when I nonchalantly circled one raised digit.

Green tendrils sparked.

Doralious froze, his shape shrinking before me in a swirl of magic. With a devious giggle I watched his muscular body wilt. Skin hardened to coarse leather. Limbs shriveled to nubs. Eyes bulged from their sockets. In mere seconds he was reduced to a polyp on the ocean floor. My very first, and by *far* the most rewarding … up to this point anyway.

Crouching down, I studied him with gleeful appreciation. One tentacle rolled back, poised in warning.

"Think of this as my *favor* to Atlantica." Throwing his own words back at him, I let my hovering appendage fall.

The decorated soldier met his end with a stomach-turning squish.

Unfortunately, the ink dissipated right about the time Doralious went *crunch*. Screams rang out. The panicked masses fled in droves.

"Yes! Hurry home, children!" I taunted. Noticing the remaining Guardsmen nervously contemplating their own escape, I clucked my tongue against the roof of my mouth. "*Tsk, tsk.* Not you, boys. I have big plans for *you*."

A rhythmic roll of my fingers and my will snaked out in swirling vines, capturing each soldier where they swam.

"*Ursela, stop!*" Triton boomed, injecting himself in a prime position to block further magical *fun*. "I'm the one you want! Leave these merfolk alone and target your rage at the one deserving of it."

"How self-sacrificing, and … *kingly*," I sneered, folding my arms in front of me.

Chest puffed, he towered over me, expelling warm water at my face with every heaving exhale. "You want to kill me? *Kill me*." My pulse lurched at his tempting offer. Still, I waited for the hook. An offer that appetizing *had* to come equipped with one. "I lost my mother, father, *and* best friend. My *sister* was all I had left. If you're telling me that she's been replaced by this *monster*, then you can go ahead and end this miserable existence for me. Spare me a lifetime of living with the ghosts of all that have died since this damnable crown was placed on my head! Free my soldiers. Take me inst—"

His noble declaration morphed into a choked gurgle. One ambitious tentacle seized his throat before I had even made the conscious decision to allow it. Watching the violet hue of twilight steal over his features, I dropped my voice to a husky whisper. "You know nothing of ghosts, little brother."

"Finish it," Triton gasped, his fingernails instinctively digging for freedom from the appendage holding him.

As if cued by the mention of them, the voices of the undead rose in a haunting symphony.

*"Kill him."*

*"Wring the life from his body."*

*"Claim the throne."*

*"It can all be yours."*

*"Urrrrssseeellllaaa."*

The desire to administer that one fatal squeeze was intoxicating. My breath quickened at its seductive pull. Somehow through the fog of bloodlust, the goading of my sinister counsel gave me pause. That was my brother. They were talking about *my brother*. The same tow-headed child that held two of my fingers in his chubby fist as we watched our mother's funeral procession swim by.

I hated him.

Loathed him for what he had done to me.

But ... I couldn't kill him.

Not yet.

My tentacle retracted, allowing Triton to eagerly gulp down a mouthful of water.

"You will die when *I* allow it," I vowed to myself as much as to him. "First, I will see you writhe. I'll watch you wriggle like a worm on a hook as you are stripped of everything just as I have been. Every morning when your lids flutter open after a fitful sleep, I want your first thought to be *'Is today the day?'* Know that you are never safe. I have proved how easily I can wipe out *any* who guard you. They'll be gone, and you'll be nothing but a merman with a pointy stick and a big title. Until then, I will wait. Watching for the perfect opportunity ... *to sink you to the depths.*"

Spinning in a fan of tentacles, fleeing Atlanticians scuttled out of my rampant path.

Swimming from the courtyard, I reeled passed the Kraken, my heart sinking in my chest. One hand brushed over his chilled flesh, saying a silent good-bye to the only friend I had in that square.

"Take me with you," Calypso rasped, jerking me from my fleeting reverie. "Let me serve you as the true *goddess* you are."

One stroke and I hovered by her side. Cradling her chin with the tip of one tentacle, I guided her gaze to mine. "Such pretty words and a charming sentiment, yet I know you for the conniving sneak you can be. Answer me this: if I *were* to cut you free, what will you do now that your army and title are gone?"

"Ursela, you have been banished from Atlantica. You need to leave the boundaries of the kingdom!" Triton huffed, struggling to reassert the authority I'd stolen from him.

"Simmer down, junior. The grown-ups are talking," I tossed over my shoulder at him, before wrinkling my nose in Calypso's direction. "You were saying?"

Full lips parted, then clamped shut again. Jutting her chin out with an indignant flair, the Caribbean beauty opted for the ugly truth. "When the mood strikes me, I shall turn my fury or favor on all those of my choosing."

Snapping upright, I glanced back at Triton, my eyebrows disappearing into my hairline. "Now *that* was a good answer," I mused, jabbing my thumb in her direction.

Purposely keeping my tone light and airy, I pretended not to notice the soldiers slinking in behind me or the inaudible ghoulish whispers buzzing a constant stream of background noise.

Curling my fingers, I engaged my magic. Wisps streamed into Calypso's pupils, dilating them to black pits eager to be filled.

"Calypso," I pressed in close to breath against her ear, "I free you from this subservient bond. From this day forth, you shall be bound only by the ocean—able to take whatever nautical form you desire."

Shackles falling away, Calypso's protective glare snapped around, thick braids lashing at her face, *"Behind you!"*

I knew the young soldier was there, could feel his presence edging closer. Still, the heads up was a thoughtful sentiment. Snatching at the water between us, I reduced him to a polyp before even acknowledging him with a glance.

"They just don't seem to be getting this," I commented to Calypso in a conspiratorial hush.

"Stand down," Triton ordered his men, most likely for their own safety.

Rising above them all with a flick of my tentacles, I jerked my head in Calypso's direction. "I would steer clear of this one," I warned my brother. "She's *feisty.*"

Echoes of my own manic laughter swept me from the only home I had ever known. Only I knew my performance for the façade it truly was: a painted mask of sculpted beach sand fragile enough to crumble at the faintest touch.

# CHAPTER TWENTY- EIGHT

loteson? Jetteson?" With one hand against the slick stone wall, I ventured into the mouth of the cave where I first found my babies.

I expected to be enveloped in a heavy cloak of darkness. I was welcomed, instead, by the soft blue glow of bioluminescent plankton. The walls had been painted with it. Spinning in a slow circle, I admired the starry night sky effect on the otherwise dismal cavern.

"Princess," Jetteson darted in, his scaly hide brushing against my cheek.

"We've been busy preparing things for you," Floteson finished, lacing himself around my now fuller midsection.

Closing my eyes, I reveled in the squeeze of their twining embrace. "My darling boys, I feared you wouldn't recognize me."

Flicking their heads, my striped babes exchanged matching guilty grimaces.

"We had to know you were well, Your Majesty," Floteson explained, his tail nervously twitching from side to side.

Jetteson's lip curled from his teeth in a vicious snarl. "We saw all our princess was subjected to by those treacherous wretches."

Them having witnessed my degradation caused a hot flush to fill my cheeks. "If you watched, you know I am no longer anyone's princess."

"Now you can be whatever you choose." Curling across my lower back, Floteson nudged me forward while trying out my new moniker. "Come … Ursela, let us show you around your new home."

"It took a great many trips since your arrest, and some awkward collaborative team work, but we would gladly endure this and more to make you happy," Jetteson gushed, guiding me down a slight incline which delved farther into the lair.

Eyes snapping open wide, my hands clapped over my mouth. Everywhere I looked, the space was decorated with my most treasured possessions from my quarters, and my Alchemist parlor. A ridge in one wall was lined with my potions and tonics. Next to that, sat my cauldron and the faded remnants of the Olympus Pearl.

Snorting an abrupt laugh, my shoulders curled in as I rushed to a heap of fabric situated in the corner. "*My bedding*! You thought to bring my wonderfully cozy bedding!"

My boys braided themselves together, beaming at my enthusiasm.

"We would've brought your actual bed," Floteson began.

"But the sea turtle we bribed to carry it swindled us," Jetteson finished.

Gathering one lush blanket in my arms, I flung it around my shoulders like a cape. Twirling with a giggle, I stopped short, the laughter dying on my lips. My vanity mirror. Mouth suddenly arid, I realized I had yet to see the result of my transformation.

Letting the blanket float to ground in a discarded mound, I moved to the mirror in a dream-like trance. Parted lips expelled a slow, easy exhale. The figure staring back at me was of fuller, more cephalopod-esque form. That part I anticipated. Unfortunately, I was unprepared for the ruthless fashion in which the devastation had robbed my entire appearance of its vibrant pallet. Long, flowing raven hair drained to a dull platinum. A once creamy complexion had taken on the shade of an overcast day. Bright violet eyes I inherited from my mother blinked back a steely gray.

Hands trembling with the shock, I pinched my cheeks to give them a dash a color. It helped … a little. Extracting a petal from a sea flower my boys had generously supplied, I painted my lips a brilliant red. The girl staring back at me would never be what she once was. On the other hand, there was nothing saying she couldn't be … better. *Fabulous* even.

Spying my fencing sword propped against the wall, my hand instinctively closed around the hilt. Twisting my bleached locks into a knot on top of my head, I administered one quick swipe of my blade. All that remained of Vanessa was sliced away, drifting off on a passing current. Curling my fingers into my short-sheared hair, I gave a pull here and a tug there. The strands darted off my head in a messy disarray. Sucking in my cheeks, I turned my head one way then the other, admiring the end result.

It was new.

It was unexpected.

It was … *fierce*.

"That's a good look for you," a deep baritone rumbled from the mouth of the cave.

Six little words. That's all it took for me to go from eased acceptance to ravenously livid fast enough to give a sailfish whiplash.

"*Triton*! Saying you aren't welcome here is a *vast* understatement."

Skirting around him with a vengeful glare, I dragged my fingers through the glowing plankton, leaving angry black slashes in its otherwise serene blue. My heart beat the drums of war against my ribs, the crescendo of thumping calling forth death's malevolent army. The walls came alive around me, writhing and churning in a sea of faces. Yanking my hand away, I flinched at the stone surface that blinked back at me with cold, unfeeling eyes.

Oblivious to the ghostly new arrivals summoned by my rage, Floteson and Jetteson shot behind Triton, pinning him into the lair.

"I didn't come here looking for trouble." Acknowledging the stunted sharks with little more than a passing interest, Triton cast his gaze to the ocean floor. Chewing on his lower lip, he watched the tip of his tail brush over a few loose stones. "Quite the opposite in fact."

"*He plays coy.*" The voices of the unseen melded together, their whispers curling over my lobes, burrowing their influence into my mind. I could make out my mother's voice among them. I would recognize it anywhere. "*The timid younger brother. Yet it was he that ordered you to be strung up. He would see you, his own sister, exxxxxecuted.*"

"Playing coy," I repeated. Swallowing hard, I attempted to physically shake off the spirits' influence. "I almost believe the act. Then, I remember you to be the same cold-hearted barracuda who ordered my body be shredded and contorted in the most painful way imaginable, and better sense prevails. I'm fickled like that."

Nodding his acceptance of the claim, Triton chose his next words carefully. "When I handed your sentencing over to the Council, I never imagined they would demand such extreme measures."

"*Lies!*" the paranormal chorus countered. "*He wanted to see you suffer, yet was too cowardly to speak the words himself!*"

Acidic bubbles churned and popped in my veins, releasing their venom into my bloodstream. "You did nothing to contest it. Quite the opposite, in fact. *You*, in all your kingly glory, called forth the creature to infect me. You see, I remember the proceedings in intricate detail. I found that moments of abject torture and anguish, such as that, provide a certain sense of clarity."

Dragging his tongue over his bottom lip, Triton forced his gaze to meet mine. "I said I never imagined, not that I didn't agree."

Behind him, Floteson and Jetteson hissed their outrage, their mighty jaws snapping at the water.

"*He admits it!*" the dead chided. "*He doesn't deserve to wear that crown!*"

Gills rising and falling in ragged pants, my blood boiled, preparing to erupt in a violent fury. "Thank you *so much* for coming all the way out here to clarify that. Now, I suggest you take your leave."

"*Blind him with ink. Trap him in —*"

Expanding his gills, he expelled a rush of water in exasperation. "Hundreds of soldiers died, Vanessa. The spell that killed them was *your* creation."

"*Say that name again and it will be the last word you utter!*" I roared, eliciting a giddy titter from those haunting faces.

Palms raised, Triton attempted to halt my outburst. "*Ursela,*" he corrected in a soothing whisper, "I didn't come here to fight, nor to apologize."

"*No one knows he's here, or else they wouldn't have let him come alone. Now's your chance … seek our vengeance.*"

The blood pulsing behind my eyes awoke a pounding in my temples. "So, this visit is for a status update? Wonderful. Let me speed this up then. You publicly tortured me and turned me into a sea monster. *We,*" with two fingers I gestured from me, to him, and back again, "are not okay."

"*Torture him.*"

"We *could* be," Triton exclaimed, edging his way closer. "We have no one except each other left. We can still be a family. The banishment must stand in the eyes of Atlantica. Even so, that doesn't mean we can't be a part of each other's lives!"

"Family," I tried on the word, wincing at its bitter bite against on my tongue. "Is that what we are?"

*"Play with him."*

"Of course!" Triton grinned. The blue diamonds sparkling victoriously in his eyes made it clear he believed me to be convinced. "I love you, you know that!"

Tentacles rolling across the ocean floor deposited me directly in front of my brother. Tilting my head, I stared up at him through narrowed eyes. "Were we family when you had me bound in the courtyard? What about when the first gruesome pop of my tail tearing apart resonated through the kingdom? Were you my *protective* brother then?"

The words struck him with the force of a harpoon to the gut, stealing the water from his gills. Hunting for words of any sort, his mouth opened and shut like a largemouth bass.

*"Kill him,"* the seductive whisper of the voices skittered up my spine, shuddering through me.

"I was alone in my torture. And you shall be alone in yours," I rasped, hands clenched at my sides.

It wasn't time.

I wasn't ready.

His offer to repair our shattered family still sliced too deep into my battered heart.

Even so, the wraiths' suggestions seeped into my veins, creating an overpowering need for carnage and chaos. It took every ounce of strength I had to keep all ten appendages firmly in check.

*"He's not fit to wear that crown. Rid the kingdom of his incompetence. Take what is rightful yours."*

"You need to leave. *Now,*" I snapped, feeling the thread of my resolve slipping from my grasp.

"I'm not afraid of you, Ursela," he declared with a sad, nostalgic smile, whisking us both back to the first time we found ourselves in that same cavern.

*"Wrap your tentacles around his neck. Choke the life from his useless carcass."*

Chin to my chest, I feared movement of any kind would unleash my brewing frenzy. Glaring up from under my brow, I forced the words through clenched teeth. *"Then you really haven't been paying attention."*

"I don't want to leave you." Tone bordering on a whine, Triton's shoulder's sagged in defeat. "Ursela, *please* ..."

As if moving by their own accord, my hands rose, curling into vicious claws on their ascent. Something ugly and twisted inside of me yearned to feel his pulse still. To experience the crunch of his trachea under my unrelenting grasp.

"Triton," I gasped in a final plea, *"get out!"*

A potent riptide of magic slammed into him, whisking him back to his domain in a bright flash of light.

Arms falling slack, I squeezed my eyes shut at my temporary victory and focused on steadying my erratic breathing.

Slimy scales brushed my bare shoulders and neck, my boys coiling around me in anticipation of my command.

"Floteson, Jetteson, follow him home," I ordered, acknowledging each of them with a tender scratch to the chin, "and ... keep an eye on our young king."

With dutiful nods, the whirled around me, then darted off to do my bidding.

*"You won't be able to resist us forever,"* the rippling wave of faces warned. *"Only through retribution will you be reunited ... with your love."*

Something bumped the halved clam shell resting on a nearby ledge, which the sharks had swiped from the vanity table of my palace quarters. A small item rolled free, catching the current to float directly into my eye line.

Breath lodged in my gills, I moved as if in a dream. Catching the thin reed between two fingers, I turned it over, admiring the whale's tail image carved into the delicate driftwood. The last time I saw Alastor, I gazed up at his handsome features while he fastened the accessory into my hair. Clutching it to my chest, I felt the scabbed wound on my heart tear open. He had only been mine for a moment, yet I held no doubt I would ache for him eternally. With him, I was safe. I was beautiful. I was *home*.

Vanessa would have screamed her throat raw at the loss of him and unleashed her fury by shattering vials with a violent sweep of her arm. My hand twitched at my side with longing to carry out that very act. Then, I remembered … *Vanessa* was dead. Pulling the reed away from my torso, I pinched it between two fingers. Eyes narrowing, a tentacle rose on either side of me, looping around each pointed edge of the painful reminder. A sharp pulse, a little pressure, and the twig snapped in two. Both fingers and tentacles let it fall away, the shards riding the tide out.

If that was all I had left to hold on to of Alastor, it was insufficient by far.

Caught up in the dark storm of my thoughts, I failed to notice the chestnut-haired beauty flitting into the cavern with tentative strokes of her tail.

It was the sweet lilt of her voice cutting through the somber drone of the dead that snapped my head around. "Lady Ursela? I-I'm terribly sorry to disturb you. Others warned me not to come, but I had no choice. I had to speak to you."

Sucking water through my teeth, I recoiled into the shadows. I had barely recovered from the ghouls' last onslaught, I couldn't fight them off again. Not yet.

"I mean you no harm!" the girl offered with a compassionate tilt of her head, extending one hand in my direction.

"It's not *me* I'm worried for," I forewarned, sinking farther into the darkened corner.

The mer let her hand fall. Lacing her fingers together in front of her, she nervously picked at her nails. "I don't believe the horrible rumors circling the kingdom. You did all you could for our soldiers." Chin quivering, her voice cracked with emotion. "What happened was simply a horrible accident. What followed … a travesty."

I tried to speak, only managing a pained whimper.

All around me haunting faces churned, their full, ghastly forms emerging from the stone.

Like hungry sharks in chum filled waters, they swarmed our unsuspecting guest. Brushing her hair from her shoulders. Inhaling her scent as if intoxicated by it.

Oblivious to all of this, the mermaid continued, "After … *everything*, I didn't know who else to turn to."

"*She was in the crowd,*" the specter of a soldier missing half of his face murmured against the nape of her neck, causing the girl's body to tremble with an involuntary shudder.

"*Laughed as you suffered,*" yet another, with blue lips and blackened gums, added.

Clinging to the reed, I prayed it would anchor me in the knowledge that this lass was young and innocent. She was no enemy of mine.

Squaring her narrow shoulders, my brazen guest ventured close enough for me to see the light dusting of freckles across the bridge of her nose. "My fiancé was killed during the battle with the Lemurians," she admitted, her face crumbling in misery.

"*Do you think her tears would taste as salty as the sea?*" a corpse in the late stages of rot pondered, dragging his tongue over the rise of her cheek.

Bringing my fist to my lips, I stifled a heave.

"Since I lost him, I can't sleep. Can't eat. The pain … feels as though it could consume me." Her desperate stare beseeched me, pleading for understanding.

Round and round, the phantoms eddied. Each more horrific than the last.

"*She knows not of real pain.*"

"*We could show her.*"

"*The poor soul.*"

"I was hoping," her request wavered with the tangible sorrow of true mourning, "you might know of a way to heal my heart and grant me a bit of peace … with *magic*. I'm willing to pay *any* price."

Shaking my head, I tried to deny my own licentious longing.

This was the beast. The infection. It wasn't me.

"*She wants us.*"

"*Needs us.*"

"*No one will know.*"

"*Plant a garden of souls that wronged you.*"

"*Let her be the* first *seedling.*" My mother's spirit broke from the pack. Her gnarled hand reached for me, beckoning me forth. Her tone made it sound like a special honor I could bestow on the humble maiden.

The shell pulsed red against my breastbone.

My fist tightened around the reed.

"Lady Ursela?" she attempted once more, my silence seeming to give her doubt if I heard her at all. "Can … can you do that?"

The manifestations drifted around her, presenting her to me as if in offering. Silence descended. The living and the dead waited with vested interest, eager to learn of my true nature.

Slow rolls of my tentacles eased me out from hiding. As my head rose, an oily slick smile spread across my face. "My dear, *sweet* child, that's what I do. It's what I *live* for."

Enjoy an Excerpt of Crane
Also written by Stacey Rourke

# 1

If his wife hadn't let her ass grow to the size of a sofa, Vic wouldn't have to cheat. Shrugging his navy blue sport coat over his shoulders, he stepped forward, allowing the hotel room door to shut behind him with a soft thump. A smug smile curled across his face, his chest puffing with pride at his own prowess—thanks in part to those spiffy little blue pills his doctor prescribed. The heels of his wing-tipped loafers clicked against the cement stairs, one impeccably manicured hand running along the handrail as he descended. The rusted metal rail squeaked its protest under the faint touch. Taking its suggestion, he retracted his hand.

Why he humored Karma by letting her drag him to this dive every week, he had no idea.

*Her firm little apple bottom isn't that great*, he mused to himself, snorting a quick, dry laugh.

Of *course* it was. She made good money with it at the Sugar Shack down by the airport. Grinding to R&B's raunchiest hits, while clad only in a sequin thong. She was a sweet, albeit naïve, girl that believed if she stroked Vic's … *ahem*, ego just the way he liked, she would someday find a fat rock on her finger and the title of Van Tassel behind her name. Hence her insistence on the flea bag hotel. She had flipped her bleached blonde waves, batted those ridiculous fake eyelashes, and pouted that she couldn't be seen as the "other woman" by the same crowd she would soon be rubbing elbows with. As if he would *ever* let that happen. Karma's airbrushed nails and hooker heels would *never* fit into his world. After all, in Tarrytown the Van Tassel name meant something, and not because of the stupid legend the residents of the small glen of Sleepy Hollow mercilessly clung to. No, as one of the founding families they helped build this town. Meaning, here, he might as well be a Rockefeller. A fact he reveled in and would *never* tarnish with outward displays of his cheap conquests … no matter how well she could wiggle.

Vic crossed the parking lot, lit only by one humming street lamp, with a wide, jovial stride. As he shook his keys from the pocket of his slacks, thumbing the button to unlock the doors, his phone buzzed from the breast pocket of his Armani shirt.

Snatching it from its resting place, he tapped to answer. "Yello?"

"Don't you sound chipper for someone working late?" Yvonne slurred, the only hint he needed that she'd already cracked open tonight's bottle of wine.

"Why shouldn't I be chipper?" he playfully asked, turning to glance back up toward the room Karma had rented. A flash of her blonde locks appeared from behind the stained drapes. He raised his hand in a casual wave, but couldn't tell from this distance if she returned the gesture. "I just finished showing a multi-million dollar estate that the buyers are *very* interested in, and now I get to head home to my loving wife."

"Yeah, right," Yvonne openly scoffed, her voice muffled by her glass as she took another sip. "We're the friggin' Cleavers. Hey, Cassidy is at the mall. I need you pick her up on your—"

Vic jerked his head to the right, in the direction of the neighboring gas station. Between the normal ebb and flow of rushing traffic, he heard the distinct snap of hoof beats pounding over pavement. "What kind of idiot would bring a horse out this close to the highway?"

"The highway? Where the hell *are* you, Victor?"

A moment ago the drum of the approaching rider had been coming from the south of him, Vic was sure of it. Yet somehow, without so much as a faltered step, it shifted to the north. "Stopped for gas, that's all." Vic paid little attention to the lie rolling off his tongue as he rose up on tiptoe and craned his neck to peer into the darkness.

"Oh!" Her momentary flash of accusation was all but forgotten at the exciting prospect of fresh booze. "Are you near Gordon Bleau's? I need a bottle of Amaretto."

Vic stifled a cringe at the thought of his wife's mixed drink induced wandering hands. If he wanted to fend off an overly Botoxed hag that reeked of booze, he'd go visit Nana at the home. Her old biddy friends loved him, and putting in his time there helped secure his spot in her will. "I'd love to, pet, but I'd hate to keep Cass waiting."

A hot, snorted breath heated the exposed skin of Vic's neck, tickling down the collar of his shirt. He spun, his heart pounding painfully in his chest, and pressed his back to the car door. Chills raced up and down his spine, electrifying his entire body. *Nothing.* There was nothing before him but that lone buzzing light and the seedy motel. "Damn it! Punk kids!"

"And they have a horse?" Yvonne's giggle morphed into a hiccup. "You better watch out, Vic. It could be one of those lesser known equestrian gangs."

The lightning that flashed on the otherwise calm night was the only omen Vic needed to spur him into action. Throwing himself off the car, his trembling fingers fumbled with the door handle. Behind him, metal hissed free from leather. Slowly—with a cold, hard fist of dread clenching his gut—his head swiveled.

"Oh," he said with a nervous lilt of laughter to the ominous symphony of black before him. "That's ... good. You got me. I really believed for a sec —"

Vic's anxious, cracking plea morphed into a scream as the figure pulled back. The blade of their arched sword gleaming gold under the yellow-hued light.

Victor's hands raised in the only defense he could offer. "No! Noooo!"

He sucked in one last gasp as metal winged through the air.

"Vic? Victor!" Yvonne screamed, panic clearing her alcohol induced haze. "*What's happening?*"

The only response she received came in the form of a ghostly whinny ... followed by a soft thump. Her shrieks were muted as the phone tumbled to the ground — right next to Vic's still rolling head.

## About the Author

Stacey Rourke is the author of the award-winning YA Gryphon Series, the chillingly suspenseful Legends Saga, and the romantic comedy Adapted for Film. She lives in Michigan with her husband, two beautiful daughters, and two giant dogs. She loves to travel, has an unhealthy shoe addiction, and considers herself blessed to make a career out of talking to the imaginary people that live in her head.

Connect with her at:

www.staceyrourke.com
Facebook at www.facebook.com/staceyrourkeauthor
Amazon Author Page:
http://amzn.to/2l8FlbH
or on Twitter or instagram @rourkewrites

If you enjoyed *Rise of the Sea Witch*, pick up these other titles by Stacey Rourke:

# The Gryphon Series
*The Conduit*
*Embrace*
*Sacrifice*
*Ascension*
*Descent*
*Inferno*
and *The Official Gryphon Series Coloring Book*

# The Legends Saga
*Crane*
*Raven*
*Steam*

# Reel Romance
*Adapted for Film*
*Turn Tables*

Made in the USA
Columbia, SC
14 January 2019